# NORTHERN
# ECHO

# NORTHERN ECHO

## Boys Don't Cry

### WILLY MITCHELL

# NORTHERN ECHO
## BOYS DON'T CRY

*Scripture quotations marked KJV are from the Holy Bible, King James Version (Authorized Version). First published in 1611. Quoted from the KJV Classic Reference Bible. Copyright © 1983 by Zondervan Corporation.*

*iUniverse books may be ordered through booksellers or by contacting:*

*iUniverse*
*1663 Liberty Drive*
*Bloomington, IN 47403*
*www.iuniverse.com*
*844-349-9409*

*Cover Art: Mind The Gap*
*Artist: Paul Giggle*

*ISBN: 978-1-5320-9852-9 (sc)*
*ISBN: 978-1-6632-1058-6 (hc)*
*ISBN: 978-1-5320-9851-2 (e)*

*Library of Congress Control Number: 2020919250*

*Print information available on the last page.*

*iUniverse rev. date: 10/08/2020*

# Jerusalem

And did those feet in ancient time
Walk upon England's mountains green?
And was the holy Lamb of God
On England's pleasant pastures seen?
And did the countenance divine
Shine forth upon our clouded hills?
And was Jerusalem builder here
Among these dark Satanic Mills?

Bring me my bow of burning gold!
Bring me my arrows of desire!
Bring me my spear! O clouds, unfold!
Bring me my chariot of fire!

I will not cease from mental fight
Nor shall my sword sleep in my hand
Till we have built Jerusalem
In England's green and pleasant land.

—Hubert Parry, 1916

Punk is musical freedom. It's saying, doing, and playing what you want. In *Webster*'s terms, *nirvana* means freedom from pain, suffering, and the external world, and that's pretty close to my definition of punk rock.

—Kurt Cobain

# CONTENTS

Acknowledgments ................................................................. xi

Prologue ............................................................................ xiii

1  Public Image ................................................................. 1

2  Adamant ........................................................................ 9

3  Mr. Jones ...................................................................... 21

4  Bill Grundy ................................................................. 33

5  Bombs ........................................................................... 41

6  Anger is an Energy ..................................................... 51

7  Careers ......................................................................... 59

8  Winters of Discontent ................................................ 73

9  The Troubles ............................................................... 89

10  Breaking Glass ............................................................ 105

11  Pedros Godropolos ..................................................... 113

12  Bright Side .................................................................. 123

13  Nimrod ......................................................................... 131

14  Enemies of the State .................................................. 137

15  White Riot ................................................................... 145

16  Charlie Harper ............................................................ 159

17  He Who Dares Wins ................................................... 171

18 Screaming Babies...................................................... 177

19 Tin Soldiers............................................................. 187

20 Yorkshire................................................................. 197

21 No Future ............................................................... 207

22 (The) William Shakespeare ........................................ 221

23 The Queen's Shilling ................................................. 229

24 End of an Era............................................................ 237

25 Grace ...................................................................... 245

26 Boris....................................................................... 255

Afterword.................................................................... 269

Author's Notes ............................................................. 273

Definitions and Clarifications......................................... 293

About the Author.......................................................... 319

# ACKNOWLEDGMENTS

I started my writing journey more than five years ago. I believe everyone has at least one book in him or her and has a story to tell. All my books so far weave fiction with real historical events, along with lifetime experiences. Each story begins in a pub, bar, or hostelry somewhere in the world, places that often are great sources of material.

I have many people to thank for their help and support along my journey so far. Thanks to my wife and my daughter for all their patience and suffering. Thanks to my mother, father, and sister. Thanks to Jay, Hans, Prentiss, Charles, Jeff, Eric, and my best friend, Gary. Thanks to Andrew Hemmings, an author and historian, and Alta Wehmeyer, an educator and creative-writing tutor, for all their encouragement and support on my writing journey so far.

To all those I grew up with, as we journeyed through our teens into adulthood, thanks for the fond memories I hold of those times. Most of all, thank you to my friend, my hero, the man himself, the legend Tim "Tiny Tim" Timpson, or just Tiny, as most knew him.

Thank you, Kerry, not only for helping me but also for supporting me and encouraging me to write *Northern Echo*. You are the best.

A big thank you to photographer, and filmmaker Paul Giggle for his contribution of the book cover art work, 'Mind The Gap'. You can check out Paul's website and his amazing work at www.paulgiggle.com.

Thank you to all who have helped and supported me along the way, all I have mentioned and all I have missed.

Thank you!

*Willy*
MITCHELL

# PROLOGUE

The train chugged southward out of Glasgow Central as I stared blankly out the window at the passing cityscape. I had an increasingly love-hate relationship with Glasgow and, in fact, much of the United Kingdom by then. I found it sad. I was a former servant to the queen who'd been in the British Army for more than a decade of my life, yet as I looked around at the shit state of the train, the other passengers, and the staff, I wondered, *What was it all for?*

The tenements, the high-rise tower blocks—I struggled to understand what made anyone want to live in them. *Maybe they have no choice. Maybe they have no path to a brighter future.* That thought also made me sad. "Poor fuckers," I whispered aloud. The man sitting across from me glanced over at me with a puzzled look on his face and then went back to reading his newspaper.

I remembered the punk rock revolution that had hit the shores of Old Blighty back in 1976. The backdrop of political turmoil, the former Hollywood actor, and the Iron Lady had united. Nations had built up nuclear arsenals, posturing and threatening to throw them at each other. I recalled the union strikes, the demise of whole industries, high unemployment, and the sense of hopelessness that had existed with Britain's youth. Many years had passed since those turbulent times, yet they were as fresh in my mind's eye as if they'd occurred only yesterday.

From that sense of having no future, a movement had arisen like a phoenix from the flames, an opportunity for the youth of the day to rise up, protest, and demonstrate their discontent through music, fashion, and a way of life that many just plain didn't understand. Many of the older generation considered punk rock nothing more than noise, and they considered the kids who loved that rebellious form of rock to be scum.

The mid-1970s had marked the beginnings of the punk rock movement. I had been in on the ground floor. The chaotic nature of punk had captivated my imagination. It had tapped directly into the rebel in me, and it had set me free to get into plenty of trouble with my equally rebellious friends. One friend in particular, Tim Timpson, whom we all called Tiny Tim or just Tiny, had pushed the so-called proverbial envelope on what he could get away with, and I'd tagged along for the ride.

Tiny was on my mind as the train left the city proper. The gray industrial atmosphere gave way to the sprawl of any big city in those days, and the scenery became more bucolic as the miles ticked by. Tiny had occupied my thoughts a great deal of late. He'd said he had something important to tell me and that it had to be in person. That was unlike Tiny. I knew in my heart that something was up and that it probably wasn't good.

The conductor entered the far end of the car and began collecting tickets. In anticipation of his arrival at my seat, I shuffled in the back pocket of my jeans and fished out my return ticket to Windermere, the tourist town where I'd grown up.

I watched the conductor make his way down the carriage. He was in his early twenties, I guessed, and wore his uniform like a bag of shite. His forage cap slanted to one side; his hair was in need of a cut, flowing out the sides of his cap; his gray-blue trousers were covered with tramlines from too many misguided ironing sessions; and in contrast, his shirt looked as if it had never seen an iron at all.

"Fucking egit," I whispered to myself, and I turned my attention to the accountant type who sat opposite me. He was oblivious, sliding an old Bic pen into his ear, seemingly cleaning out his earwax. "What the fuck?" I stared at him as he slowly became self-conscious about what he was doing and apologetically placed the scabby pen on the table between us. "For fuck's sake," I said. He picked up the pen and jammed it into his jacket pocket.

Nearby I saw an old couple holding hands, a handful of football supporters going to some game somewhere, and a woman with two bairns screaming their heads off. She was smoking Marlboro Reds and drinking a can of Stella, yelling at the two children in her barely understandable Glaswegian drawl.

"Fucking classy." I had a habit of talking to myself, often aloud.

The conductor arrived. "Tickets, please."

I waited for the accountant to rummage around in his briefcase and eventually find his rail pass. He was a frequent traveler heading to work down in Manchester, Birmingham, or even London for the week, I guessed. People's lack of savvy pissed me off; the conductor had been calling for tickets for at least the past three minutes.

"Fucking egit." I glared at him, and he just looked away, doubly embarrassed and self-conscious.

As I settled in after giving the conductor my ticket, my thoughts again returned to Tiny. Our meeting would be at the Royal Oak, which had been a favorite haunt of ours for many years. Tiny was a friend, protector, promoter, and hero—my hero. My best friend's wife had been taken away by cancer. She'd been too young to die and too beautiful, both inside and out. I swore I saw her in every train station, airport, and shopping mall, following me, staring at me, smiling, never saying a word. She'd joined the numerous others on the growing list of lasting memories of people who had passed away. The list grew longer by the year, and the names on it lingered with me as the faces faded into the oblivion of the passing decades.

I had left Glasgow on the 12:40 p.m. from platform 1 and headed south to Oxenholme Station. After a fifteen-minute wait there, I was then on the old bone shaker into Windermere, the last part of the journey, which brought back memories—some good, some bad, and some conveniently forgotten—and whisked me back to my youth.

I hadn't made that journey for more than thirty years— thirty-three, to be precise—and that was my first return to the northern town where I'd grown up, on the same train I had left on way back then.

As the train wove its way past Kendal, Burneside, and Staveley toward Windermere, I felt pain and anxiety rising from the pit of my stomach. It was like traveling back in time to a place far in the past, a place full of happiness and joy yet sadness of times, memories, and people long gone.

The familiar downpour of rain was there to greet me like an old adversary as I stepped onto the once-familiar platform and walked to the big red double-decker to take me down to Bowness. I sat on the top deck, as I had years earlier, and looked out the rain-spattered window as we passed through Windermere, close to the Odana Café, the Windermere Hotel, the Elleray Hotel, an old friend's place, and the Queen's Hotel. We went down past the clock tower into Bowness, past my old family home, the old cinema, the Nisi Taverna, the Old England Hotel, and the Stag's Head to the lakeside, my final stop.

It was like going back in time. Things had changed but not too much; it was pretty much the same place I had left all those years earlier. I recalled my mother and father waving me off at the train station when I'd left to join Her Majesty's British Army to find some glimmer of hope in what had seemed hopeless times back then.

That day was a typical February Sunday afternoon in the north of England: cold, wet, and miserable.

Tiny had sent me a text late on Friday night, asking if I would like to meet up "one last time." I assumed the text was fueled by alcohol or some other substance; nevertheless, we had always promised each other that in times of need, we would answer the call.

All those years later, I was confused. I felt unclear on why I had never returned, but deep down, I knew the answer to that—a secret buried deep within, conveniently and deliberately parked away in the depths somewhere, never to be spoken, never to be heard, rarely coming to mind apart from the occasional times of loneliness and the frequent times of darkness. Churchill had called it his black dog. I called mine the black bastard; he was both dark and extremely cruel.

It had grown over the years, becoming deeper. With each passing day came another event, loss, death, mistake, regret, or suicide. They all piled up one after the other. Most of the time, from the outside, people saw me as strong, but inside, I was vulnerable. I put on a good show. I had learned how to do that, usually passing off tragedy and sadness with humor. That was how we'd dealt with it in the army. It seemed to work, at least on the face of it.

Although Tiny and I had maintained our bond from a distance, we were also torn apart by our secret, which neither of us could ever share with anyone else. Not ever. I'd tried for years to run away from the secret, our evil deed. The fear of facing up to what we had done kept us apart. We'd talked regularly at first, but over the years, our communication had subsided as we compartmentalized our memories and our lives.

Pushing that thought to one side, I realized there were many good memories too. We were brothers-in-arms on our journey of discovery and partners in crime.

The music of Morrissey, former front man, singer, and songwriter for the Smiths, played in my head from the moment the train pulled into the station and during the ride down the hill, ringing in my ears, haunting me. "Trudging over the wet sand, back to the bench where your clothes were stolen"—the lyrics reminded me of "the coastal town they had forgotten to close down." The lyrics suited my mood that day.

I sat on a bench overlooking the lake, with the wind blowing and the rain now just a light drizzle, looking over the water to Belle Isle, to the distant shore. I gazed at the mountains serenely rising above, the hills and the dales, the rich green forests coming down to meet the shore, and the ducks and swans gathering around me, expecting food.

I realized I probably had been a little harsh on that place of obvious beauty; however, years ago, I had escaped. I had moved on from the lack of options and opportunity and the fear of having no future in growing up in a northern town with little hope.

I grabbed a bag of crinkle-cut Worcestershire-flavor Seabrook crisps—my favorite—from my hold-all and started to share my snack with the appreciative birds around me. I had a couple of packs and was happy to share my food. It was like comfort food for them as much as it was for me, I thought.

The crisps served as another reminder of my youth. I recalled Tiny, some of the other boys, and me in the Air Training Corps, with our uncomfortable wool tunics rubbing and irritating our adolescent skin. Our commanding officer, a distant past relic of the Royal Air Force, complete with potbelly and mustache, marched us around the ATC hall in our big boots and blue berets two nights a week. Truth be known, the only reason we went was for the Seabrook crisps—and to fire the big elephant guns and attend the summer camps where we got to fly things.

I sat back and lit a Marlboro Light; zipped up my padded North Face to the top, feeling the sharp wind on my face; and smiled to myself, thinking about how time blurred memories and how being back there was stimulating recollections long since hidden.

The tourists had long gone for the winter. The piers before me usually were bedecked with a multitude of rowboats for hire, but that day, just a couple bobbed and clanked in the wind with that familiar and strangely comforting sound.

I looked at my watch and realized I was colder than I had thought and felt the draw of an open fire and a pint of Jennings to warm me up. I started walking up the hill to the old familiar Royal Oak.

As I walked, my mind finished the song in my head as I passed the abundant gray slate of the buildings, which likely were warm and toasty inside but added to the grayness and cold outside, especially on a day like that one: "Every day is like Sunday, silent and gray."

Tiny and I had agreed to meet at one of our old haunts. I walked up the hill, past Saint Martin's Church on the left, and turned right, and mounted above the road, looking down like some old wise man, stood the Royal Oak, with its familiar sign: an old British cutter ship at full mast, perched on the crest of the ocean waves. The place had picnic tables at the front for summer days, a back bar, a front bar, a pool table, blazing fireplaces, and Jennings. I was relieved to get out of the cold and into the warm comfort of the bar.

I looked around and noticed Tiny sat around the corner in the back bar, a more secluded and quieter option. He greeted me with his big signature grin and familiar bear hug. We ordered two pints of Jennings Best Bitter and took our first sips in the silence of old friends before exchanging the usual pleasantries of two old friends who hadn't seen each other for a while, catching up on what we had been up to and on family and friends.

He sat across from me. He still had his big frame; square shoulders; equally square chin; loveable, boyish smile; and huge personality, yet I could see he had dwindled, and the Tiny who sat on a stool before me was not the same Tiny I had known in the past.

As if it had been only yesterday, I recalled his green PVC pants, his Mohican, his eight-laced Doc Marten boots, and his friendship guiding me through the labyrinth and the dangers that had existed throughout our youth in the north of England.

That night, I saw a sadness in his eyes I had never seen in Tiny before, but I recognized the look, which I had, tragically, witnessed in others before and was certain I would again.

We both remembered the landlords of old: Neil and his wife, Carol. Their trinkets and entertainments we knew well remained: the leather yoke from the annual gurning competition, the yard of ale atop the bar, and the mayor's medallions, all reminders of the annual kangaroo-court-style, beer-infused mayoral challenge and crowning of the successor and the nonexistent civil duties for the town for the year until the next time, when it happened all over again.

We looked down the list of engraved names on the trophy and recognized many of the old heroes of the town. Neither Tiny nor I was on that list.

"Remember this fella?" He pointed at the name of an old familiar friend: Mayor James Gregg.

"Big Bertha—of course I do," I said, remembering the night he'd gotten crowned. "Downing the yard of ale faster than anyone and nailing the best gurn?"

"He had a distinct advantage there, the ugly bugger."

"Come on. He's got a face only his mother could love."

We raised our glasses. "Here's to the mayor, Big Bertha! The mayor!" we echoed as we clinked our glasses and took big gulps of our ale.

We sat there as old friends in silence, digesting the memories, the night ahead, and where we had found ourselves all those years later, silent in our secret.

"What's going on, Tiny?" I asked the obvious question.

Tiny looked at me and then, like a little boy, looked away, as if he hoped the question might disappear. It was evident something wasn't right. I had known the man since I was eight years old. He always had been a leader, always at the front, always fun, but that night, something about him was different from the Tiny I'd known in the past.

We both took another swig of our Jennings, and I looked him in the eye again. "What the fuck's going on, Tiny?"

He looked at me, started to well up, and took another swig of his beer. I ordered two drams of whisky: Liddesdale, a favorite of days gone by.

"Do you remember the time you got onstage with Charlie Harper and sang 'Crash Course'?" He grinned with his one-tooth-missing smile, reminding me of the old Tiny Tim I had come to respect and love over the years.

"Aye, I do. Do yer remember the time in Manchester, at the Hacienda, and the fight outside, stuck between the fucking Perry Boys and the Bikers?"

Tiny nodded with a distant smile and then looked me in the eye. "Hell yes, I remember that. Good old times, Willy." We clinked our whisky glasses and took a sip each.

"What about that time we went to see Adam Ant, and they didn't turn up?"

We echoed together, "Gone to fucking Top of the Pops."

"Fuckers."

"Yeh, then that arrogant fucker Terry Hall in the pub after?"

"Bloody Specials thought they were fucking special."

"Fuckers."

"Yeh, but to be fair, Ghost Town was a legend of our time."

We both nodded in agreement; it was hard to disagree.

"Remember that time when you jumped off the stage in Blackburn and crowd-surfed like a true trooper?" Tiny paused, clutched his midriff, and winced. He did not say a word, but his face told the story.

"What the hell, Tiny?"

He looked at me, and his manic, lovable smile turned once again to sadness and pain. "It's not good." He looked at me, not seeking an answer and not looking for any sympathy.

"What have they said?"

"Cancer. Pretty bad." He laughed with his typical shrugging shoulders, the deep giggle that was his trademark.

I looked at him again, wanting more information.

He said, "Terminal."

"Oh fuck, Tiny, is there anything I can do?"

"No, Willy, fuck off. Just being here tonight is good enough, unless you have a new body to give me, a new pancreas, or a suitcase of cash." He laughed again, trying to dispel the seriousness of his situation.

We sat in silence, sipping our beers and whisky for a few minutes in the silence of comrades. I had witnessed that silence before, on a Sunday afternoon in the Game Cock, in Hereford, before secret soldiers went off in their unmarked uniforms or no uniforms at all to undefined destinations and conflicts, never knowing if they would return or not or if they would see each other again. Silence was the binding that kept them together without the need for detail or unnecessary words. What was the point? That was their fate.

"Fancy one last bash down the Stag's Head or the Wheelhouse?" Tiny asked hopefully.

"Are yer sure yer up to it?"

"Fucking right I am. I was born up for it."

"It's Sunday night, Tiny—are they open?"

Tiny grinned. "Of course they are; it's fricking Valentine's night," he said with his big smile painted across his face. He had done his research. Tiny always did. It was always important for us, especially Tiny, to understand not only the *what* but also the *why*. That was a shift in how people thought during the punk revolution—our revolution.

He slapped me on the shoulder and, given his size, muscle, and enthusiasm, nearly knocked me off my stool. There was a reason he was called Tiny Tim, and it wasn't due to his lack of size. Not that he was overweight—far from it. Tiny was just a big unit, solid, as broad as he was tall and as wide as he was wise.

We finished our drinks and walked down the road toward the Stag's.

On our way across Lake Road, Tiny said excitedly, "Let's go up the clock tower and ring some bells one last time together," referring to the old familiar Saint Martin's Church.

We entered the front gate to the pretty, ornate church and graveyard, a place we both remembered as kids for weddings, christenings, funerals, and a little mischief back in our time.

"I wonder if it's still here." Tiny fished around in the wooden slats that formed a false window to the left of the bell tower door. "Got it!" he said with a big smile as he pulled the ancient key from the slats. He put it in the equally ancient door lock and turned it counterclockwise, and we both heard the familiar movement of the old lock. Tiny opened the door, still grinning, reemphasizing his point. The moment was not lost on me.

He led the way up the stone spiral staircase, barely fitting his shoulders through the narrow entrance. "Do you remember this, Willy?" he shouted back. "Fuck, we used to have fun. What the hell happened?" He reached the top of the bell tower.

As we stood there, Tiny clutched his midriff once again. "How long?" I asked.

"Not as long as I'd fucking like." His response was semihumorous but leveling. "C'mon. Let's sparkle these bells for a few and then leg it and get back to Patrick and the Stag's before the bizzies arrive."

"Fuck it. Why not?" was the only response I could muster.

We both looked at the bell ropes hanging down from the belfry and glanced over at each other, signaling when we were ready to begin. The mischievous tension between us was a return to familiar ground for both of us. Brothers-in-arms, we were suddenly kids again.

We tugged, heaved, and pulled and rang out a dubious tune across the rooftops of the town.

"They told us we couldn't fucking play!" Tiny shouted with a grin.

After a few minutes of pandemonium, we looked at each other again with another familiar look: it was time to bug out before the local police arrived. Back down the narrow stone spiral stairs we went, back to the door, and as per etiquette, we carefully stashed the ancient key back in its hiding place behind the mock slat window for the next visitors.

It was a handy little secret that most of us knew about and created great shelter for a mooch, a couple of tinnies, or even a place to get some sleep when locked out or too inebriated to make it all the way back up the hill and home.

Off to the Stag's we went with the sirens of the local bobby and blue lights behind us. It was an old but still amusing play!

"Just like old times, Willy," Tiny said. "The best times of my life."

I nodded in agreement, looking at the familiar ground, lost for words and remembering our secret and regretting our self-enforced separation over the years.

We crossed through the graveyard to the back entrance of the church, to the back gate, and across the street to the Stag's. Tiny doubled over again, wincing, clearly in pain.

"Tiny, what the fuck?"

"Fuck it. Let's go for a drink" was his only explanation and response.

I respected his silence on the subject; after all, it was clear that things were not good, and I didn't want to ruin what I assumed might be our last night together. I recognized how important it was for Tiny to go out with a splash. Fading away was not Tiny's style.

"I'm sorry, Tiny."

He looked at me. "I'm sorry too. We shouldn't have gone to Paris. It was my idea."

"Fuck off. I didn't mean that," I said as the painful memories rushed back.

"What did yer mean then?"

"That I haven't been back since I left. That we drifted apart."

He looked at me again with sadness in his eyes. "Aye, me too, Willy. I missed yer like hell. But at least yer here tonight." He slapped me on my shoulder.

We walked into the quiet side of the Stag's Head, and the old familiar face of Patrick, the longtime manager, was there to greet us, not looking long for that life himself.

"Fuck me. Willy Mitchell, where the hell have you been all this time?"

I avoided the question. "Two double Liddesdale, Patrick."

"I see nothing changes," he said sarcastically as he poured two generous glasses from the bottle. "Welcome home, Willy."

I raised my glass and turned my attention to my old friend Tiny Tim. Flashing blue lights were visible through the windows as the police searched for the errant bell ringers.

We were alone.

"We could've reported it," Tiny said.

"Aye, yer right. We could've, but we didn't. Neither of us can turn the clock back."

He nodded. "That is certainly true, my friend."

We talked for a while, recollecting old adventures and times long gone, a lifetime away. The local police walked in to check out any budding campanologists in the bar that night. Tiny and I just kept chatting as if oblivious to the two officers.

They walked past the two of us, likely thinking we were clearly too old to be playing those sorts of antics, looking for potentially more youthful suspects. On the way back around, one of the officers paused and greeted Tiny, who was well known to all in the area, including the local constabulary.

"Evening, Tiny."

"Evening, Officer." Tiny smiled without looking the officer in the face.

"Having a good night, Tiny?"

"Aye, always, and you?"

"Always better seeing you," the officer responded, looking me up and down. "You gentlemen hear them bells ringing earlier?"

Together, practiced, in unison, we said, "What bells?"

Tiny added, "I think you lot must be hearing things, Officer. You can get medication for that, yer know." He smirked in a playful way. "No stray cats to rescue tonight, Officer? What about that parrot of yours?" he asked, referring to the escaped exotic bird that, for some reason, hung out on the chimney tops above the police station and had done so for years. Even I remembered the red-and-blue parrot.

The officers just smiled and walked to the door, speaking into their radios before they left just to make sure we heard them.

"Nothing here, sir," one said. "Just a pair of old boys at the bar—that's all." He opened the door to leave and shouted back, "Good night, gentlemen!"

As the door closed on its spring hinge, Tiny shouted after them, "Fucking tossers!" making sure to yell loudly enough for them to hear. The blue lights outside turned off, and Saint Martin's and the Stag's returned to peacefulness.

We had grown up in an era when there was mistrust with all levels of the establishment, including the police. Especially as we'd skirted close to the law for much of our youth, our relationship with the boys in blue always had been somewhat strained.

Tiny nodded at me with a big smile, as if checking in to see if I was still by his side, clearly in pain.

We had one more, and I could see that the lights in Tiny's eyes were dimming. "Let's get yer home, Tiny."

"No, fuck off. Let's get a bottle and take a boat ride," he said.

"What? Like a proper Valentine's date?"

"Aye, something like that, you silly fucker."

I succumbed, and we walked down to the lakefront. As we had done many times before, within minutes, we climbed onto one of the rowboats at the pier, pulled back the protective tarpaulin, unleashed the boat from its moorings, and drifted away into the dark and still waters of the lake, just me, Tiny, the cold depths, and a bottle of Liddesdale.

"I'm gonna miss you, Willy. I'm gonna miss everyone. What the fuck?"

"I am sure you will be fine. Doctors nowadays."

"I am done, my friend. It's over."

"What the hell does that mean?"

"I'm done, dusted, on my fucking way out."

We sat in silence as I rowed the boat over toward Belle Isle, a popular haunt from years gone by. As kids, we had enjoyed that romantic and stunningly beautiful part of the world, on the steps of William Wordsworth and Beatrix Potter, playing our own version of *Swallows and Amazons*.

"I've never forgotten that night in Paris," he said.

"I've tried nothing but to forget," I responded.

"He gave us no fucking choice, Willy."

"Well, he did sort of bring it on himself."

"And us. Living with the guilt all these years and the fear that the bizzies could come knocking at the door at any moment."

I nodded in agreement. I had felt the same way at first, but over time, through the years that had come to pass, as the fear had subsided, my guilt had lingered like a weight on my mind in my darkest hours. "Hindsight's a wonderful thing, Tiny."

"Why didn't you ever come back, Willy? Until now, until it's too fucking late."

The question was hard and harsh, and the answer was impossible for me to express, but I knew the distance was a safety blanket, and over the years, the blanket had become thicker, warmer, more insulating, and harder to let go of.

"I dunno, mate. It's just how it played out, I guess." I didn't have a better answer I could think of, never mind articulate to my best friend.

"We should've just come clean and claimed self-defense or something like that."

"Fuck off, Tiny. They would have locked us up and thrown away the key back then."

We had talked about that at the time and, on our journey back to the north, ruled it out as an option. Life had told me there was no point in mulling over decisions made, actions, and events of the past. It was a pointless waste of energy.

"Fuck all we can do about it now, Tiny. It's gone, in the past, forgotten. At least we didn't end up in some fucking prison cell somewhere."

"Or the Foreign fricking Legion." Tiny smiled his big, broad grin. His comment was a dig at my running away to join the army.

I continued rowing around the back of Belle Isle, where the calmer, tranquil waters were protected by the island from the wind and the currents. It was nearly silent in the light but cold breeze. The winter stars in the cloudless sky above sparkled down on the ripples in the water below. The foul weather had obviously pulled out, leaving in its wake the cold kiss of February.

"Willy, you're a writer."

"Well, a couple of novels, I guess."

I was embarrassed at the label. It felt too elevated, too grandiose. I had thought about it a lot and realized my writing was not for me or for money or fame. I had come to the conclusion that my writing, good, bad, or indifferent, was about telling stories that deserved to be told, to memorialize them for the future in the hope that the next generation would read them and somehow learn and grow from the stories. I hoped so especially for my son and daughter and their children and beyond.

"I want you to tell our story." He looked at me hopefully.

"What? Everything?"

"Why the fuck not? It's a fucking tragedy, Willy, just like William fricking Shakespeare."

"What? Like fucking *Romeo and Juliet*?" I joked.

"Well, it is Valentine's Day!" He smiled his old Tiny smile.

He was right. As I looked back at our lives, I realized our story was a tragedy. We'd been two young kids growing up in one of the most idyllic settings in the north in the United Kingdom and even the world, with the countryside as our playground, but in a period when there was little hope or visibility regarding the future.

Then had come the distancing over the years of two best friends; one had stayed, and the other had left. The distance and time had grown, and now there we were all those years later, with the end of days nearing for Tiny, back together under terrible circumstances.

I'd had plenty of time for reflection on the train on my way down and since my arrival back in that northern town.

My own life had been packed away on the train and sent south to the army, and after doing my time, years later, I'd returned to normality. Then life had just taken over: one failed marriage, another on its way, two kids, two mothers, and not a pot to piss in. But still, I had hope, and my lust for travel remained as strong as it had been all those years ago.

"Where did all those bloody years go, Tiny?" It wasn't really a question.

"How life can change in the flip of a coin," he said. "Tell our story, Willy. Otherwise, what the hell was all that about?"

"Tiny, calm the hell down. What the fuck are you on about? You'll be fine, my friend. Doctors and health care nowadays." I was deliberately trying to stay positive and not sure I was doing a convincing job.

"Willy, I am fucking dying—one step away. This is my song. I want you to promise me. Tell our story, our last song."

We fell into silence once more until Tiny started to sing his own version of "My Way" in a Sid Vicious sort of style with hints of the Clash and Kirk Brandon's Theatre of Hate howl—all bands that Tiny and I knew well, remembered, and admired.

We stayed out there on the icy but beautiful waters for another hour or so, and when the conversation turned into gibberish, I got Tiny back to shore and called him a taxi to send him safely back home.

As he got into the cab, Tiny leaned out the window and shouted, "They'll never take me alive!" while punching his fist in the air—a stark reminder of his situation, a memory from the past of previous exploits and adventures, and his final ask of me. "Willy, promise me you'll tell our story. The world deserves to know it. We deserve it. I fucking deserve it. You promise?"

I nodded and saluted as Tiny was whisked away while shouting out the window, "You're a fucking legend, Willy!"

I watched as the taxi made its way back up the hill. The song he had quoted played in my head: "I'm leaving on the fast train. Don't ask me when I'm coming back again. I reckon it's only a matter of time before the law kick in the door."

The next morning, I headed back to Glasgow, and that was the last time I would see Tiny Tim alive, at least in that world. I would see him in the next, I hoped.

# I

# PUBLIC IMAGE

WM

Years earlier
December 11, 1983
King George's Hall, Blackburn

**THE LAST CONCERT TINY AND** I went to together was a memorable one and typified the era and the tail end of the punk rock revolution.

The expectant crowd gathered in the old dance hall long after its heyday, a mix of color and of Doc Marten boots, leather, chains, skinheads, Mohicans, piercings, and tattoos. They were from all walks of life, the sons and daughters of barristers, policemen, clergymen, train drivers, teachers, and council workers, all with one thing in common.

Coming out of the punk rock movement, they had their own interpretations, but the themes of rebellion and abandonment and distrust of the establishment were a common thread as they tried to understand their place in the world, a modern world of apparently no future and little hope.

It was a seasoned and experienced audience that night. They had all clearly been around for a while, and they knew the score; the menace of potential violence at any moment filled the air. They had grown up in it.

Tiny and I had hitched a ride down to Blackburn earlier in the day. We had set off early because of the unpredictability of getting a ride, but we had struck gold when we were picked up by a mate's parent, who happened to be traveling down to nearby Preston on business. He took us all the way into Blackburn's town center, where Tiny and I hung out for the afternoon.

Once a proud mill town built on the wool trade, Blackburn now was a shadow of its former glory. Rows of redbrick tenements stained with the soot of the coal of industry were long gone. We had been there many times before but never with so much time to venture out and about.

"What a fucking shithole," Tiny said as we walked down the main street.

I couldn't disagree. It was a far cry from home, with its shuttered-down shops and the locals staring at our leather jackets, studs, and haircuts and Tiny's green PVC trousers. We just stared back at their kaftans, turbans, and yasmaks with equal indifference.

We found the shop we were looking for: Pink Punk. Tiny had done his homework again. We took a look around to see if the store had any of the latest fashions on the racks and shelves and quickly worked out that it was a waste of time. It was one thirty in the afternoon.

"C'mon, Tiny. Let's head to get a bite to eat and a pint."

The Sir Charles Napier was right in front of us and close to the evening's convert venue. We walked in, sat down at the bar with the local drunkards, winos, alcoholics, pensioners, and unemployed with their flat caps. They all turned and stared as we walked in, and we stared right back.

"Told yer we should've gone down to Manchester," Tiny said.

"C'mon, mate. We got lucky, and we're here now; let's make the most of it." I looked down at the bar menu and could smell the stale fat in the fryer in the kitchen in the back. "Smells fucking beautiful. What do yer fancy, Tiny?"

"Anything that isn't fucking fried!"

We looked through the menu, and although there were plenty of choices, it was obvious by the pictures that the food was all out of a freezer. We opted for two microwaved cheeseburgers and fries.

"Fucking fantastic. What beer do they have?" Tiny said.

I looked across the bar at the hand pulls and settled for a couple of pints of the local Thwaites Original. The barman, with a dirty beer towel slung over his shoulder and a cigarette hanging out of his mouth, obliged and dumped the two glasses in front of us. I just stared over at him.

"You bring me to all the fucking classy joints, Willy!" Tiny said. We clinked our glasses and took big slurps of our ales.

"At least the beer's half decent." I smiled at my mate.

Tiny just grinned back. He had a grin for every occasion, and he was giving me his "I told you so" grin.

We could hear the whir of the microwave in the back, and I imagined the two cheeseburgers side by side, spinning around inside on a glass plate. Three minutes later, we heard the *ping*. Tiny and I looked at each other to confirm the recognition of the event unfolding. The barman wiped his hands on the stained beer towel on his shoulder, went back to the kitchen, returned a moment later carrying two plates of food, and placed them in front of us. Tiny and I looked down to inspect the food.

"Would you like anything with that?" asked the barman.

"Do you have a fucking sledgehammer?" asked Tiny.

The barman just looked right back at us. "If you don't like it, then just fuck off!"

"Classy," we both said in unison.

It turned out we were both hungry, and the burgers, although a bit rubbery around the edges, when smothered in Heinz ketchup, were somewhat edible.

"This burger is wubbery," Tiny said in his best Chinese accent. "Aw, fank you wery much." He bowed as he told his joke.

The barman, overhearing the joke, just stared, lit another cigarette, and poured himself a shot of whisky.

It was a long afternoon. We ate and left and headed over to another boozer, the Blackburn Times, which was right across the road from King George's Hall. We played all the remotely punk-related music on the jukebox, played pool, and set on our way to getting slashed for the afternoon—but hopefully not so much so that we missed the gig.

Later, I woke up in the corner of the pub. We had fallen asleep with our heads on the table. Everyone had left us alone; we were in a dark corner and probably somewhat intimidating to the older clientele in the bar. I jumped up, realizing the time, and nudged Tiny—probably a little too hard, as he fell off his chair with his legs sprawling and arms waving, thinking he was in the middle of a fight with an unknown adversary.

He realized where he was and that it was me.

I smiled at him. "C'mon, yer silly fucker. Let's go before we miss 'em."

He jumped up, and we were out the door and on our way across the street to see the Godfather himself.

We made it just in time. The band took to the stage, shrouded from clear view, but there was no sign of their charismatic front man, an Irishman with bright red hair, a manic look, and crazy antics. They started a riff on the bass to temper the crowd, and as the rhythm resounded across the venue, it raised the expectation and anticipation of the audience even further.

A tunnel built in the center of the stage, like a football tunnel, pumped out liquid smoke as the sickly yellow and red lighting added to the atmosphere, like a gas attack. The smoke caught the back of the throat like some sort of poison, and the bass guitar carried on with its almost hypnotic repetitive melody.

*Dum, dum, dumdum, dumdum dundum, dundum.*

A sea of bright pink, green, and red hair and spikes; shiny tops of skinheads; and goth black and crimson were spattered around the audience, who stood like worshippers facing the stage, many of them mimicking the sound of the bass guitar. As usual, Tiny and I stood shoulder to shoulder.

A fight broke out between two rockers jostling for position at the front of the stage, a bottle got smashed, and others joined in. The fracas broke up as one of the Mohican-donning rockers stumbled away with blood dripping from his head. Tiny and I steered clear of getting drawn into the melee.

The smoke still bellowed, the lighting continued to strobe, and the bass guitar continued its hypnotic rhythm.

*Dum, dum, dumdum, dumdum dundum, dundum.*

After what seemed an age, just as the crowd became impatient, the band appeared from the depths of the smoke, with the bass player continuing his riff. The tunnel lit up, and the excitement in the crowd rose. Tiny looked over at me with his big grin.

*Dum, dum, dumdum, dumdum dundum, dundum.*

Eventually, there was movement from deep within the tunnel, and slowly, out walked the lead singer with his signature bright red spikes, a pair of round steampunk sunglasses, and what looked like a pair of baggy white pajamas with Japanese characters daubed on them.

He came to the front of the stage, staring out across the crowd, as the rhythm of the lone guitar continued. The crowd roared, and the singer just stared back at them as the bass continued its drone.

Anticipation and a certain uneasiness grew as the man with the red hair and pajamas, the Godfather of Punk Rock himself, just stared for what seemed an age through his tinted shades, until he eventually spoke with his usual manic, crazy, unpredictable, and overpronounced roll of words, as if he were some sort of crazy witch doctor.

He gave one last menacing stare at the audience, and the crowd erupted as the words rolled out: "Why don't you lot just fuck off?"

# 2
# ADAMANT

WM

Ten years earlier

1973

Yorkshire

**I SAT AT THE KITCHEN** table with my father, mother, and sister over a lunch of fish 'n' chips with alphabet spaghetti. It seemed there was a big family announcement brewing as I nibbled on my meal and avoided the putrid tinned excuse for spaghetti, watching and listening carefully.

As we ate, my mother started explaining. "Well, children, your father and I have been looking at the local school options for when you get to secondary age," she said, looking at my father for his support.

"Well, yes, we are not sure they are the right place for you to be educated," my father added.

I had heard stories of kids being sent to boarding schools, and that had been my fear over the previous weeks as I listened at the top of the stairs to my mother and father discuss schools while watching the ITN *Ten O'Clock News*—a ritual of misery back then, as there was not much good news to be heard, or at least that was what I gathered at the time.

Ironically, Peter, Paul, and Mary were blasting out an old classic, one of my mother's favorites, on the radio on the kitchen counter: "Leaving on a Jet Plane." That added to the atmosphere and my dread in fearing the worst.

My friend Jeffrey had lasted only a year at some boarding school in Scotland, learning only two things: (1) boys from Scotland hated boys with English accents, and (2) his head was the perfect fit for an Adamant toilet—enough to plug the flush away and nearly enough to drown him. I closed my eyes briefly, thinking of the scene of my friend upside down with his head in the toilet, and then quickly returned to the conversation at hand.

"And you know we really like the Lake District—the scenery, the countryside, blackberry picking, the lake, the boat," my father said.

My sister and I nodded. We both loved our trips to the lakes and our boat, which my father had named after my sister, despite the long, arduous single-road hike across the Pennines amid the smell of clutches burning out and the evidence of cars stranded on the side of the road. I could smell a similar odor as we sat there, thinking it was my memory making connections with my imagination.

After leaving the Ford Motor Company as sales director, my father now owned a couple of garages that did car sales, service, and petrol, and as far as I could see, he was doing pretty well for himself. We had a new car every few months, always some top-of-the-range model, usually with leather and usually fast. My favorite was the Ford Capri, which was bright orange, with a vinyl roof and a three-liter engine. As I sat in the back, egging my father on, with his cigarette dangling from his mouth, we got over a hundred miles per hour. It was my first time going that fast; hence, I created my connection to that hero of a car.

A few months later, one Saturday morning, when I learned my father was about to sell the Capri while I was with him at the garage, I locked myself in the car, refusing the prospective buyer access to the car. It was too precious; the Ford Capri and I had a bond. However, my effort was in vain; the car went and was replaced by some other top-of-the-ranger.

So as my family sat there, I thought the discussion was a move to send us to boarding school in the lakes.

Suddenly, my mother looked around and jumped up from her seat in a panic. "Walter! Walter!"

I hadn't seen Mum so animated since the rabbits had had babies—a lot of them. This time, the chip pan was on fire on the stove. Mother had forgotten to turn it off.

My dad had been in the army during the war, part of the Royal Electrical and Mechanical Engineers. He had been part of the Normandy landings, and although he only told me the good stories when I was that age, in that moment of panic and apparent danger, I recalled a story he had told me about the fuel lines of his dual-engine landing craft coming undone and causing them to slow down with all the might of the German guns and armaments coming down upon them.

Of course, he'd managed to fix it, and as I watched the now raging fire from the chip pan, my father, as cool as a cucumber, opened the kitchen window wide; wet a towel; threw it over the pan; picked up the pan, with the flames fighting to get through the wet towel and back to the oxygen; and threw it out the window onto the back lawn. The panic was over.

That was my dad—always the fixer.

After a few minutes of waiting for Mum's hyperventilating to slow down and for Dad to make sure the fire was fully out, the kettle was on for a cup of tea, and the family announcement resumed.

In all the panic, I had managed to avoid the tinned spaghetti and had thrown it away in the bin amid the confusion. My father took over the conversation from there.

"Well, kids, your mother and I were thinking. We've found a beautiful house in Bowness-on-Windermere, between the town and the lake, with good schools—"

"What about the garages, Dad?" I asked, interrupting. I spent a lot of weekends there, hanging out with the mechanics, helping with the petrol deliveries, and watching the salespeople and their techniques and the flow of fancy cars. I had gotten connected to the business, and I liked my trips as the garage owner's son.

My dad looked at me and smiled. He knew how much I loved the garages and that one day I wanted to work there—I had told him plenty of times.

"We have a buyer for the garages. I am meeting them on Monday to do the deal."

"So we are moving then?" I asked, trying to mask my disappointment and my enthusiasm. I didn't like my current school. In fact, I'd hated it from day one; the teacher had had to drag me kicking and screaming from my mum. In one playground incident, I'd run after a plane in the sky straight into the climbing frame and split my chin open, leading to a trip to the hospital and six stitches. Then there were the bullies. I had pushed them off a wall one day when they were teasing me, unintentionally breaking one of their arms in the fall. As a result, I'd gotten the cane right across my hand, which really hurt, never mind the humiliation of it.

Apart from the potential horror of a boarding school in Scotland, it seemed to me almost any change was good right now.

We were moving, and that was that.

We moved that summer, and soon it was my first day at my new school, courtesy of the Church of England. My parents had decided to move away from the hustle and bustle of the metropolis and to the idyllic world of *Swallows and Amazons*.

Courtesy of Marks and Spencer, I was outfitted like Little Lord Fauntleroy in my color-compliant uniform, but I added corduroy to my shorts, suede for my shoes, and leather for my coat, and thanks to my mother, I had a Paul McCartney bowl haircut to top off the look.

I stuck out like the proverbial sore thumb.

The kids in my class were the children of farming stock, restaurant owners, chefs, builders, rangers, gamekeepers, and poachers. I was the exception, not only the son of a businessman but also from the other side of the Pennines.

The combination of my background and dress kept away the boys, who were not sure what to do with me, but it was an attraction to the girls, even at that tender age. Seemingly, the difference piqued their interest, a phenomenon I would experience at various points in my life and one of my first lessons that being different was actually okay after all.

Alison Appleby was the first girl on my radar—or, rather, I was on hers. Hers was the first love letter I ever received— maybe my only love letter. She was sweet, a local farmer's daughter, and sent a proposal of marriage. I blushed, too shy to address her, and we never mentioned it, but during class, I often found her staring, smiling, and fluttering her eyelashes at me. I would smile back and blush again. I was, after all, only eight!

That said, I did have some exposure to romance, as I already had read the novels about Tom Sawyer and Huckleberry Finn and Tom's girlfriend of sorts, Becky.

I was fond of my first teacher, Ms. Coward. She was old, or at least that was my perspective—back then, anyone over thirty felt old. As my mother often told me regarding the sense of one's own age, "If the schoolteacher, policeman, and doctor look young, then that probably means you are old." I wouldn't fully appreciate those wise words until much later.

Ms. Coward taught us English, reading, writing, and cursive. I could write the alphabet in one motion, without leaving the page, joined up. Every time I did so later on, I thanked her for that life skill, not that I used it much.

She persuaded me to enter a writing competition, and I ended up winning. I was a published author, although in a somewhat limited fashion: "Happiness is like a disease; it spreads." One line, seven words, and a great impact, or at least I thought so at the time. I was famous, at least for a day.

I received the handwritten note in an envelope from my newfound admirer.

> We have forty acres and hundreds of cattle and sheep. One day I would like to marry you, have lots of children together, and live happily forever on my farm. SWALK.

I was only eight; nevertheless, it was invigorating that someone thought she might want to marry me. Not that I really understood what that meant or the implications—that was a lesson I would learn later in life.

"What does SWALK mean?" I asked Nikki and Jacqui Swanson, a pair of sisters I had taken a liking to.

Nikki and I sat together each day at lunch, taking in the culinary delights. Our favorite was steamed pudding and pink custard on Thursdays. I half hoped for a similar letter from Nikki, for her cuteness and ski-jump nose. Her older sister, Jacqui, had the ability to hold her nose, blow, and squirt water from her tear ducts. I thought it was a cool trick and spent many hours trying to replicate it myself, but to no avail. Jacqui was talented, and her sister was cute.

As the sisters listened to my question, they giggled and made me feel embarrassed in realizing my naivete, and they both said together, "Sealed with a loving kiss!"

My embarrassment was full beam. I looked away, thanked them, pushed my love letter into my pocket, and went to find somewhere to hide on the playground.

I came across a boy from my class, Timothy Timpson. He was nicknamed Tiny Tim by the other kids. Not that he was small—far from it. It was a play on his name and the character from Charles Dickens's *A Christmas Carol*.

I hadn't really connected with any of the boys, but I hadn't had much chance to talk to Tiny yet. He was also alone, looking on as the other boys played football. As I approached, he had a big grin on his face, giggling in a deep and hefty manner. He had broad shoulders and a big mop of dark hair, and I already knew I liked him from class. I introduced myself formally, reaching out to shake his hand. That was what my father had taught me and what I had learned while observing the salesmen plying their trade at the garages. It seemed the right thing to do.

Tiny looked down at my hand as though I had just thrust a burning firework his way and, for an awkward moment, didn't know how to respond. Eventually, he reached out, nearly crushing my fingers in his grip. As soon as he let go, I quickly retreated from the handshake, trying not to show any pain.

"I know who you are, posh boy. Willy Mitchell," he said, patting me on the back and almost knocking me over. "Everyone knows who you are. Not much goes on in these parts without word spreading. They call it the jungle drums," he added, smiling away.

I looked around, thinking about drums in the jungle, Michael Caine in Rorke's Drift in *Zulu*, *Tarzan of the Apes*, *The Jungle Book*, and many legendary phrases, including, "Don't throw those bloody spears at me!"

He said, "You know, word gets around. That's all. Don't fret. The name's Tiny. Tiny Tim."

We hung out, watching the boys play football, until the whistle blew, and it was time to get back to class. We walked back together—as friends, I hoped.

I liked our new home. It was a cool twelve-bedroom Victorian Lakeland Slate home. It had formal gardens to the front, a conservatory, a reception lined with mosaic, a formal dining room overlooking the lawns, a snug living room adorned with fancy chandeliers, and even a bar. It also had a huge kitchen with an old original AGA stove, and I had my own bedroom at the top of the house.

It seemed my parents were using the proceeds from the sale of the garages and our home on Shell Lane to refurbish and upgrade the residence to turn it into a bed-and-breakfast inn. My father always had been entrepreneurial, and opening up a swanky little inn for the elite set of well-heeled tourists made perfect sense in the Lake District. As a little kid, I thought the prospect of living in a tourist attraction seemed exciting.

Each day, the property was a throng of construction workers fixing the place up, including an old man I befriended named Billy. He was really old, at least as old as my grandad. Billy always wore a tweed suit to work, with a white collarless shirt, a matching waistcoat, a flat cap, and round-rimmed spectacles, and he always had great stories to tell. I always liked a good story.

Billy was like a character from a Tintin book. Each day, when I got home from school, I would seek him out in the hope he would share one of his tales.

He had a metal tiffin in which he packed his lunch each day, hot or cold. It had three layers to compartmentalize his daily delights. He said he'd bought the tiffin from a Chinaman, a fellow construction worker, while working on the Sydney Harbor Bridge in Australia.

He also had a teakettle he'd purchased from the same coworker way back when. It was of similar construction to the tiffin: plain metal, with a handle on top, the size of an old-fashioned pint milk bottle.

Billy would show me his trick of whirling the lidless flask around his head without losing a drop of tea. It was kinda cool, or so I thought back then. I later learned about gravitational effects and g-force in physics, and the trick made more sense. I was always one for understanding not just the *what* but also the *why*.

Billy had been all over the place. In the Great War, he'd fought the Hun in the Red Fields of France. He had also served in World War II and been a prisoner at Colditz. In between, he had traversed the globe to Australia and China, sailed through the Panama Canal, seen the ancient pyramids, and even been to New York on his way back home. My eyes were alight as he told me his tales.

Billy was no ordinary construction worker, and I would sit with him, often for hours, as he glazed windows, built a dry stone wall, or lunched from the delights of his tiffin. He would pour me a mug of his milky tea and usually give me a digestive biscuit treat, sometimes a chocolate-covered one.

Billy reminded me of my own grandpa, whom I would hang out with back in Shell Lane as he planted sunflower seeds and told me stories of his own travels, including stories of a meeting with Harry McNish, the 1914 Shackleton expedition, the *Endurance*, Elephant Island, and the *James Caird*.

I missed my grandfather, and I would miss Billy when he was gone. I was not fully aware of the true implications of human mortality, of the finality of death, but my grandfather's passing marked the first emergence of my thinking on the subject. Death would become a sort of strange, unwanted, and even hated companion for its constant presence in the shadows of my well-traveled and adventurous life. As an eight-year-old, I was oblivious of what my future might hold. I lived for the moment, as most young boys did.

# 3
# MR. JONES
**WM**
1974
The Lake District

**MY DAD ENJOYED FORMULA ONE** racing, and his hero of the track was Emerson Fittipaldi in his black John Player Special Tyrrell.

It was okay to advertise cigarettes back then, and Gillespie's, our corner shop on the way to school, had individual cigarettes for sale, including a match to light them, available to the kids as they stopped by to get football cards, Marvel comics, Tintin episodes, sweets, and candy.

Fittipaldi was joined by other drivers of the day, including Niki Lauda, Mario Andretti, and British driver James Hunt. My dad and I religiously watched the races together on our television at home.

Every Saturday was wrestling, and we would watch the likes of Giant Haystacks and Big Daddy romp around the ring in their strange outfits and with even stranger moves.

We also watched boxing, the heavyweights, including one of my father's most admired people on the planet, Muhammad Ali, and the famous Rumble in the Jungle. "Float like a butterfly, sting like a bee" was my father's adopted saying from Ali and one he would repeat to me often through the years.

My new friend Tiny started coming around the house, first to meet Billy and then more and more to hang out, watch TV with my dad, and listen to music in my room. Tiny did not talk much about his home, his parents, or his own family. It wasn't that I didn't care; I just never really thought to ask.

I had a skylight in my room that led up to the roof. Tiny and I would go up there secretly and sit on the slates, looking out at the world below and around us. We would lie on our backs, looking at the stars in the sky, and allow our dreams to take us to distant and different lands.

"What do you want to do when you get older?" I asked Tiny as we lay on the roof one night. There was a long pause. I guessed he was thinking; we were looking at the stars, distracted. Time didn't matter much back then.

"I don't know, Willy. One day to get out of this place and travel the world."

I saw the stars above in front of me and considered his response. "Me too. I can almost reach them, see them, and be in them. That's where I want to be one day. In the stars."

The next day, back at school, it was a Tuesday, a spring morning. After assembly, Mr. Jones, the headmaster, was going to conduct rehearsals for the school choir. Tiny and I were both interested in joining. We both fancied ourselves as would-be musicians, but in the absence of talent, if that pursuit failed, as it likely would, then singing was the next best option.

The whole school lined up in rows like soldiers. Tiny and I stood next to each other, both hopeful, keen to get into the choir and gain access to the privileges it brought, including trips away from school, free passes on some of the more mundane classes, and avoidance of the dreaded swimming lessons.

Mr. Jones was a Welshman and a keen brass band musician, conductor, and choir man.

Mr. Jones sang everything. Even when he was just talking, telling a story, or telling someone off, the words came out as if he were singing. He was a harmonious orator, I thought at the time.

The school started to sing: "And did those feet in ancient time walk upon England's mountains green? And was the holy Lamb of God on England's pleasant pastures seen?"

Mr. Jones walked up and down the rank and file like a sergeant major, listening intently to each pupil as we sang out the words to "Jerusalem," occasionally tapping kids on the shoulder as an indication they hadn't made the grade, and they would walk out of the assembly hall with their heads bowed in shame and their dream of being in the school choir shattered.

I could hear Tiny belting out the words next to me. After our rehearsals in my bedroom, I was a bit skeptical if he would make the cut, but I didn't want to dampen his enthusiasm. He sounded more like a football or rugby supporter singing the national anthem in the stands before a big game.

"Bring me my bow of burning gold! Bring me my arrows of desire! Bring me my spear! O clouds, unfold! Bring me my chariot of fire!"

As stirring as it was in the moment, the school choir candidates were thinning, and quickly, only about a third of the original choir parade remained. As Mr. Jones had thus far skipped past Tiny and me, I was beginning to think we had gotten away with it and might just get through. We were building up to the finale as Mr. Jones homed in on me and Tiny. I puffed out my chest and belted out the words as if I were Pavarotti himself.

"I will not cease from mental fight, nor shall my sword sleep in my hand, till we have built Jerusalem in England's green and pleasant land."

Mr. Jones listened intently for a few seconds, leaning over uncomfortably close. I could feel the heat of his breath, which smelled of coffee, and the pressure. I glanced my eyes left without moving my head, facing forward, trying to get some sign from him.

After what seemed like an age, he looked at me; smiled; tapped me on the right shoulder as my indication I had not made the cut; and, in his deep Welsh male choir voice, said, "Nice try, my boyo. Maybe next year."

That was it. I was devastated and made my walk of shame out of the assembly hall and back to Ms. Coward's class—no privileges for me. Dreaded swimming lessons were still on the agenda.

Those rejected rallied together and took herd comfort in collective failure, including Tiny, who was kicked out moments after I was.

"I told you we couldn't sing." Tiny grinned and slapped me on my shoulder, nearly knocking me over.

Later that afternoon, we had our cycling-proficiency class. Tiny and I collected our bikes and wheeled our way to the running track and sports field at the back of the school and joined the others. Girls were in one group, and boys were in the other.

While waiting for the instructor, we raced around the running track on our various makes and styles of bikes. I had a top-of-the-range road racer with low-profile tires and ten gears—anything my parents could do to make me stand out even more. The rest of the kids had bikes of various styles and costs, including hand-me-downs and bikes begged, borrowed, and, in some cases, maybe even stolen—an array of grifters and choppers. Tiny had a black-and-red chopper that was ideally suited for his character and stature.

After a couple of laps, we assembled, ready for the serious lesson in front of us: how to stay alive and not get squashed on the roads.

A couple of weeks later, Tiny somehow snagged a bulk order of topless glamour playing cards, which made their way around the school, and those who managed to get a pack privately prized the novelty. Truth be known, we had no idea what they were, as none of the people we knew looked even remotely like that anyway. They might have been pictures of aliens from outer space as photos of the fairer sex. They had no meaning or resemblance to anything we could relate to, apart from Ms. Atkinson later on.

A few weeks later, passing our cycling-proficiency test was a big deal; it was our first license to take to the roads. At least our parents had some confidence that we wouldn't get squashed or killed on the streets of our little northern town.

We dabbled in competitive games, but the more serious stuff would come later, in high school. Tiny, a boy called Batey, and I ran the four-hundred-yard dash. I steamed around the final bend, puffing like a steam train—always a source of amusement for Tiny and a lasting memory. Nevertheless, I won!

My family's house was now almost finished. My storyteller and friend Billy had left, and I missed him, his stories, his adventures, his kettle trick, his tea, and certainly his chocolate-coated digestive biscuits.

My father was putting the finishing touches on the house, carpeting, painting, displaying pictures, and unpacking boxes of our Christmas ornaments.

Tiny and I would go to the local auction house with him to buy new furniture and odds and ends to dress the house. After all, we had a big house to fill. I loved the thrill of the auctions—the sight of my father raising his paddle in the air, bidding, and the feeling of success as the auctioneer's hammer came down with a call of "Sold to the gentleman in the corner, number seventeen hundred!"

Tiny and I often went to the bric-a-brac shop down the street, an old Nissen hut converted into an emporium of old and fascinating things. It provided hours of amusement as we sifted through old medals from the First and Second World Wars; old contraptions, trying to work out their purposes; Singer sewing machines; typewriters; old coins; stamps; and military hats and clothing from both sides of the lines. One day we spotted a not-too-old record player in its own carrying case, which looked like a miniature suitcase. I mustered my savings and made the purchase, deciding it would be better than borrowing my mother's old player for us to listen to our music at night. It also had a built-in radio, which was kind of cool back then.

Our first Christmas, Uncle Tommy and the rest of the clan descended upon us. The house was big enough to accommodate all my aunties and uncles, my cousins, and my grandma, plus my mother, father, sister, and me—twenty-eight of us in total. Little did I realize that was a dry run before welcoming paying guests to stay at our home, which was now being renamed Elim Bank Hotel. A new sign was stored in the garage, and there were two hanging attachments: Vacancies and No Vacancies.

Having the family around was always fun. With all of us together, occasionally, inevitably, Uncle Tommy would at some point kick off with one of his brothers, and usually, my grandma would put him in his place, often with the use of her handbag as a deterrent around his head. "Och, Tommy, behave, will yer?" she would shrill.

Nevertheless, I liked my uncle Tommy. He always had a good story to tell about his exploits, wild times, travels, and secrets. Uncle Tommy had three girls in the quest for a son and heir, and in the absence of that, he took a liking to me as the next best thing.

He became a civil engineer eventually but spent many years as a mariner. He always had a story in him, especially after a couple of whiskys. I always got the sense my family was full of secrets, and I sensed that if anyone new those stories, it would be my uncle Tommy.

After the break and into early spring, the dreaded Swim Day arrived. Tiny and I had heard some insights and horrific stories from the older kids: the cold, dark depths; the brutal march across the yard; the stern lecture beforehand; and the shock of the ice-cold water.

"Why can't they have a heated pool like elsewhere?" I asked my mother.

She just shrugged, as if to say that was just how it was.

That was the way of it back then, especially with my mother's side of the family. You were simply to accept and be grateful for what you got dished up—not just for supper but in life too—but at the same time rue what you didn't have without expecting it or trying to do anything to attain it. In other words, you were to put up with it and complain but not be prepared to put the effort in to chase your dreams.

There were a lot of people like that in those days. "Mediocrity is a disease that spreads" was my revised version of my previously published line.

My father, however, was different. Although he had been through a lot, he was always striving to be better and to grow, seeking progress, but at the same time, he was happy with what he had, taking comfort in the knowledge "It is better to have tried and failed than to have never tried at all." He often said that to me in his regular life lessons.

On the dreaded day, I trudged up the hill from our new home, a two-mile walk, with my backpack full of kit, books, pens, and my speedo and towel. I was about to experience the horrors of swimming lessons in those days.

I met Tiny in class, and he looked as apprehensive as I felt. Notably, a handful of kids called in sick that day.

As spring was barely breaking, we were unceremoniously ordered to the changing rooms to shyly don our swim trunks, and with rolled-up towels underneath our arms, wearing speedos and white plimsolls, we frog-marched to the outdoor pool across the other side of the campus.

That was the north of England, not the south of France or Portugal, where my father often took us for the holidays. The temperatures were brutal.

Twenty-two nine-year-old girls and boys marched across the playground from one end to the other, almost naked and with no protection from the elements. I thought that was bad, but it quickly got a lot worse.

Tiny and I exchanged nervous glances. Tiny was as white as a sheet.

As the teacher opened the padlocked gates to the pool for seemingly the first time that year, we walked inside onto a concrete rectangle. The still, deep blue water below looked like the depths of some faraway polar ocean.

"Right, boys and girls, welcome to your first swimming lesson," the teacher said, and he went on to describe the danger of the lakes that surrounded us both in the summer and in the ice of the cold winters.

"Learning to swim is fun, but it also may one day save your life." He gave his stark warning.

I was so cold I couldn't think straight, never mind listen. My teeth chattered uncontrollably as I stood on the side of the icy depths.

The news wasn't getting any better. "This is an unheated pool and therefore is very cold, and you will need to immerse in the water together and embrace the shock of the cold. Lean against the side, lift your legs, and start kicking."

I looked around at my classmates, and they looked at me. It was the first time in my life I had witnessed looks of fear painted across faces.

"Five, four, three, two, one," the teacher called out, and then the whistle sounded.

One by one, we jumped in. I was the last one. I braced myself, jumping feet first, and the rush of cold around my body hit me like a brick wall. I surfaced as quickly as I could—it seemed like a century—and grabbed the concrete edge and started kicking frantically in a vain effort that my bodily movement would warm me up in the insanely cold water.

The thirty-minute lesson lasted forever, and no one was more relieved than I was to hear the whistle and scramble out of the pool to the relative warmth of the spring morning and escape the horrors of the water below.

We grabbed our towels; wrapped them around ourselves, feeling the warmth and the familiar and comforting smell of our mothers' chosen washing powders; and scampered back to the changing room. We were delighted to get back into our clothes. We took no showers, and the lasting odor of the excessive chlorine lingered for the remainder of the day.

It was like a dawning, a harsh welcome to a new world. I felt it was the first time in my life I had faced the harsh reality and brutality of life, but then I realized that wasn't true; I had a predating memory of such atrocities from my previous school.

Back in Yorkshire, during a summer break, my sister and I volunteered to babysit the class budgerigar for the holidays. One morning about ten days in, I came downstairs to find Percy lying at the bottom of the cage, praying to Allah. He lay on his back with feet in the air, dead.

My mum threw a hissy fit, and upon my father's return from work, we sat as a family and agreed to buy a replacement. We did, no one ever noticed, and Percy II made it into the *Yorkshire Book of Records* as being the oldest living budgerigar in the history of the world, or so we joked.

My sister told me I had been adopted as a young child and said my real mother was a witch. She would tell me her cooked-up tales as I fell asleep in the bottom bunk of our bedroom.

I was mad keen on football and would kick my ball all day long against the wall, dreaming of playing for Manchester United one day—back and forth, dribbles, free kicks, penalties. One afternoon, my sister came outside for the third time. "It's time for tea," she said, and she snatched my ball from me. My reaction was to punch her, and I broke her nose. Blood was everywhere. My father was summoned from his work, and upon his emergency return home, he belted me, buckle end first. I would never forget that, and my sister never fully forgave me either. But I was only seven or eight years old; I didn't know what I was doing.

In our new house, I found a sense of contentment I had lacked earlier. Perhaps it was the routine of a somewhat settled life with my family. Of course, I was still just a boy. The troubled times of my adolescence remained years off in my future. I would sit in my new room with my newly acquired record player, listening to my mother's old records of the Beatles, Elvis Presley, Buddy Holly, and such and my newly acquired *Jeff Wayne's Musical Version of War of the Worlds*. I immersed myself in the story, imagining myself fighting the alien invaders from distant planets.

By helping my mum and dad out with family chores, I earned some money, and I purchased my first two real records: *Hotel California* by the Eagles and "Bohemian Rhapsody" by Queen. I was transcended to a far-off land, to some other place that played like a movie in my head.

Maybe it was the lack of TV choices, *War of the Worlds*, Tolkien, or all of the above, but I dreamed in Technicolor. I could visualize the scenes and places and, without the use of any substances, transport myself to a different place. I was actually there in my mind, and my imaginings and reflections began to shape me as a person, as the man I would someday become after spinning out of control in my teens.

# 4

# BILL GRUNDY

WM

## December 1, 1976
## Thames Television

**I WAS NOT SURE EXACTLY** when I heard my first f-word. My mother did not swear at all. My father never swore; *bloody* and *bugger* were about as flowery as it got. It might have been Tiny when he called in sick to avoid the prospect of our second swimming lesson, saying, "Fuck that for a game of soldiers." Or maybe it was Bernard Manning, the Mancunian comedian, who famously got banned from television for a joke. I was watching that night to hear him say, "I got home from the pub the other day and said to the wife, 'Hey, luv, we've won the lottery; pack yer bags.' The wife said, 'That's great news, luv. Where're we going? Costa del Sol? The Caribbean? The Maldives?' I said, 'Listen here, luv. We've won the lottery. Pack yer bags, and fuck off!'"

It was an awkward moment in our front room. I looked around at my mother and father to gauge their reactions. My father just stood up, turned the television off, and announced that it was time for bed.

There were many defining moments in those days. There was much doom and gloom, and with just three channels to choose from, our television was our window to the world. We had no internet, no on-demand streaming, and no YouTube. Maybe you had a video recorder if you were lucky enough; otherwise, you had to be in front of the box at the right time, or you would miss the program.

The newspapers were the second source of information, if a story was big enough to be featured. One story appeared across the front pages of all the red tops: the Sex Pistols and punk rock had made the mainstream news and caught the attention of society.

The band Queen had apparently been booked to appear on the *Today* show, but because of Freddie Mercury's toothache, Malcolm McLaren managed to get the Sex Pistols in their place as substitutes.

Chaperoned by McLaren, the original Pistols lineup of Johnny Rotten, Paul Cook, Steve Jones, and Glen Matlock transitioned from the green room into the studio to meet their interviewer, Bill Grundy, on *Today.*

The four sat down, and fellow punk rockers Siouxsie Sioux, Steven Severin, Simon Barker, and Simone stood behind them.

Tiny and I watched in our family room.

> GRUNDY. [*Looks to the camera.*] They are punk rockers. The new craze, they tell me. Their heroes? Not the nice, clean Rolling Stones. You see they are as

drunk as I am; they are clean by comparison. They're a group called the Sex Pistols, and I am surrounded by all of them.

JONES. [*Reading the autocue.*] In action.

GRUNDY. Just let us see the Sex Pistols in action. Come on, kids.

The screen cut to footage of the band at one of their gigs—the crowds, fans, spiked hair, fashion, piercings, safety pins, studs, and swastikas. I was fascinated. My father had fought against the Nazis in the war, and I had never seen that symbol outside a military context before.

The clip showed the lead singer, Johnny Rotten, with his manic ginger spikes, shouting out the lyrics into his microphone. The song was "No Fun": "Yeah, all my friends, no fun. Fuck my friends; they're gone. They all left one by one, and now the summer's done; they don't need more fun. Ya, I drive around on my own. I'm rich, but my AC broke."

The footage cut to the audience freak show, including the rear end of what I assumed was a woman with a black thong. Tiny and I were mesmerized. What was this?

"Don't check no mail. No phone. And I tell them I'm not home. And I keep to myself, fuck with no one else. And I know it's my fault, but I don't care. And I keep to myself. Who are we to pretend? And I know it's my fault; it will never end. Yeah, all my friends, it's no fun."

Rotten kept repeating the chorus to "No Fun" as the clip faded back to the studio.

GRUNDY. I am told that that group [*hits his knee with sheaf of papers*] have received forty thousand pounds from a record company. Doesn't that seem, er, to be slightly opposed to their antimaterialistic view of life?

> GRUNDY. Really?
> MATLOCK. Oh yeah.
> GRUNDY. Well, tell me more then.
> JONES. We've fuckin' spent it, ain't we?

MATLOCK. No, the more the merrier.

Swear words on television back then were taboo. I tuned back in, as I didn't want to miss a word. I had never seen anything like it. What was this?

> GRUNDY. I don't know. Have you?
> MATLOCK. Yeah, it's all gone.
> GRUNDY. Really?
> JONES. Down the boozer.

I had heard my uncle Tommy refer to the *boozer*, and it stimulated an image of him fighting with his brothers and of my grandma batting him on the head with her handbag.

> GRUNDY. Really? Good Lord! Now I want to know one thing.
> MATLOCK. What?
> GRUNDY. Are you serious, or are you just making me, trying to make me laugh?

It seemed to me the interviewer was trying to pick a fight, and I wondered, without knowing the background and the original lineup, why they were even on TV.

> MATLOCK. No, it's all gone. Gone.
> GRUNDY. Really?

MATLOCK. Yeah.
GRUNDY. No, but I mean about what you're doing.
MATLOCK. Oh yeah.
GRUNDY. You are serious?
MATLOCK. Mmm.
GRUNDY. Beethoven, Mozart, Bach, and Brahms
have all died.

I was on the edge of the sofa, taking in every moment, trying to work out what on earth I was watching.

ROTTEN. They're all heroes of ours, ain't they?
GRUNDY. Really? What? What were you saying, sir?
ROTTEN. They're wonderful people.
GRUNDY. Are they?
ROTTEN. Oh yes! They really turn us on.
JONES. But they're dead!
GRUNDY. Well, suppose they turn other people on?

Then, under his breath, just in earshot, Rotten responded.

ROTTEN. That's just their tough shit.
GRUNDY. It's what?
ROTTEN. Nothing. A rude word. Next question.
GRUNDY. No, no, what was the rude word?
ROTTEN. Shit.
GRUNDY. Was it really? Good heavens, you
frighten me to death.
ROTTEN. Oh all right, Siegfried.

The interviewer then turned to the four who stood behind the Pistols, including Siouxsie Sioux.

GRUNDY. What about you girls behind?
MATLOCK. He's like yer dad, inni, this geezer?

GRUNDY. Are you, er—
MATLOCK. Or your granddad.

Grundy then addressed Sioux directly. "What on earth is going on?" I said, thinking out aloud.

GRUNDY. Are you worried, or are you just enjoying yourself?
SIOUX. Enjoying myself.
GRUNDY. Are you?
SIOUX. Yeah.
GRUNDY. Ah, that's what I thought you were doing.
SIOUX. I always wanted to meet you.

She was clearly being sarcastic in a polite yet sort of disrespectful way.

GRUNDY. Did you really?
SIOUX. Yeah.
GRUNDY. We'll meet afterward, shall we?

Sioux pouted back at Grundy—another insult back. Jones picked up on Grundy's comment and piped up.

JONES. You dirty sod. You dirty old man!
GRUNDY. Well, keep going, chief. Keep going. Go on; you've got another five seconds. Say something outrageous.

This was TV like we had never witnessed before. I couldn't believe my eyes and ears that it was even allowed to be aired in those days. Normally, overly conservative, overly polite commentators would use phrases like "a bit annoying" or "the crowd was a little flustered" in even the most extreme circumstances of riots, bombings, or even war. This interview was different and obviously out of control.

> JONES. You dirty bastard!
> GRUNDY. Go on again.
> JONES. You dirty fucker!

All the punk rockers in the studio laudably laughed with big smirks on their faces.

> GRUNDY. What a clever boy!
> JONES. What a fucking rotter.

I couldn't believe my ears. "What a fucking rotter!" I started to see the funny side of what I was watching. Being able to say what you wanted in front of a figure of authority. Tearing up the rule book. Throwing it away. Just because someone wore a suit didn't mean he deserved respect. I thought about some of the teachers at my school.

> GRUNDY. Well, that's it for tonight. The other rocker, Eamonn—and I'm saying nothing else about him—will be back tomorrow. I'll be seeing you soon. I hope I'm not seeing you [the band] again. From me, though, good night.

The screen went blank at the end of the show and the end of the performance. I shook my head and turned to Tiny, who was equally dumbstruck, and we went to the kitchen for a glass of milk.

The next day, I grabbed my father's newspaper and read the article on the front page: "The Filth and the Fury!"

Until that point, the word *fuck* had only ever aired twice before in the history of British broadcasting.

The phones in the studio blew up, and with just twelve telephone lines into the studio, the call center couldn't cope with the volume, and calls ended up getting diverted to the green room, where the Sex Pistols and the others were waiting to leave. They started answering the calls of complaints and hurling abuse down the phone lines.

Malcolm McLaren was as white as a sheet, shaking his head, cursing at the group's performance, until the next day, when they were all over the newspapers. Then he took credit for his own genius idea.

The episode caused one of the biggest stinks in British television history.

The airing of an ill-advised meeting between a belligerent TV host and a rebellious young band, which turned into a foul-mouthed encounter, on teatime TV fundamentally changed British broadcasting, catapulted punk rock into the mainstream, and marked the beginning of the end of Bill Grundy's career.

Tiny and I just rolled around laughing our heads off. We had never seen anything like it, and we loved it. We were hooked! Fucking rotter!

# 5
# BOMBS

WM

1977

## Great Britain

**BY MY TEENS, I WAS** fascinated by the news and current affairs. The mid-1970s were a turbulent time in the United Kingdom, as they were elsewhere in the world, so the news was full of all kinds of stories. Great Britain was going through its darkest period since the Second World War. Despite leading the victory against the Nazis in Europe just thirty years earlier, the United Kingdom was considered the Sick Man of Europe, which was unbelievable to many, as the nation had made so many sacrifices to save so many lives over the past two world wars.

Watching the ten o'clock news was like watching a series of dramas unfold, better than most of the television shows. I would suffer my mother's choices of *Upstairs, Downstairs* and *Are You Being Served?* and would quietly enjoy the humor of *The Two Ronnies*, although to me, at that time, they were just a pair of old men trying to be funny. The highlight of my television viewing was the ITN *Ten O'Clock News.*

Of particular concern to me and my parents was the Provisional IRA. Its so-called freedom fighters kept on bombing things, blowing stuff up, and kidnapping and killing people. There was some monster they called the Yorkshire Ripper going around killing women with hammers. The miners, the car workers, the firefighters, even the undertakers were on strike, and unemployment was at its highest level since God was a boy. Yes, the news was filled with violence and death, and I found it depressing, but I still liked to watch. Mayhem captured my attention and imagination. The input was negative, of course, yet it gave me a sense even at that young age that life was no cakewalk for anyone.

The IRA might have been busy detonating high explosives wherever they could do the most damage, but they weren't alone. Tiny and I made our own sort of bombs. After all, we were boys growing up in the surroundings of fields, forests, and secluded places in the countryside. There was plenty of opportunity to get into mischief. We just needed the creativity.

One day we were with the Gascoigne brothers in the local park.

"So how big a bang do these babies make?" Tiny asked as Kelvin clubbed together a dozen matches with the red phosphorous tips all tightly together before wrapping them in tinfoil from my mother's kitchen.

"Yer know, loud enough." Kelvin giggled. His brother had also made one. Tiny and I just watched as they pushed them into the cracks of the slate wall.

"Now what?" I asked, a little nervous that we might damage the wall, injure ourselves, or catch the unwanted attention of the local bobby. The Gascoigne brothers had already been in trouble, and the police had visited their front door. My mother had warned of the dangers of a repeat at our house.

Kelvin lit a match and held it to the clump of matches, which fizzed to life like a Roman candle.

The three of us watched Kelvin's bomb-making attempt; our faces showed how underwhelmed we were.

"Was that fucking it?" asked Tiny. "You dragged us down here to show us that?"

"Wait!" Conrad shouted. "Watch this little beauty."

We all watched as he lit his own match bomb.

This time, with the aluminum foil packed around the matches tighter, there was a much bigger flare, but it was nowhere near the rocket-style expectations we had.

"Thanks for that bomb, boys!" Tiny shouted at the brothers as they continued in their bomb-making efforts. We trotted off across the park to the big conker tree by the swings, where we threw sticks and rocks at the branches to dislodge the dangling seeds of the horse chestnut.

A dozen of the ripe green-spiked shells fell to the ground. Tiny and I gathered them together and started peeling to reveal the hard brown conker within.

"Look at that beauty." Tiny held out his hand with a conker about half the size of a golf ball.

I looked over and said, "Impressive," speaking in a deliberately unenthusiastic way. Tiny was already the conker champion, and I suspected he had some secret to his preparation. It had long been rumored that he steeped them in vinegar and then baked them to make them as hard as bullets, but the rumor had not been proven yet. I had tried it at home myself, only for my dad to find them smoking from the AGA and stinking up the whole house.

I was settled in at school by then. I was fitting in better. I had gotten rid of my Paul McCartney haircut and my fancy Marks and Spencer clothes. Thanks to Tiny, my fashion designer, I had moved on to much more creative means of dress and adornment.

We would go to the local jumble sales, pick up secondhand clothes from the bric-a-brac shop, and repurpose old Teddy Boy stuff from Tiny's uncles. We watched for the latest trends and music in the NME magazine. We spent a bunch of time at Snaith's Action Replay record shop, spending our savings on the latest tunes.

But we also made bombs.

Years later, in the army, in a cadre in Castle Martin, South Wales, I learned how to make improvised explosive devices, or IEDs, out of old mortar shells and ammo cases filled with nuts, bolts, and screws, fueled by plastic explosives with the use of det cords. We had also made incendiary devices using old egg timers and razor blades. When the timer went off, the blade would spin and slice a plastic pouch of antifreeze to mix with potassium permanganate and burst into an almost inextinguishable flame. Two great learnings courtesy of Her Majesty if I wanted to blow something or somebody up or burn something down.

At least Tiny's and my exploits were a little safer and less destructive for the most part.

However, some of my forays with Tiny, even as we moved into adolescence, involved criminal activity. For example, one night on the lake, we snuck out of our bedrooms in the wee hours and stealthily ventured down to the docks, where we liberated a rowboat and rowed around the back of Belle Island to the yacht-mooring area. We spotted our target: a double-masted sailing yacht with a hatch cabin and a simple padlocked door on the back. We pulled the rowing boat alongside, tied it to the yacht, and boarded. The padlock was easy to snag open, and we made our way inside to see what bounty the yacht might behold. It was packed up for the winter, and we found a pair of sleeping bags, a signal torch, and some tins of baked beans and Fray Bentos pies in the cupboard, which we left. Then we found the booze cupboard, which we stacked into an old canvas hold-all.

In the kitchenette was a two-burner Calor gas cooker.

"We'll have that little beauty," Tiny said as he pulled out the hose from the counter and removed the cooker. "That'll come in handy for next week's camping trip at Steeley's." We grinned at each other in the dark.

Conscious that there was a night patrol on the lake, in order to avoid a knock on the door in the middle of the night, we got our bounty into our little rowboat; made the cabin look as if it hadn't been touched, at least from a distance; and slid back into the dark.

We decided to make camp on one of the nearby islands, got out the two sleeping bags and a couple of pillows, and opened a bottle of Jameson whiskey from the yacht.

"Just like fucking pirates." Tiny raised the bottle and grinned.

We enjoyed adventures in the nearby woods as well. We once built a big campfire behind Steeley's. He had been collecting wood for weeks, and it was piled high, about six feet tall. We invited a group of mates from school, mostly burgeoning punk rockers in various states of evolution. A couple of them had Mohicans, studs, leather jackets, the odd piercing, and an occasional tattoo, and almost every one of us wore Doc Martens. About twenty of us gathered with Steeley's beatbox blaring out the latest tunes on a compilation cassette he had put together.

We got one of the older mates to buy a ton of beer. We had a grill and some burgers and sausages and, for some reason, at least a dozen catering-size cans of Heinz baked beans.

As the beer flowed and some smoked dope, Tiny and I found some old tins of paint in the outside store and threw them onto the fire. We listened to the crackling and expansion of the tins and the whoosh as the lids burst and the contents met oxygen, sending flares up into the night. We found some spray cans of WD-40 and found they made good flamethrowers. We used lighters to ignite the vapor when we depressed the red button on top of the can, and flames roared outward for several feet, or at least that was what it seemed like then. Of course, we had no clue what damage we could do to ourselves if one of the cans blew up. The ignorance of youth.

As the kitchen closed down, there were ten tins of beans left, and as the party had become somewhat oblivious to their surroundings, Tiny and I placed the tins on the fire, retreated, and watched.

"Fucking watch this." Tiny smiled with his arms folded across his chest.

We could hear the metal creaking and expanding as the beans inside heated, expanded, and let off steam, until one by one, in a matter of thirty seconds, they all exploded, splattering baked beans all over the woods and the audience within.

"Fucking hilarious!" Tiny and I rolled around on the floor of the wood in uncontrollable laughter. I didn't think we had ever laughed so hard.

Steeley came out of the darkness with beans dripping from the top of his head. The frames of his glasses were broken and slanted. "What the fuck, boys?"

Tiny and I laughed even harder.

Those were heady days, and they laid the foundation for what was to come. I didn't lead an ordinary boyhood. The world seemed to be increasingly harsh and unwelcoming to me. Yet there were some good things happening too. Liverpool continued to dominate the football league with their tenth winning season, with the mighty Manchester United managing to snatch a victory against the Liverpudlians with a 2–1 win at Wembley. Red Rum won the Grand National for the third time, Her Majesty's ship *Invincible* launched, and that year was the year of the queen's Silver Jubilee.

Queen Elizabeth II—or, as our Australian cousins called her, Betty Two Strokes—born in 1926, was crowned on June 2, 1953, reigning after the death of her father in February a year earlier. It was a great excuse for the British people to get out on the streets and celebrate and to take our minds off all the misery that prevailed around us.

Excitedly, the people of the nation made preparations to line the streets from London to Birmingham, from Nottingham to Manchester, from Liverpool to Leeds, and even to our small northern town. At school, we prepared, making plans. Marching bands played, and we made flags and learned our recent history and the history of the monarchy. It was a time to pull up our socks, keep calm, and carry on.

Unemployment was high, and prospects were low for Britain's youth of the time. Amid disillusionment about the apparent decline and what seemed the demise of the British Empire, we slid into a depressive mediocrity.

A depressing, dead-end life was the reputation we had built for ourselves as a nation. We'd gone through the Great War, World War II, and now an economic decline that loomed large in the mind of most everyone who needed to work, which was most of us. We as a nation were on our knees. We had forgotten our soul, our drive, and our unwavering rebuff for defeat by anyone or anything at any time in our history.

As my friend Billy the builder would have said, we had lost our gumption.

The jubilee was a perfect time to find it, dust it off, try it on, and wear it with pride.

It was, however, a perfect storm. With little or no future, disillusioned, angry youth with little to do and no prospects led to the rise of a voice, an opportunity to, through a new form of music, be heard, make a point, and not just suck it up and complain but maybe make a difference.

The National Front were marching, protesting, and rioting on the streets of London, and in contrast, the

Campaign for Nuclear Disarmament was protesting the arms race between the Soviet Union and the United States, with the United Kingdom caught somewhere in the middle.

The Clash released their first album; Marc Bolan, lead singer of T-Rex, died in a car crash; and Queen released their "We Are the Champions" anthem. Meanwhile, the Sex Pistols got fired by their record label, EMI, after only one single release, due to their disruptive behavior on ITV's *Today* show and their misbehavior at London Heathrow a few weeks later.

"Disruptive behavior" was the phrase of the day as the middle class pushed back against the mood of the nation and its youth. The phrase made it to the north of England; to my school; and, much to my dismay, to my own school report—a charge I didn't deserve. My mother's, my father's, and my protestations, it stood and remained. My first high school report didn't get me off to the greatest of starts.

Our mate Johnny's older cousin returned home on leave from the army with a couple of thunder flashes and set one of them off underneath an upturned trash can. It let off a huge bellow that reverberated from the glebe and, amplified across the lake, could be heard for miles around, including at the local police station. Flashing blue lights descended upon us as we scarpered in opposite directions and made our escape via the various secret routes we had discovered.

Johnny's cousin got in serious trouble for that and ended up in the Colchester military prison as a result.

As the season opened up again, there was another explosion that could be heard across the lake. Tiny and I went down to investigate, and in Shepherds Boat Yard, Tiny and I saw a yacht we had been on a few weeks earlier in the middle of the night with its cabin blown right off, apparently due to a gas leak.

# 6
# ANGER IS AN ENERGY
# W⧸M
Fifteen years later
1992
St. Angelo Barracks, Enniskillen,
Northern Ireland

**I STRETCHED OUT ON MY** sorry excuse for a bed in my sorry excuse for a room in St. Angelo Barracks, a shithole of a place occupied by the Irish Guards for their first ever tour of the province. I had already been there for six months and had just one month left until I headed back home to the United Kingdom, back to my first wife and a troubled marriage with few miles left on the odometer. As I reflected morosely on my life, I thought about the events that had led me to where I was. Feeling guilt about the murder rush back in despite the passage of time, I made a conscious effort to push the painful moment out of my mind.

I thought of punk rock's mantra: "Anger is an energy." I thought that was about the truest thing I'd ever heard. I certainly believed it at the moment there in my bunk.

I sat up in bed, swung my legs over the side, and put both feet on the cold concrete floor. I picked up a letter from Tiny. It was addressed to the British Forces Post Office to protect my whereabouts.

When things got down and dirty, the powers that be sent in the troops. I loved the thrill of the hunt and the adrenaline rush of the firefights I'd been in, but for the most part, time in the military was nine parts boredom and one part absolute terror. I liked the terror part, which made me feel alive. I didn't so much like the boredom part, which made me sometimes want to have a blowout, which I occasionally did.

Before my deployment to Ireland, I had an incident with my sergeant major at the time. On the ranges, during our annual personal weapons test, or APWT, he took the piss out of me at the results of my practice rounds, not realizing I was fucking around, shooting at other people's targets, random objects, and even a goat that had somehow gotten onto the range.

Wearing my sand-colored beret, I was proud of my soldiering skills and, I admitted, somewhat arrogant. I told him to fuck off under my breath and proceeded to re-earn my marksman's badge over the forty minutes. "Fuck you!"

That night, he invited me and my wife to the sergeants' mess, and after dinner, he and I sat at the bar together. He'd been winding me up all night. The Skull, as he was called, was from some shithole former mining town in Wales. He was completely bald, and when he shouted, as his job often demanded, the veins in his head would pop out.

By that time, I was a full-fledged boxer, having boxed at light heavyweight level for the army and for my regiment, and rugby player. I was full of testosterone, fitness and energy, and a fair amount of skill. That night, port-fueled anger drove me to an altercation, and my reward was being sent to that shithole in Northern Ireland. I'd been in the army long enough to know better than to mouth off to a superior officer, but on that occasion, I couldn't help myself. I often joked that my stripes were on Velcro because I never knew when I might have to give them back. I had to do that a lot.

There had been incidents in childhood: my sister and the football, the bullying as a kid, and my rising through the ranks at high school as I defeated one challenger after another despite never once looking for it. Throughout the punk days of concerts, breakouts, and fights, Tiny and I, back to back, were not starters but were finishers.

I never really understood where it came from. My mother was not violent. My father, although he had served in the war, never showed any signs of violence, yet it was something I felt was somehow engrained in me. Maybe it was the Scotsman in me; the mix of the Glaswegian and the Border Reiver; and my ancestor Jock of the Park, his infamous half lugs, and his battle cry of "How dare you fucking mess wi' me!"

I turned the envelope in my hands, getting ready to open it, and on the back was *SWALK*. "Silly fucker,'" I said out loud to myself, as I had a habit of doing.

There had been the bullworker incident with the Blues and Royals, who'd decided it was a good idea to pick on me on Regimental Day. There had been the monkey wrench incident with three marines who'd tried to do the same.

Just a few weeks previously, I'd faced a big fucking Irish Guard, Queen's Troop—the tallest, though all were over six foot; the fittest; and, apparently, the hardest. I had put a stop to that legend on Paddy's Day. He had smacked me for no reason as my fellow soldier friend Moxy, a Blue and Royal, and I were chasing the jackpot on the fruit machine, the only day of drinking on the entire tour, and I had retaliated with a premium uppercut that had launched him off the top stair of the portacabin down to the ground in convulsions and out for the count.

I was in my prime and had the skills and the experience.

I grabbed a knife and opened the letter, and out dropped a rock of hashish—what looked like Moroccan black, from my limited knowledge. "Silly fucker," I said, and then I opened the letter.

> Willy,
>
> I thought I would send you a quick note to see how you're doing; it has been a while. God, I miss you, man!
>
> I called Christine the other week just to check in, and she told me you guys had a bit of a fallout. You should really look after her, Willy; she's a cracker and a sweetheart, and I have no idea how your ugly mug ever managed to land that one! But anyway, she sends her love and told me to tell you that she misses you and hopes you get home soon. She told me she was going to treat you to a holiday when you get back! Lucky boy! Can I come with you?

Same old, same old at this end. You know nothing ever changes around here! Still doing some building work, fixing fences, dry stone walls, and a couple of scaffolding projects. I'm doing some work with Biddy Baxter's old man and also the Stafford brothers.

On weekends, I team up with Big Bertha doing some bouncing at the Wheelhouse and occasionally the Stag's for Patrick. It's good—extra beer tokens! They both say hello!

I included a little treat for you. I hope it gets through customs! Careful, though—it's strong stuff. Just find a pin or a needle or any skinny, pointy object. Stick the rock on the tip, light the rock, stick it under a glass, and enjoy! I included the instructions on how to smoke hash under glass because I know you don't like doing drugs and don't know shit about stuff like this. Figured you might want to try some of the good shit, though.

All quiet on the western front. Hopefully catch up soon.

Cheers!

T.

I looked at the piece of dope wrapped in cellophane, reread his letter, and paused at the bit about Christine. I loved her too, and I regretted my actions that night long ago and truly hoped we would be together forever, as we had once promised.

"All quiet on the western front" was code meaning he had not heard anything with regard to the terrible occurrence in Paris. I hadn't heard from the homicide police either, thank God, but I had followed the newspaper reports about Parisian authorities investigating the mystery of a Russian punk rocker and a member of their own gendarmerie found dead in a wheelie bin.

In walked my roommate, taking a break from guard duty. "What's that yer got there, Willy?" He pointed at the letter on my lap. "A love letter from the missus?"

I shook my head. Norm was a likeable yet annoying sort of guy from Egremont or Whitehaven or some other god-awful town in the north of Cumbria with more sheep than people, where even the humans resembled sheep more than their own species.

"What's that?" He pointed his self-loading rifle at the lump of dope. "That's fucking weed, isn't it?" He had excitement in his voice. "Come on, Willy; break it out. I'm in need of some of that."

"But you're on guard tonight, yer silly fucker."

"Aye, I am, and putting up with that silly fucker Captain fucking Jacobs."

I knew whom he was referring to. In fact, everyone knew of Captain Jacobs, a Rupert who was convinced the next stray mortar coming over the perimeter fence had his name on it. He had taken to wearing his tin hat permanently, and at the slightest noise, bang, or even someone sneezing, he would dive for cover under the nearest table, vehicle, or rabbit hole.

"Imagine him in World War I! He'd be a fucking wreck."

"C'mon, Willy; crack it out."

I unpeeled the rock from its plastic wrapping, found an old glass, lit the Moroccan black, and put the glass on top, which filled with smoke. Norm and then I deeply inhaled the aromatic, pungent fumes; held in the smoke for as long as we could; and then repeated. Within five minutes, we were both absolutely wankered.

As I slid to the floor, losing complete feeling and control in my legs and, in fact, every part of my body except my head, I listened to Norm and his increasingly paranoid and frantic rants.

"Yer see, Willy, I haven't heard from my missus since I got here. Until last week, that is. Then I got a fucking letter to tell me she has fucking shacked up with fucking Jim Simpson!"

I looked over at him. "Who the fuck is Jim Simpson?"

Norm looked back at me as though I were crazy. I felt totally compos mentis apart from the paralysis I was experiencing from the neck down. I'd smoked weed before, albeit just once or twice and never as a habit. It just didn't do it for me the way it did for some of my other mates. But that was nothing like the high I got from the hash.

"Jim fucking Simpson is the geezer fucking my girl at home, Willy! I need to get home now and go see her. I need to get the fuck out of here!"

"What the fuck are you going to do, Norm—fucking swim?"

"No, I tell yer what I'm gonna do, Willy. I'm gonna go now and see Captain fucking Jacobs and get him to sign release papers tonight. Trust me, I will be gone by the morning."

I did my best to dissuade Norm from his suggested action, especially since he was on duty, had a fully loaded assault weapon in his hands, and was as high as a fucking kite.

As always, Norm ignored me. He went to see Captain Jacobs and held him up at gunpoint all night until he secured his release back to the United Kingdom, across the water—but instead of his hometown in Cumbria, he had the pleasure of going to Her Majesty's military prison in Colchester.

That night reinforced a valuable lesson I'd learned long ago. It was a simple one, but amazingly, few people seemed to get it: think before you act.

# 7
# CAREERS

**WM**

## Back to my youth

**WE NEEDED TO UNDERSTAND BOTH** the *what* and the *why*. That was the difference back then. That was how we were challenging the status quo: we did not just accept what we were told but asked why and demanded the answer. Too many people just accepted the status quo, got what they were given, and never questioned why.

Mr. Stephens was my careers teacher. I had a one-to-one meeting with him to try to work out my path in life. As high school progressed, I still had no real direction. I didn't know what I wanted to do for work, and I didn't much care at that point. I was curious what my careers instructor had to say, but only to a point.

As I entered his office right on time, he greeted me and told me to take a seat. I obliged as he shuffled through some papers in front of him—trying to familiarize himself with my case, I assumed.

"So, Willy, I see you like rugby, box, and play football; you like your music; and all the reports say you are very bright but somewhat of an underperformer for your potential. How do you feel about that, Willy?"

I didn't know how to answer. *Underperformer. What the fuck?* "I'm not sure I would classify myself as an underperformer, sir." I looked at him and smiled my best sarcastic smile.

I wanted to do well. I found the academic lessons easy for the most part—in fact, a breeze. I had no problem with exams; I passed everything and never failed once. I had opted in for all the appropriate lessons, including math, physics, chemistry, technical drawing, French, and German. I had opted out of biology, as the thought of dissecting frogs and mice put me off. *Why would anyone want to do that anyway?* Another unanswered question.

For the most part, I was pretty quiet and withdrawn. I had a bunch of friends but was only really close with Tiny. I was sociable, fit in, and was pretty popular, but the string of contenders I faced continually changed my life. I was always challenged and often scared as hell, but I never gave up and had never lost. I was prepared to do almost anything to win in a fight.

"I don't know, sir. I think I am actually pretty capable," I said.

Mr. Stephens just looked at me with his half-moon spectacles at the tip of his nose. He pulled out a pamphlet, *Careers with the Royal Mail*, and handed it to me.

I slowly and reluctantly reached out and grabbed it. "What's this, sir?" I was struggling to hold my smile.

"It's about careers with the Royal Mail," he said, matching my sarcasm.

"I can see that, sir. But what's this got to do with me?"

He paused for a moment, and from his expression, he clearly was struggling with the question. "Well, Willy, you might want to consider joining the Royal Mail." He smiled back at me.

"Oh, thanks a bunch, sir. Will there be anything else?"

He was already packing up his papers. "No, that's it, Willy."

"Thank you, sir."

I got up to walk out of his office and headed to the door. Under my breath, I mumbled, "Thanks a fucking bunch!" I shut the door behind me. "Fucking tosspot!"

Not long after my brief and unhelpful conversation with Mr. Stephens, Tiny and I climbed out of the skylight in my bedroom to light up a couple of smokes. We were still kids for the most part, but we were also worried about the state of affairs in the United Kingdom at the time. As we smoked up a fat joint, we talked and reflected on the future.

"What the fuck is going on with this country, Tiny? It's going to fucking pot!"

Tiny broke into laughter. "It's going to fucking pot," he said, pointing at the joint in his hand. We both fell into uncontrollable laughter at my unintentional joke.

"I was actually being fucking serious, Tiny. These people are fucking up our futures, and we're letting 'em get away with it!" I said, with Tiny nodding and grinning at the same time. "Even the fucking gravediggers have gone on strike— we are burying bodies out at fucking sea!"

For both punks and politicians, fear, despair, and the destruction of old taboos and social and political norms made way for new openings and new ways to do things—not necessarily to completely rip up the rule book but certainly to give it a major overhaul.

The bands of that time were singing a new song, no longer just being rebellious. The strength of the political commentary and demands for change were growing and not just in punk rock but across Britain's youth at that time.

"Tiny," I said as I took a long toke on the last of the joint, "we're all headed to hell, and we know it. Still, I think there's room for us to change for the better. I just know there is." I passed Tiny the roach.

"Yeah," Tiny said as he inhaled the last of the weed, "and like pigs can fly, man! Like pigs can fly." He passed me back the last bit.

I sucked up the last of the smoke and tossed the roach. "Fuckin' A. Right, man! Like when pigs fly, maybe we can get the fuck out of this shithole little dump of a town."

The summer passed, and we all headed back to school. I welcomed the change from having little to do but chores and hang out to actually having to use my mind. I didn't like the boring stuff, such as swimming lessons, but I did like learning about history and social justice. I yearned to understand where we as a nation had been, so I could understand where we were in the present and where we might be bound for in the future. In a way, I thought if I could understand my country and why it was in the shitter, I might be able to understand myself and why I felt like I was in the shitter the entire time, with no hope for the future except for more of the same old shit piling down on my sorry ass.

I loved getting together for a daily game of football at lunch. We had fun, spent a lot of energy, and honed our footie skills further, all of us with ambitions to play for Liverpool or, in my case, Manchester United one day—that was our lofty hope of escape.

We all believed that could happen with the help, support, and coaching from Mel Jefferies, the local football coach with bowed legs, an athletic frame, a generous smile, a kind heart, and gray hair of wisdom. He believed in us too. That was refreshing for us, as Mel was one of the few who did.

For us, footie was everything. It was our only hope of getting out of there, or at least that was what we thought at the time. Later, music became a possibility but not for long. That really wasn't a dream, given our talents or lack thereof, thanks to Mr. Jones.

I never wanted trouble, but I was learning that it had a habit of finding me. I just wanted to do my own thing and be left alone. I was independent, and although from quite a different family background, I, like Tiny, saw little of my parents. They were always working or preoccupied with something else. The only real time we spent together was around the TV or if I was helping my mother cook or my father fix up his latest car project in the garage. In both cases, I was just the assistant: "Pass me this. Pass me that."

I was okay with that. I liked my independence, and I was discovering myself through my own independence. The constant camping trips, messing about on bikes and boats, climbing the hills and dales, football, rugby, boxing, and the ATC were things of independence. We were thrill seekers; we didn't care. I never knew if that was the influence of the punk rock movement or my ancestry or a combination of both.

One lunchtime at school, we were playing our daily football game. I was in midfield, received the ball from the goalie, and passed it out to Tiny on the wing. It came back into the middle, to Dean; there was a short pass back to me; and I smashed it into the goal, beating the keeper—my fourth goal of the game. We were ahead 8–2. The ball went beyond the two piles of sweaters that were our posts.

One of the older kids picked up our ball and walked slowly back to our pitch. I expected him just to pass the ball back to us, but he held on to it in his arms like a rugby ball.

"Can we have our ball back, please, Brian?" I knew his name because his younger brother was in our year.

"No, you'll have to come and get it, Mitchell." He knew my name too, evidently.

"C'mon. Just give us the ball back, will yer?"

"I heard you are quite the cock around here." He was referring to cockfighting. "Heard you broke poor Billy B.'s nose last week." He was close now, about six feet away, and still advancing slowly.

I shrugged. "We both know Billy picked that fight. I didn't want anything to do with it." He was now in range. "Brian, just give us the fucking ball back, will yer?" I tried to grab the ball from his grip, but he wouldn't let go. The red mist was growing inside me. "Brian, give us the fucking ball back."

He still refused. My fist, already clenched by my side, went up for a right hook, a left uppercut, and then a killer right to the bridge of his nose. *Crunch.* Blood splattered onto the grass, and he fell down, defeated. I added another broken nose to the growing count.

By then, there was a crowd gathered. Tiny grabbed my shoulders, spun me around, and walked me away from the scene. "C'mon, Willy. Let's get the flock out of here." It was the first time I'd heard that saying, and it kinda stuck with us from there on out.

We slid around the back of the school, to the bike sheds, where he pulled out a couple of Gillespie's specials, and we lit up. After my latest altercation, I felt physically sick. My heart was racing as though it would pop out of my chest, and I thought I was going to puke.

"You, my friend, are a fucking legend." Tiny grinned. "Do you know who that was?"

I nodded. "Yeh, Gordon's brother."

"Not just Gordon's brother but the hardest kid in the third grade and, for that matter, fourth grade too."

He was referring to the British grade system and, therefore, the fifteen-year-old grouping. However, his comment didn't make me feel any better about it. That probably meant I would face someone from the fifth grade next and then a sixth-former after that.

"When the fuck will it stop, Tiny?"

He just shrugged. "Until you lose, Willy, I guess."

After that day and Tiny's observation, I contemplated staging a public loss in an effort to put a stop to the procession of contenders, but when it came to the moment, the red mist prevailed. It was simply not in my genetics, makeup, ancestry, or whatever it was to allow myself to lose.

Throughout my life, the contenders got bigger, meaner, and harder, but no matter who they were, I would never, never, never give up. Maybe I was inspired by Sir Winston

Churchill, probably the greatest leader of all time and certainly one of the greatest Brits of all time.

The school year dragged on, and winter set in. Northern England in winter never ranked as a pleasure spot. The cold, rain, and darkness could depress even the hardiest of optimists. There wasn't a great deal to do. We were creative in the way we entertained ourselves, especially when the darkness, wind, and rain prevailed. As opposed to the summer months, when there was plenty to do with the influx of tourists and out-of-town restaurant and hotel workers, in the winter, there were fewer people and fewer choices.

A pal of mine, Denny, invited us all to his house for a Ouija board session day while his parents were away for the weekend. We had no idea what that was, but it sounded interesting.

A couple of Mancunians were there when we arrived, and they seemed to know what they were doing. I saw a ring of letters and numbers on the mahogany dining table; a mirror at each end; and, in front of each, a black candle lit and flickering in the still of the stone Victorian house.

Tom and Dave had done this many times before, and they explained what to expect to the newcomers.

I grasped the concept. I thought of the people I had already lost at that tender age: my grandad Willy, my cousin Susan to cancer, Phil to motorbikes, and Diane, a girlfriend who tragically had lost her life on a night I was due to meet her for a date.

The words resonated in my mind and around the room: "Ouija board, Ouija board, would you work for me? I have got to say hello to an old friend."

I was always more into lyrics than just the music itself. Great music and crap lyrics or vice versa didn't work for me, but when the combination was right, magic happened.

That night was a different form of magic, as we went on to find a bunch of lost souls, including a former history teacher at the school, Diane, and someone called Zatyn. The candles inexplicably blew out, the glass shattered, and all the occupants of the house were terrified, including me. I looked over at Tiny, and tears rolled down his face. That was the only time I ever saw him cry.

After we made our excuses to Tom, Dave, and Denny and promptly left, outside the old house, I took a look back at the house and saw a figure in the top window staring at me. It was a dark humanlike face looking down on me, staring at me with its dark eyes, staring right through me and into my soul, it felt like.

Not feeling too brave at that point, I legged it all the way home and did not sleep a wink. I assumed it was Satan himself, and he certainly looked how I'd imagined!

I had another go at hosting a party back then. My parents went away for a weekend, leaving me and my older sister in charge. I managed to persuade her that throwing a party was a good idea, and she reluctantly agreed.

That Saturday night, half the school and their friends turned up with tinnies and bottles of various substances. My sister and I had strategically placed refuse bins around the house for ease of disposal, in the vain hope we could keep the place in at least some semblance of order.

As the party kicked into gear, there was a full house. Maybe a hundred-plus people rampaged through the house, playing records on my father's expensive and precious mahogany-lined stereo and smoking cigarettes and other substances around the house. As things later progressed, there were the obligatory party drunk, the suicidal girl, several who succumbed to alcohol and were close to alcohol poisoning, and one fight. Having gotten everyone home and the house cleared eventually at one o'clock in the morning, my sister and I surveyed the damage with horror.

We had a lot of cleaning, tidying, and fixing to do before our parents got home that evening.

Thankfully, our parents were running late on their return from London, but that still didn't give us enough time to mend the huge cigarette burn on my father's prized walnut coffee table or do anything about the two shattered Wedgewood ornaments. We threw them away, hoping no one would notice their absence.

Like a pair from the Von Trapp family, we lined up on our parents' return, hoping they wouldn't notice anything, which, of course, they did. We tried to explain it away without much success.

My so-called disruptive behavior was once again called into question.

Like the violence, I never understood my rebellious streak. Maybe they were related.

Years later, in the army, in the Lothian Barracks in Germany, after the bullworker incident, I was on Guards Orders, which meant reporting to the guardhouse several times during the day: before breakfast, after lunch for duties, and in the evening for parade in my dress number twos. My duties for one afternoon were to sweep the leaves on the outside perimeter of the camp.

As I set about the task, I had anger inside me; after all, the incident had been based on my self-defense against two pissed-up old soldiers wanting to do damage to me. With the assistance of a bullworker, I'd deflected their assault, and they both had wound up in hospital for a few weeks.

As I swept, I came up with my plan: I would just keep sweeping leaves for as long as it took before they came to find me. I made neat piles of leaves every fifty yards, and sure enough, later that night, around ten o'clock, the guard commander pulled up beside me in a Land Rover.

"What the fucking hell do you think yer doing, Mitchell?" the commander said, not doing well to hide his amusement.

"Sweeping leaves as ordered, Corporal Major, sir!" I stood to attention and overplayed military-drill discipline, with the broom gripped like a rifle beside me. I thought that added to the humor of the moment, and I believed Corporal Major Harry Hunter thought so too.

"You stupid fucking boy, Mitchell. Get in the fucking back, will yer?"

On the ride in the Land Rover, Harry Hunter counted the piles of leaves neatly and meticulously piled up every fifty feet. "How long have yer been up to this malarkey, Mitchell?"

"All day, sir, since lunchtime."

"Did you realize you had guard parade at nine o'clock?"

"Just carrying out orders, sir!"

"Aren't you the one who taught Jones and Fleming a lesson the other night?" He knew full well that I was.

"Well, I wouldn't put it like that, sir. It was more like self-defense."

Harry Hunter was part of a powerful group of senior noncommissioned officers at the time. All of them had a trademark swallow tattooed on the crease of their thumbs. No one ever quite knew why, but did know, along with the likes of Tommy Quinn, Danny Bond, and Ken Hampton, they were all as hard as fucking nails and be shouldn't messed with.

By the time we got back to the guardhouse, I knew I was safe, and I knew my plan had worked. I guessed Harry and his fraternity had done worse things in their time, and although some were more senior than others, Harry was the regimental corporal major in waiting, so he carried a bit of clout.

"Get yerself to bed, son, and be at Major Barclay's office for orders at eight o'clock sharp." He looked at me and winked. "You got it, Mitchell? Eight o'clock sharp, and no sweeping fucking leaves."

The next morning, Harry was there, as was Major Barclay, the squadron officer in charge, behind his big mahogany desk, which looked as if it had come straight from some expensive town house in Knightsbridge—and it probably had.

"Mitchell, I have had a special request from Mr. Hunter here. I understand you got yourself in a spot of bother the other night. I also understand you have a liking for sweeping leaves and following orders to the letter." He looked up at me from behind his desk as I stood in front at attention.

"Yes, sir!"

"You see, Mitchell, this regiment has a lot of friends in very high places, from Kensington, Knightsbridge, Pall Mall, and the palace itself all the way to Detmold here in Germany."

I had no idea where this discussion was leading.

He pulled a document from his tray and opened the brown cardboard folder. "You see, Mitchell, you've boxed for the regiment, played rugby for the regiment, and been on the downhill ski team, and apart from a couple of minor indiscretions, your service has been exemplary." He nodded back at Harry Hunter knowingly, and Harry rolled his eyes. He was referring to an incident in which my mate Gary and I had been caught wearing *Never Mind the Bollocks* T-shirts and Union Jack shorts in a banned nightclub, in breach of the regiment's strict dress rules of a suit or sports coat and slacks.

"As you were sorting out our two regimental bullies last week, I received your new posting orders," he said.

"Yes, sir." My mind was racing.

He read from the documents before him. "You will report for duty with the 29 Commando Royal Artillery and 9 Parachute Squadron Royal Engineers at Airport Camp, Belize, to undertake jungle warfare training. This will be a six-month posting, and from there, you will report to the 22 Special Air Service, Sterling Lines, Hereford."

Harry Hunter nodded and winked again.

"Now, get back to your normal duties; you are dismissed from order. Keep your nose clean, and good luck in your next endeavors."

"Yes, sir!" I saluted and spun around, and Squadron Corporal Major Hunter led me out of the office.

By then, I was officially a rebel with a cause. At least someone appreciated my rebellious streak.

# 8
# WINTERS OF DISCONTENT
## WM
### 1978 to 1979
### Great Britain


**MY YOUTH UNFOLDED IN ONE** of the grimmest periods in British history. They were dark days indeed—literally, as the National Grid infrastructure needed upgrading, and union striking was rife, a combination that led to power outages across the nation during what turned out to be the coldest winter in sixteen years.

There was a global recession, and Britain was hit as severely as most. The British government was trying to control inflation, and the unions wanted higher wages.

Great Britain was debt ridden, including still paying back the United States for its support during the last war. Between the United States and Canada, Britain had borrowed more than £5.5 billion and would not pay it off for another thirty years and, by that time, would have paid back double in servicing the debt.

The freezing conditions across the nation, including blizzards and snow, made some lines of work impossible to complete. The weather affected the high street and shoppers' willingness to put their hands in their pockets, adding further to the economic pressures of the time.

Ferreting his way and rising to power in the National Union of Miners was Arthur Scargill, who had been leading change in the union movement for many years by that time. He led strikes and was credited with the innovation of flying pickets, whereby he would organize buses of strikers from one pit to another to bolster the militant crowd and pile pressure on the owners to submit to their demands.

Coal was a major industry for the nation back then, as were car and truck making and fisheries. Coal was needed to keep the lights on and keep the wheels of the nation turning.

January 22, 1979, was the biggest individual day of strike action since the general strike of 1926.

The train drivers, the nurses, the waste collectors, and even the gravediggers went on strike. The country was being brought to its knees slowly by its workers. Leaders like Scargill were draining the life out of our nation and denying kids like me and Tiny any chance or hope of a future.

We had been through so much as a nation. We had defeated the Germans twice, including Hitler, and now we were self-imploding and destroying ourselves.

"It's time we did something about this, Tiny."

He looked at me with his usual cheery expression. "We gonna rob a bank? Like the great train robbers or something?"

"Na, mate, I'm fucking serious. The world is going to fucking pot!"

"You wanna smoke some weed?"

"Tiny, be bloody serious, will yer?"

"What do yer suggest, Billy Boy?" He knew that name wound me up.

I ignored his reference, but I did not have a response to his question. I did not know what the answer was. I knew only that things were desperate, and things had to change.

I, like many others at that time, was sick of the middle-class stuck-in-the-muds and their boring, mundane lives and acceptance of misery. They were not prepared to do anything about it, just letting our country slide.

"It's them that's responsible, you know?"

"Who?"

"The old fuckers. The bastards in charge. They need to get a fucking grip before it's too late."

Tiny nodded and agreed. "But what the hell can we do about it, Willy? Seriously?"

"Maybe we should rob a fucking bank after all!"

We had been to see The Clash a couple of weeks ago, and they'd played a tune they were threatening to release, "Bank Robber." Tiny and I broke into song. Then there was Ronnie Biggs himself, the Great Train Robber, and the Pistols song "No One Is Innocent." I cranked up my record player, pulled out *The Great Rock 'n' Roll Swindle*, found the track, and blasted out the tune in my room. Tiny got out his little brown bottle, shoved it up his nose, took a large sniff, and fell into his oblivion as Ronnie Biggs sang his socks off—well, sort of.

Tiny and I broke into song and belted out the chorus as if we were on the stage of the Hammersmith Palace.

Tiny was less self-conscious about his little-brown-bottle habit; it was becoming the norm, and it really bothered me. I didn't like to see him getting high on coke, speed, or whatever his little brown bottle held at the time. It didn't seem like the drugs did Tiny any good at all. In retrospect, I would realize they were slowly killing off his spirit, robbing him of any ability to escape from the confines of the small town where we grew up and the confines that grew within him of his own unwitting accord.

The career discussion I'd had with Mr. Stephens stuck with me as the winter progressed. I didn't like the idea of a boring job in the Royal Mail or any other silly segment of the economy that required nothing more than buckling under to authority and bowing to the big, bad badass man with all the bucks—the world of business, politics, and high society that seemed to rule the entire bloody planet.

One early evening in the late winter of 1979, I found myself ensconced in the Odana Café with Tiny and another friend, Kerry. I was hot under the collar about the apparent universal judgment that I was worthy of little more than a menial job that would numb my mind until I dropped dead at an early age due to alcohol, illegal or legal drugs, or eating the wrong end of a loaded pistol for tea.

"What a fucking tosser!" I shouted to Tiny and Kerry as we sat at a table. A mug of tea sat in front of each of us, and a plate of chips to share sat in the middle. "The guy doesn't even fucking know me and is condemning me to a life of no ambition."

"Hang on just a fucking minute, Willy. My old feller is a postie," Kerry said.

"That's not the point, Kerry. I love posties. I have a great deal of respect for them, and I also have a lot of respect for your dad—of course I do—but the real point is, this fucking tosser and tossers like him are the reason we are in such a bloody state in the first place."

Tiny and Kerry both nodded in agreement, mostly because they couldn't be bothered and had had enough of my going off, I thought. They had heard me all the way on the bus. I would have one last rant and call it a day.

"He doesn't even fucking know me, understand me, or have any fricking clue what my ambitions are for the future."

"What else did he say?" asked Kerry, now obviously losing interest.

"Yeh, come on, Willy. Calm the hell down," Tiny said. "What did you expect anyway?"

Tiny was right. What did I really expect anyway? We were deep in a land of mediocrity, and stacking shelves at Walter Willson's was okay, a life as a civil servant was okay, and eating the same meal-menu cycle week in and week out was okay. Going to bloody Butlin's on your fucking holidays or in your caravan was okay. Scratching to earn a living and survive after the taxman gouged your pay packet was okay.

I had one final go. "Guys, there has to be something better than this." I looked around the Odana and all its mediocrity.

I looked back at the pair of them. "Fuck it. Fancy getting the train down to London tomorrow?" *Fuck it! Why not?*

There were lots of opportunities to explore and find oneself in the hills and countryside around, although other opportunities were distinctly lacking at the time. It was not just a regional thing, but Great Britain at that time wasn't known for its ambition and opportunities.

As my teen years rolled on, I knew I had to break the cycle I was in. I had to disassociate with the notion of being posh; it was a label of being different to the rest and therefore a focus for bullies. I knew I didn't like being bullied, and I knew it was a cycle I needed to tackle before it got out of hand.

I was determined to make changes, and amid our various camping expeditions in the glorious and free countryside that surrounded us—the fells, the dales, the forests, and the lakes—I made the decision to invest a portion of my savings in getting rid of my Paul McCartney bowl haircut and getting something a little more cutting edge, and that was what I did. Tiny and I started to truly dress the part of the punkers. Hair was just part of the trip.

I had much the same haircut for years but with some interesting and occasional deviations along the way: short back and sides; a crew cut; the occasional Mohican; the Cramps' gothic look, including the blonde fringe; and even noughts and crosses shaved in one iteration. However, I defaulted back to the original look after.

On the advice of Tiny, I made the investment in some new clothes and some old clothes from the local jumble sale too. The use of stitching, strategic tears, bleaching, dyeing, spray paint, and marker pens built up my new wardrobe. I took great care in the creation of my wardrobe, like a fashion designer making a statement through the clothes I wore.

I invested in a studded buckle belt, some rebel T-shirts, and my first pair of Doc Martens—black with eight holes and bright red laces.

Complete with my new makeover, that was the new me, but at school, the uniform of gray, blue, and a blue-and-gold tie prevailed. The later addition of a red Harrington jacket was about the only point of individuality acceptable.

The problem at high school was that my sister, who was two years above me, had already secured a reputation as a rebel, and that reputation evidently rubbed off on me, as I discovered on my first day of school. Mr. Snowden incorrectly accused Tiny and me of wrecking the bathrooms in the first-grade wing. The truth was that the culprits ran from the bathroom as we entered, but we both knew that being a grass was not okay. We kept our mouths shut; took the accusation on the chin; and, despite our pleadings of innocence, were overruled.

I concluded that growing up was not easy.

Pink Floyd's *The Wall*, featuring "Another Brick in the Wall (Part 2)," became a favorite for many of the kids of that age. It was a song of rebellion against the establishment, our teachers. It was a time of noncompliance or differentiation— being different and bucking the trend of obedience at all costs. The last thing on my mind was working for the Royal Mail or any other establishment entity.

Our fathers had fought in the Second World War and grandfathers had fought in the First World War, and we knew the tales of army generals, such as Haig, sending them over the top just to be slaughtered by the German machine guns. The Maschinengewehr 08 was capable of blasting out an incredible 450 to 500 rounds a minute at an effective range of more than two thousand yards.

Those stories, and the millions slaughtered on the Red Fields of France, inspired a nation of the working class to vow never to blindly follow the mindless orders of the higher class in such lunacy and eventual death to so many.

We were not of that generation and never would be; we would have our own minds and our own points of view and not just do what we were told because someone in a position of authority told us to.

Compared to the older generations around us, we were different. Our parents, our teachers, the newsreaders on TV, the union leaders, the politicians—everyone, it seemed, had given up and were content with a future of mediocrity at best.

An attitude of rebellion was growing in me and the people around me, and as we pursued our adolescent flirtation with punk rock, it became clear that rebellion wasn't just a state of mind but was growing into a movement. It extended far beyond punk rock. A collection of youth growing up with no hope were not just lying down and taking it but were prepared to actually do something about it.

During the queen's Silver Jubilee in 1977, the streets were decked with Union Jacks, trestle tables, egg and cress sandwiches, sausage rolls, cheese and pineapple on sticks, tea, lemonade, and strawberries and scones. We waved our little Union flags, streamers, and balloons and thanked our queen for the glorious past twenty-five years of her reign. As I grew older, I remembered those heady times. I embraced them even two years later.

The Sex Pistols continued their own disruptive behavior. They hired a barge in London and famously belted out "No Future" and "Anarchy in the UK" on the River Thames as they sailed through the capital with their rebellious and maybe even mutinous message to the country and the world. They finished their set with "God Save the Queen."

The great days of the empire had waned. The unions had taken over, and the Japanese, the Russians, and Europe were all vying for their own positions and challenges to the commonwealth. It felt as if the country had resigned itself to a future of mediocrity—that was, until 1979, when Margaret Hilda Thatcher, the Iron Lady, became the first female prime minister of the United Kingdom. As many people hated her as loved her. My parents were in the latter group, supporters and fans, and I tended to agree. She had the ability, talent, wherewithal, and, most of all, courage to reverse the decline of our glorious nation, unlike the plethora of career politicians who were resigned to mediocrity and steady decline into our future.

Along with the help of the United States and the Allies, we had saved and liberated our European cousins from the devil, and now, thirty-five years later, that had been long and conveniently forgotten.

In the search for a savior, I turned to my music and books and the hidden learnings within. I was not clear on what I was searching for a savior for, but I had an intense desire to be free—free from all the mediocrity and decline. I wanted to be part of the future, not the problem, cocreating the solution, not the past.

As a child, I took up reading with my first book, *Charlie and the Chocolate Factory*, recognizing the differences between Charlie and his golden ticket and the other spoiled kids who expected everything they deserved and deserved everything they got.

Other books that really made an impact on my life were *The Hobbit* and *The Lord of the Rings* and the escapism they represented. With whole worlds, languages, adventures, enemies, friends, and an opportunity to find adventure and explore, they were a perfect escape from my surroundings as a child. To wander the countryside in the context of Bilbo or Frodo was exhilarating.

Wilbur Smith and his tales of the origins of South Africa and the pioneers of that hard and harsh continent fueled my wanderlust.

Like reading, beyond the music, lyrics interested me, as did storytelling, such as the epic story of *War of the Worlds*. When it was originally released in 1898, H. G. Wells caused a panic, as people thought it was real.

I liked the classics of Bowie and Morrissey, an often-underrated lyricist whose humor got mistaken for depressive tones. In fact, I always found quite the opposite. "As Anthony said to Cleopatra as he opened a crate of ale" and "I booked myself into the YWCA, and do you have a vacancy for a back scrubber?" were just two examples of his poetic wit.

Then there was the new version of rebellious music against the state, against depression, and against a life of never-ending unemployment opportunities. It was antiwar, antiestablishment, and antinormal and said, "Fuck the world," which came through strongly in the tempo, mood, dress, and lyrics.

As I weaned myself off my mother's Beatles and Elvis collection and off Simon and Garfunkel, I found myself introduced to Queen and "Bohemian Rhapsody," the Boomtown Rats, and the Sex Pistols.

Kieran Galloway was a gamekeeper and poacher who had a kennel of lurchers, hunting dogs. Tiny and I would borrow them to go hunting, lamping, and ferreting and bring back our spoils to skin, gut, feed to the dogs, or make a hearty rabbit stew.

Growing up in the north of England, just below the Scottish border, wasn't all that bad. In the summer, we spent as much time in the great outdoors as we did at home.

Learning from books, courtesy of Ms. Atkinson, and others' experience, including Kieran's, we learned to catch pheasants; snare more rabbits, gaff, and salmon; and explore the opportunity of sustenance from the resources around us.

Fattened raisins were the key to catching pheasants. We'd soak them overnight to fatten them up and add a touch of port or cherry brandy from my father's cocktail bar. In the morning, we'd either (1) roll a chip cone and place a fattened raisin in the bottom, and when the pheasant plucked the raisin, it was blinded and would not move, or (2) thread a horsehair through the raisin, and as soon as the pheasant felt the blockage in the throat, it was paralyzed. Either way, just picking up the pheasant was far easier and cleaner than other alternative methods.

The arts of ferreting, gaffing, and snaring were more complex and needed more practice, skill, and experience to reap the rewards of success.

The ferrets and polecats were mostly feisty and nippy and, in my experience, rarely did what was asked or expected. Netting a rabbit warren was the preparation work. We'd carefully peg a small net over each of the escape holes. Most warrens had many, so it usually took some time. Once that was completed, we'd take the ferret out of its bag and release it into the main entrance, which usually was denoted by the amount of evident foot traffic. Then we'd wait, with the theory that the nets would catch fleeing inhabitants.

We would wait and wait, until we realized we would have to dig the errant ferret out in order to get home for tea. A beacon on its collar would allow us to find where to dig, and after hours, usually, we would retrieve the ferret and go home for tea.

Gaffing was also an art. A gaff looked similar to a shortened oar with a split and teeth designed to bear down on top of salmon and, once engaged, into its teeth, denying the fish escape. It was a rudimentary and ancient instrument. We stood in midstream at the height of the season, and the salmon would abound, almost threatening to knock over the less experienced—like us. In fact, they often did, but the prize of taking those beauties to prepare at home was worth it, although the criminal risks of what was considered poaching were high.

Then there was the art of snaring. That was truly tricky. Steel wire was strategically placed in loops or in straight lines on runs, and then came the mystery of which type of animal we might, if lucky, find upon our return the next morning. That was our least successful hunting activity, with the slingshot, air rifle, and shotgun being the most successful, in that order.

In my pursuit of new thrills and spills, I also took up boxing and the sport of rugby.

Boxing was at the local recreation club, at the youth club on Tuesdays and Thursdays. The boxing club was run by a legendary Great Britain Olympic coach who was the father of two of my schoolmates. The smell of sweat and leather was memorable, with sessions of weights, medicine balls, sit-ups, and press-ups, followed by skipping on the spot and learning the different hand movements and rope-spinning techniques over time.

Then followed, at the end of each session, sparring, when similar-size, similar-weight attendees would be paired off and put in the ring to beat the hell out of each other for three minutes. We were young, and it would take time to be more practiced and measured, as opposed to, due to the fear of conflict, hitting as many times as quickly as possible without any regard to style, technique, or actual effectiveness. That would come later.

A group of the best of us, or those stupid enough to accept the challenge, were invited to partake in a boxing evening at a local fancy hotel with an audience of fat businessmen wearing penguin suits, smoking cigars, and betting on the outcomes in the ring. It was the scariest moment of my life to date. Five hundred men, almost savage-like, were shouting, cheering, jeering, and hungry for blood, barely visible from the ring through the clouds of smoke and the lights dazzling. For the most part, we tried our best to stick with the style and the technique, but the heightened pressure made the most inexperienced, which included me, default to haymaking.

I was young. I would get better with experience, and those experiences later allowed me to fare well in my future pugilistic endeavors.

Rugby, for the most part—largely because of Sparky, our head coach; Steve; and Joe—was much more fun. That was when I first heard the saying "The sum of the parts is greater than the whole." The game was truly a team sport; each member, whether a forward or a back, was reliant upon the other fourteen on the field to secure success. I also heard another saying for the first time: Sparky's self-made catchphrase "Pain is only an illusion."

The sense of team and camaraderie was a refreshing contrast to that of boxing and a welcome one. Paddy, Hunts, and Tim were the standouts on the team. Dave and Simon were a year younger but clearly talented. Batey was reliable and steadfast, no matter the odds. Consty, the tallest of all, was a tower of leadership and strength.

One of our early games was in Barrow, on the cliffs above the Irish Sea. It was cold, wet, and miserable in the depths of winter, with a severe storm overlooking the ocean—probably my most miserable game ever. Freezing cold, rain, sleet, and high-force gale winds made it almost impossible to pass or kick the ball, and Johnny, on my wing, with his soccer gloves protecting his hands, shivered. We were relieved when the referee decided to abandon the game ten minutes into the second half. We complained that he had not made that decision before the first whistle blew.

A few years later, I would be back at the Royal Oak, sipping down pints of Jennings, listening and watching in awe as the town's First XV sang in dulcet tones after a hard-fought game, nursing their wounds, clinking their glasses, and singing "Moon River."

As I stood there with my heroes in the Royal Oak, with my misty eyes, I wondered where Moon River even was—wider than a mile and crossing her in style. And what was the rainbow's end? What were the possibilities in front of me at that time, despite all the doom and gloom in the air? Who knew?

Moon River, wider than a mile!

# 9
# THE TROUBLES
**WM**
1979

**I WAS BECOMING INCREASINGLY WORRIED** about Tiny. He never talked about his personal feelings much. He spent more and more time at our house, camping, and at other friends' houses. I was trying to work out if he actually went home at all anymore.

His little brown bottle was making an appearance more and more—poppers for a short buzz. They would take you to another planet and back but were not as bad as the hard stuff. He liked weed and would smoke at least a joint a day, which was fine, I guessed.

We tried magic mushrooms once, and that was enough for me. We also tried speed one night in my bedroom and stayed up all night listening to music and making stuff—it was bizarre. After eventually crashing out at seven o'clock in the morning, we awoke to see all our craft work from the night before: things made out of cardboard; random drawings; paintings of imaginary album covers for our band, Contraband; socks stuffed with other socks to make sculptures of sorts; and ramblings of lyrics and poems.

I realized how mind-bending the stuff was, and I knew how dangerous that was.

My father was more than twenty years older than my mum; he'd been in his fifties by the time my sister and I came along. He had been there, done that, and gotten the T-shirt. It was hard to do anything but respect my father, his wisdom, and his teachings.

Apart from those experiments as a teenager, thankfully, I never got into drugs of any kind and was never tempted by the ubiquitous tattoos either. For the most part, I managed to escape those forms of self-harm. I was not sure why I was able to do that, because I was indeed troubled. Perhaps my inner compass was already acting on me in a positive way, despite the negativity that surrounded me.

Tiny was a happy kid. Apart from his fear during the Ouija board incident, I had never seen him upset. Tiny was always happy and a joker, always had that signature grin on his face, and always saw the bright side in everything. That was why he was a puzzle in my mind. How could someone seemingly so happy be so sad?

Some of the kids got into crazy stuff, sniffing glue and other adhesives or chemicals. There was cocaine and heroin. I had even heard of some injecting straight alcohol into their bloodstreams. It was shocking, really, for an idyllic northern tourist town and for kids so young. Thankfully, I stayed away from most of it, valuing my body, mind, and life obviously more than some.

Tiny turned up at my house one day. I saw him walk in from Lake Road and head round to the back and the kitchen door. He was wearing a new donkey jacket I had never seen him wear before and a bright orange reflective strip with the big letters *SLDC* on the back. He wore his green PVC trousers and a pair of cherry-red Doc Martens. I ran to the back door to meet him. As I opened the door, he stood on the step in front of me with his wide Tiny Tim grin, looking as proud as punch.

"What is it, Tiny? Did you just get an audition for one of Santa's little helpers?" I couldn't help myself. "Or was Noddy looking for a stunt double maybe?" Tiny's smile slowly evaporated. "What about Coco's assistant at Barnum and Bailey?" I fell on the floor, rolling around laughing my socks off.

"Fuck off, Willy. I'll be off then," he said, straight-faced, and he started to turn around.

I jumped up, realizing that was maybe only the second time I had ever seen him anywhere close to being upset. "Hey, Tiny, I'm sorry. Come on inside, mate." I needed to turn him around in all senses of those words.

I got him inside, and he calmed down. We went up to my room and had a smoke on the roof. I had tobacco, and Tiny's was mixed with copious amounts of weed.

"So what's the story with the jacket, Tiny?" We lay on our backs on the slate, puffing smoke rings into the early evening sky in a silent competition of whose lasted the longest and was the biggest, most perfectly shaped, and weirdest shape.

"Look at that one, Willy; it's a fucking perfect double-decker bus, I tell yer."

I looked at Tiny's latest production and had no idea what he was talking about. "I reckon that weed must be extrastrength tonight!"

"Me dad got it for me."

"What—the weed?" I said, still in humor mode.

"Na, yer silly fucker. The jacket, yer fucking egit!" He looked over at me.

"I gathered that. I saw the South Lakes District Council on the back," I said, trying my best to keep a straight face.

"What's so fucking funny, Willy? Why is that so fucking funny? We aren't like you, yer know. Sitting here with everything, with the world at yer fucking feet." He sat up and gestured with his hands, as if showing that everything before us was mine.

"Fucking hell, Tiny. Where the hell did that come from?" I was lost. I never for one moment had realized that could be an issue. I waited for a few minutes for him to answer, but he didn't, and I thought I'd best leave it alone.

He decided to stay the night, and we went down the road to pick up fish 'n' chips. My mum and dad were working late, my mother in the kitchen and my father behind the bar, serving the guests. Tiny and I watched TV, eating our meal out of the newspaper wrapping, me with tomato ketchup and Tiny with HP sauce.

"I don't know how you can eat that stuff." I pointed to the brown sauce splattered all over his fish 'n' chips. "It fucking stinks."

"Horses for courses, Willy. That's what makes the world go round."

"What—HP sauce?"

"No, that everyone's different, and we all like different things."

"What—like yer fucking Noddy suit this afternoon?"

He threw the HP bottle at my head; fortunately, I was quick enough to roll my head as it went flying past my ear at a rate of knots. It was a friendly exchange.

I tidied up the newspaper and got rid of the condiments, as my parents would be in shortly to watch the news. It was good I acted quickly to clean up the mess, because my parents strolled in right as the ITN news came on. Tiny and I were as interested in the world news as my parents—maybe more so. It was our window to the outside world. We both had growing concerns about the state of the world. The music and the lyrics of the day encouraged it—repression, conflict, fears of nuclear war, capitalism, the rich getting richer, the middle class and poor having little or no chance of a future. The songs were of frustration and liberation, pointing out that doing nothing was not the answer. At the end of the day, if those in charge—our parents, the unions, the leaders, the teachers—weren't prepared to do something about it, then the youth at the time were. After all, it was our future, not theirs.

Earlier in the day, there had been some breaking news about an explosion in Ireland, and as Alistair Burnett and Sandy Gall introduced the news, the headline was the death of the queen's cousin Earl Mountbatten of Burma at the hands of the Provisional Irish Republican Army in Southern Ireland.

Tiny, my mother and father, and I sat around our lounge, listening to the report. The scenes could have been from the waters less than a mile from us but, thankfully, were across the Irish Sea and on the west coast of Ireland.

Apparently, for more than thirty years, Mountbatten had holidayed at his summer home, Classiebawn Castle, in the fishing village of Mullaghmore, County Sligo. According to the newsreader, it was twelve miles from the northern Irish border and County Fermanagh, known as a cross-border refuge for the IRA.

Lord Louis, as the IRA referred to him, was lobster potting and tuna fishing on a thirty-foot wooden boat, *Shadow V*, with his eldest daughter, his son-in-law, their twin sons, and his daughter's mother-in-law, Lady Brabourne.

Just a few hundred yards from the shore, the IRA terrorists detonated the fifty-pound bomb they had planted the night before, causing a massive explosion, and the boat was blown to smithereens, along with its occupants. The footage showed the debris scattered across the waters and a fleet of Irish fishermen trying to help the rescue.

Mountbatten was dead, as were one of his nephews and a young crew member. Lady Brabourne and the others were seriously injured.

Various people were quoted in their outcries, including Jimmy Carter, president of the United States; the pope; and, of course, Prime Minister Margaret Thatcher, the Iron Lady, who said, "His death leaves a gap that can never be filled. The British people give thanks for his life and grieve at his passing."

The IRA issued a statement afterward, saying,

The IRA claim responsibility for the execution of Lord Louis Mountbatten. This operation is one of the discriminate ways we can bring to the attention of the English people the continuing occupation of our country ... The death of Mountbatten and the tributes paid to him will be seen in sharp contrast to the apathy of the British government and the English people to the deaths of over three hundred British soldiers and the deaths of Irish men, women, and children at the hands of their forces.

I looked over at my dad, who was shaking his head.

Mountbatten was a war hero, a naval man, and had been the last viceroy of India. He obviously had been around a bit and had a lot of respect and medals to go with his service.

"Who are these IRA people, Dad?" I asked.

He looked at me and shook his head. He had already told me his stories: the Normandy landings, the invasion, the liberation of France, Germany, North Africa, and Field Marshal Rommel. He then had gone on to Palestine to keep the peace, only for his friends to have their throats slit or be strung up in shop doorways, thanks to another set of terrorists, the Palestine Liberation Army and Yasser Arafat. He was a veteran of conflict, and he despised terrorists of all kinds.

"They're just bad people, Son."

"Why are they fighting? What are they fighting for?"

He shook his head again and looked me in the eye. I could tell it was one of those Dad moments wherein he would dispense his wisdom. He had been through more than most in his life, and I respected his opinion.

"Thing is, Son, anyone who says they understand Ireland doesn't really understand Ireland."

I looked at him, puzzled.

"It's so complicated, Willy. There are more sides to it than a fifty-pence piece," he said, referring to the seven-sided coin that was half a British pound.

I remembered another Dad moment he had shared with me when telling his Palestine story: "Never trust a Welshman; he will steal from you. Never trust an Irishman; he will lie to you. And never trust an Arab, because he will kill you."

My father had some prejudices of his own, and by the looks of things, he had some basis of justification.

The news on the box went on to describe how, that same morning, an IRA group had ambushed and killed eighteen British soldiers at the gates of Narrow Water Castle, just outside a place called Warrenpoint in County Down.

"What's the difference between Northern Ireland and Ireland?" I asked.

"Well, that would be to do with King William of Orange and the Red Hand of Ulster," my dad said.

Again, my confused look prompted him to continue. He told me that in 1921, under the Government of Ireland Act, Northern Ireland was partitioned to remain as part of the United Kingdom. The majority of those in the North were Unionists and loyal to the queen, Protestants, but there was also a minority of Republicans who wanted a united Ireland, Catholics. "Ever since that day, they have not gotten along, and now, worse than ever, they think the solution is to kill each other and us."

"And what do King William of Orange and the Red Hand of Ulster have to do with it?" I asked.

He looked at his watch; it was 10:45 p.m. "Getting time for bed, you two. I'll go through it in the morning."

Tiny and I called it a night and headed up for our rooftop smoke. When we climbed up through the skylight in my bedroom, we emerged onto the roof to observe a clear sky filled with twinkling stars. The natural beauty stopped me in my tracks for a moment before we sat down and lit up for our last smoke of the day.

"Why the fuck do people want to kill each other?" Tiny posed the question of the night.

I thought for a while as we did our smoke-ring ritual. "I really have no clue. I think it's ultimately about money, power, and a greed for both."

"My dad reckoned he was a pedo anyway."

"Who—Mountbatten?"

"Yep. A proper kiddie fiddler."

"Okay," I said slowly. "What's that got to do with the IRA?"

I liked that Tiny never said anything without doing his research and forming a point of view.

"Well, that's how they operate over there."

"What do you mean?"

"Well, Willy, everything is never quite as it seems."

He went on to explain his analysis of the IRA and told me they were funded originally by a loan from the Russians and then supported by the Germans in World War II and then by the stupid Americans. Their power base was really about destabilizing the United Kingdom under the guise of religious and territorial freedom, he said. In reality, they were nothing more than gangsters and murderers.

"Never trust the fucking Russians. Or ze Germans. Or the Irish."

His words reminded me of one my own father's teachings.

Two smoke rings floated into the night sky, intertwining with each other to form what looked like a head and a halo in the dim light that shone through the skylight.

"Fuck me—did you see that?" I said.

"Awesome!"

We lay there in silence as we watched the smoke rings fade away and disappear.

Tiny continued. "See, the Ruskies have something called maskirovka."

"Maskirov what?"

"Maskirovka. It is the art of deception, misinformation, lies, and smoke and mirrors. Nothing is ever quite as it seems."

"So what's that got to do with Mountbatten?"

"Amongst other things, they are law keepers and assassins."

I was totally confused at that point. "What the fuck are you talking about, Tiny?"

He went on to explain that many of the bombings we had seen on the news had been either an insurance job, a power play, or, in some cases, a paid assassination. In Northern Ireland, the IRA was a rule of law. They would punish their own if they stepped out of line. They employed the tactics of finger breaking, the Belfast grin, kneecapping, and murder.

"What the fuck is a Belfast grin?" I could tell he was enjoying his Tiny moment and the fruits of his research.

"It's where they slit you with a razor blade on each side of yer mouth, leaving you with a permanent scar as a warning to you and to others."

"Fuck me. That's fucking awful. Do they really fucking do that to people?"

Tiny just lay there and nodded. "Yep."

"So yer reckon they took out Mountbatten 'cause he was a kiddie fiddler?"

"I reckon it's not beyond the realm of possibility, young Willy."

Tiny was only a couple of months older than I was, and he liked to use that phrase when he had the upper hand.

I decided not to address his outburst from earlier that afternoon. I was still confused. I'd had no idea my best friend had issues about what I had versus what he had. Then again, I realized we lived in a big fuck-off house, although it was shared with visitors, compared to his relatively tiny three-bedroom affair up on the council estate in Windermere.

Tiny's father had started work at the council after a short stint in the army's Parachute Regiment. He worked hard, played hard, and, from what I gathered, drank hard too. Tiny's mother worked at Walter Willson's, on the checkout. They had a car, but it certainly wasn't my father's fancy BMW or my mother's Mini.

I also realized our boat, our caravan, and our annual holidays in Portugal were all alien to and different from Tiny's world. I was oblivious to my family's good fortune, because it had always been there. My dad, ever the entrepreneur, had done well for himself through hard work and good sense. Yet the differences were real and well defined, even if I didn't see them. Later, of course, I realized that mine was a life of privilege, in spite of the troubled nature of my youthful self, and that the lives of most people I knew bordered on quiet desperation 90 percent of the time. As I thought about it more, his reaction started to make more sense to me.

We finished our smokes in relative silence, each of us lost in his own thoughts. Then we went to bed.

When we got up the next morning, we went downstairs to eat breakfast. My dad explained that back in 1674, King Billy—King William III—of England, Scotland, Ireland, and France was a staunch Protestant fighting the Catholics and somewhat of a folk hero of the people in Northern Ireland and in Scotland.

Tiny, my dad, and I sat at the table in our kitchen while my mother cooked us bacon and eggs, toast and marmalade, orange juice, and a pot of tea. I looked over at Tiny and realized now that this wasn't breakfast at the Timpson household, and maybe it was one of the many reasons he spent so much time at our house.

We had seen the rivalry between the blue of Rangers and the green of Celtic and the rivalry between the Old Firm in the Glasgow derbies. I had also heard my grandma's tales about my grandfather, a dockworker on the River Clyde and a Protestant. He had a lead weight in his flute, and as they marched with their orange sashes, they would bash the Taigs on the head as they passed by.

"Okay, okay, and what about the Red Hand of Ulster?" I asked.

My father laughed and told me to go to the library on my way home from football practice, which I did. I was hungry for more detail.

We were keen to learn stuff then—not in a formal way, not in a classroom with information dished up like cold stew, but through interest, inquisitiveness, and exploration.

As a teenager, when I learned about other religions beyond my Church of England for the first time, I was angry I hadn't known earlier, because maybe if I'd had the choice, I'd have chosen something else instead, such as Judaism or Buddhism or, as I ended up, nothing at all. I maintained belief in right and wrong, good and evil, boldly and rightly, bravely and truly.

Apparently, the story of the Red Hand of Ulster was about two chieftains fighting over land in the north of Ireland. They agreed to a race in their ships, and the first to touch the shore with his hand won the race and the prize: the land. As they approached, one in front of the other, the trailing chieftain chopped off his hand with his sword and threw it ashore, making his claim that he had won the race, hence creating the legend of the Red Hand of Ulster.

We finished eating and went on our merry way. Time passed, and I didn't think much about Lord Mountbatten and the bleeding Irish terrorists, but the troubles came back into full relief when Mountbatten got a rather grand send-off at Westminster Abbey with full royal attendance, military honors, and thousands of mourners, according to the news reports.

Six weeks later, Sinn Fein vice president, a Mr. Gerry Adams, said of Mountbatten's death,

The IRA gave clear reasons for the execution. I think it is unfortunate that anyone has to be killed, but the furor created by Mountbatten's death showed up the hypocritical attitude of the media establishment.

As a member of the House of Lords, Mountbatten was an emotional figure in both British and Irish politics. What the IRA did to him is what Mountbatten had been doing all his life to other people; and with his war record, I don't think he could have objected to dying in what was clearly a war situation. He knew the danger involved in coming to this country.

In my opinion, the IRA achieved its objective: people started paying attention to what was happening in Ireland.

That was a bit harsh, I thought at the time.

On another of our exploration trips to the library, I found out the Irish situation had attracted funding from enemies of the empire for many years. During the First World War, the Russians had sent a shipload of guns to fight the British and even provided a loan that seeded the IRA. Other enemies of the state, including Libya and Iran, had supported the cause. Then there were the Americans, living in their bubbles, thinking they were sending their dollars across the pond to fund a fight for liberation, when in reality, they were funding violent gangsters and terrorists in the name of freedom. Many celebrities allegedly took sympathy sufficiently to fuel the fight.

During the troubles, more than one thousand British military and Northern Ireland security forces lost their lives, including more than 360 Republicans and 160 Unionists. The biggest loss was civilians, at two thousand, and there were more than eight thousand arrests.

Overall, there were more than three and a half thousand dead and more than forty-seven thousand injured.

The standout figurehead of the punk rock movement was from Irish roots himself, and I wondered what his point of view was on the events. Later that year, I would find out, as I was at a Chelsea concert at some shithouse pub in Preston, watching the mosh pit from the back, when Tiny tapped me on the shoulder and gestured for me to look next to me, and there he was with his ginger spikes, steampunk shades, and blue suede shoes.

No blacks, no Irish, and no fucking dogs.

# 10
# BREAKING GLASS
WM
November 22, 1980
Lancaster University

**TINY, KERRY, A FEW OF** the boys, and I headed down to Lancaster to see Hazel O'Connor and a supporting band called Duran Duran, whom we had never heard of at the time. It was an easy hop on the train from Windermere to Oxenholme and then down to Lancaster and a thirty-minute walk to the university and the concert hall.

As we walked into the vast hall, we saw that it was a different crowd, a metamorphosis from punk, softer and flamboyant, not the pinks and reds of the punks but black and blond, with the addition of makeup, including eyeliner and lipstick on the girls and the boys.

"What the fucking hell is this you've bought me to?" asked Tiny as we navigated through the crowd and moved toward the stage as the opening band was about to start.

We stood there nervously. It was a different type of atmosphere altogether. Girls held the hands of other girls, and boys were with boys, making out openly as they stood in the crowd, waiting for the band to start. None of us said a word. I daren't.

Dressed in baggy pants, fancy cotton shirts, dyed hair, and makeup—and the lead singer with a military-style French-cavalry-looking cropped jacket with gold buttons and stripes—Duran Duran took to the stage with their soft, tuneful, and likeable style of music, dancing in some sort of bebop way, swaying their arms and swooshing their legs in time with the music. Tiny, Kerry, the boys, and I just stood watching in silence.

It was a new development in the evolution of our music scene, one that would be termed *New Romanticism*.

When their set was done, the New Romantics moved toward the back, and we moved farther toward the stage for the main act of the night, relieved we were now surrounded by our own tribe and the absence of the tactile balance of the audience.

Hazel O'Connor came out to rapturous applause, wearing a skeleton suit; lit up on the dark stage; and began her feature song, "Eighth Day." We stood there and listened; the lyrics rang in our ears as she, like an automaton, sang the prophetic words and mesmerized us, especially me and Tiny.

It was like an interpretation of the Old Testament, an updated version of the creation of the world, a new spin, with an eighth day added to the story.

In the beginning was the Word.

Man said: "Let there be more light.
Electric scenes and laser beams,
neon brights the light-abhorring nights."
On the second day, he said: "Let's have a gas.
Hydrogen and cholera and pest.
Let's make some germs;
we'll poison the worms.
Man will never be suppressed."

I wondered, *Could this be a glimpse into what the future might hold as the few control the many? As we continue to build nuclear bombs, pollute, and destroy the world to the benefit of the politicians, the rulers, and the rich, fat cats who control business and probably the world?*

And he said: "Behold, what I have done?
I've made a better world for everyone.
Nobody laugh; nobody cry.
World without end, forever and ever.
Amen, amen, amen."

Who was the *he* she was referring to? I wondered. Was it the Americans, the Russians, or some other hidden forces working behind the scenes, pulling the strings? This was a different narrative, planting the seed of fear in the other extreme.

We had been on an evolutionary revelation, protesting against all that was wrong, off the rails, and in need of fixing in the world, but this was raising a dark specter of what could be, and the pendulum was swinging to the other extreme:

complacency was a killer, but so too could be progress in the extreme.

On the third, we get green and blue for pie.
On the fourth, we send rockets to the sky.
On the fifth, make the beasts and submarines.
On the sixth, man prepares his final dream.

The song was a futuristic look at the dangers before us—not just for the United Kingdom but for humankind. Was what she was professing possible? Maybe and maybe not, but it raised the stakes in giving back the control or at least a voice to the people, the youth, to at least have an opinion, have a say, and have a future—not the future of our parents and grandparents but our own future.

In our image, let's make robots for our slaves.
Imagine all the time that we can save.
Computers, machines, the silicon dream.
Seventh, he retired from the scene.

I looked across at Tiny and Kerry, and like me, they were enthralled in what they were hearing—not just a whine about where we were but a prediction of a potential future and a scary one at that. It reminded me of some of the prophecies of *War of the Worlds*, and I wondered if the woman onstage had also listened to that and if it had influenced her conclusion.

On the eighth day, machine just got upset.
A problem man had never seen as yet.

No time for flight, a blinding light,
and nothing but a void, forever night.
He said: "Behold what man has done;
there's not a world for anyone.
Nobody laughed; nobody cried.
World's at an end; everyone has died.
Forever amen (amen), amen (amen), amen
(amen)."

It was a noticeably quiet journey home; we were all caught up in our own thoughts. Tiny even stayed off his little brown bottle as the train made its way north, and we changed at Oxenholme onto the bone shaker. All of us just stared out the window, looking into space, reflecting on what we had just witnessed.

It all reminded me of a poem I had heard at a Crass concert that spoke of freedom, oppression, and staying silent in the face of all that was wrong. It disgraced those who remained silent, and it prompted people to share their voices, have their say, and stand up for what was right and each other. It was antiracist, but more, it was a call for the oppressed to speak out.

The poem was written by German theologian Martin Niemöller just after World War II.

First, they came for the Communists,
I did not speak out because I was not a Communist.
Then they came for the Socialists,
I did not speak out because I was not a Socialist.
Then they came for the trade unionists,

and I did not speak out, I was not a trade unionist.
Then they came for the Jews,
I did not speak out, I was not a Jew.
Then they came for me, and there was
no one left to speak out for me.

It was an ode, an admission of guilt of Niemöller on behalf of himself, the clergy, the intellectuals, and the German people themselves, who just stood by and watched as Hitler rose to power unchecked, ransacked Europe, and inflicted unimaginable cruelty on minorities, Jewish people, and anyone who stood in his way.

It reminded me of *The Kings of the Wild Frontier*, in which Adam Ant told the story of the Red Indians, the Native Americans, and the slaughter of people and their culture and their erasure forever.

A new world was in the making, and a new way of thinking was challenging the status quo, yet we were trying to work out what the new world might look like. Chaos prevailed; there was no master plan and no vision for the future, just an intuitive sense that the direction we were heading in was not the right one.

I got home alone, went to my room at the top of the house, and climbed out of the skylight onto the roof, my little place of seclusion. Apart from Tiny, nobody knew about it. I was up too high to be noticed, watching the world below.

It was cold, and the November stars were bright in an unusually clear night sky. I could hear *War of the Worlds* playing on my record player below. I took a snort of one of Tiny's little brown bottles he kept in my room as a reserve.

I inhaled all the way and then did it again and again and just lay on the roof, looking at the stars, fading away into oblivion.

Forever and ever, amen!

# II
# PEDROS GODROPOLOS
**WM**
1980
Bowness-on-Windermere

**I MET MY VERY OWN** Becky at my first job, at Lake Road Café. She and Louise were servers, and I was the newly appointed scone maker. Tourists back then liked their scones and jam and tea—and a lot of them at that.

Making scones sounded like an artful thing to be doing at my grand old age, but sadly, in reality, it involved opening a bag of mix, adding water, mixing it, rolling it, cutting the dough into rounds, and baking it. It was no more technical than that, really.

I would proudly present my perfectly formed scones and seek the approval of my Becky and her friend, and sometimes she'd smile and sometimes flutter her eyelashes. I was truly, madly, and deeply in love with the girl, with her almost elven looks. She reminded me of one of Tolkien's characters from Middle-earth, and perhaps she was.

My next part-time employment was at the local butcher shop. I was in charge of all things sausage-like, including the famous Cumberland variety and brawn and black pudding too.

Mr. Barnes at first tried me out at the front of the shop, a customer-facing role, but we both soon realized I was more of a back-room boy and didn't possess the patience required to deal with finicky and fussy customers. A boss and mentor of mine later in life would joke that business would have been easy without people and customers. I liked that, and maybe that was why the faceless internet would become so successful. People could take it all online. An online sausage shop! Maybe someday!

In my sausage world, including early morning starts, I often was the first one into the butcher's back of house, which was actually below the store. Each morning, when I opened the walk-in fridge at five thirty, the stares from the half dozen pigs' heads were enough to make anyone gip! But after a while, as with most things, I got used to it. "There is nothing so vile that the human form cannot become accustomed"—I remembered the old saying from one of my father's teachings relating to the horrors of prisoners of war neck deep in rancid water and rats, courtesy of the Japanese.

Cumberland sausage was my favorite task. The hand-cranked sausage maker resembled a big stainless-steel syringe. I'd fill it full of the carefully prepared and mixed filling of pork meat, breadcrumbs, herbs, and spices; place the pusher plate behind; and load the nozzle with intestines, and a steady crank would produce a line of sausage at the end, ready to link into a work of art and the finished product for the display and the fussy customers above in the shop.

I learned that if I left air pockets in the meat, cranked the handle as hard and as quickly as I could, and then pointed in the direction of my target, it made the perfect weapon of choice for pranks during those early mornings, shooting out sausage meat at high velocity.

After a while, with my pranks unnoticed, I must have been doing okay, as I was promoted to the privilege of taking up a knife and becoming a proper butcher, wrestling with what seemed huge body parts and turning them into roasts, chops, dice, or mince to feed the townsfolk and their families.

The ungodly early mornings and the solitude with the animals downstairs in the cellar got to me in the end. Across the street was a Greek restaurant owned by a Pedros Godropolos. They were looking for someone to wash up. No more early mornings, more fun, better wages, more hours, tips, and an attractive Liverpudlian waitress called Lilly sealed the deal for me.

My first night, I was partnered with Bob, the kitchen porter, who was from Exeter and had a southwestern accent; a Brylcreemed dark, almost black, coif; and tattoos. During that first evening, amid pots, pans, plates, and glasses, I learned that my new work partner was convinced he was a reincarnation of none other than Elvis Presley. I politely nodded, listened, and hummed as he went on with his theory, realizing that it took a certain sort of person to become a career-long kitchen porter.

I must have been doing okay, as I kept getting quickly promoted, and within a matter of a few weeks, I was assigned to meatballs and the tedious job of rolling them into their perfect spheres. Then came the *dolmadakia*, wrapping perfectly formed parcels of meat in vine leaves, and then came the real questionable honor: I was promoted to gutting and preparing the fresh squid, with their googly eyes, squid ink, and the disgusting smell that lingered.

Then came my real break: I got promoted to commis chef and was given the honor of making my return to the front of house—a customer-facing but not customer-dealing role. I had already decided that was not my forte. I stood in a galley kitchen alongside the head chef, Mel, helping him and supporting him. I was in charge of the meze and Greek salad.

Mel, more formally known as Melbourne Simpson, had an unusual first name, I thought back then. It turned out he'd been conceived in his namesake city in Australia. I thought it funny that although his mother had been just passing through and that, technically, he had never been to Australia, his longing to one day return to his so-called homeland was a far cry from his Wigan-accented roots.

"I'm gonna find me an Australian girl and get a visa to go live in Australia," he said.

I looked at him sideways amid my creation of our staple Greek salad, chopping and carefully placing the feta cheese on top. "You don't see many of those in these parts," I said.

Mel nodded. "She's out there somewhere," he said with a sense of certainty and his distinctive Wigan accent.

Newly promoted, I didn't want to disagree.

It was Saturday night, and we were busy—one of our records, in fact. At the pinnacle of our endeavors, Mel and I previously had cranked out more than 140 covers in just one night, and that night, at that pace, we were threatening to exceed that number.

Pedros himself ran the bar. He would dispense the beer, wine, and cocktails; issue the bills; and take the payments. It was largely a cash business in those days. He was the owner and didn't trust anyone else with those duties, apart from maybe Sue, another Liverpudlian besides Lilly who worked there.

It turned out the name Pedros Godropolos, which was emblazoned above the front door, was a loose translation of Peter Godfrey, the Irishman before me behind the bar.

Peter, otherwise known as Pedros, always wore his chef's whites and clogs. He hailed from County Cork, Ireland, and was the son of an Irish rear admiral.

"Does Ireland have a navy?" I asked, much to the boss's amusement and displeasure at the same time.

That night, in the middle of service, there was a kerfuffle behind the bar amid a restaurant full of customers. Peter was on top of our latest recruit, the head waiter, who was from Trinidad and Tobago. He had his clog off, beating Winston repeatedly over the head. Winston had been caught with his hand in the tip jar.

Mel and I helped Pedros relieve Winston of his duties and sent him packing into the street, never to return. Employment law was thin on the ground in those days, especially in the restaurant business and especially in our restaurant.

After the shift, just short of our record night, with the customers gone home, Peter, Mel, a handful of the team, and I gathered at the bar. Peter would give us our first drink for free while distributing the tips. Mel would generally buy the second round, and then it was every man and woman for him- or herself.

In exchange for a round of drinks, I was challenged to down a tablespoon of Tabasco hot sauce neat, and of course, I obliged, much to everyone's amusement. Upon swallowing the ungodly fire sauce, I turned red and then purple and then ran to the bathroom to rid myself of the poison I had just consumed. After about an hour and four more beers, the pain subsided, at least until the next time I went to the bathroom.

I managed to get Tiny a job. He replaced me as partner to Bob Elvis Presley in the dishwash. In the lull moments, we would go out back in the trash area and grab a smoke. The restaurant business was a source of income for locals like me and Tiny, but there was a plethora of Scousers, Mancs, Glaswegians, and out-of-towners. Out in the back, as we smoked, some were on weed, and some took a snort of some white powder or other. On one occasion, I witnessed one of the Scousers chasing a dragon.

I turned to Tiny. "What the fuck is he doing?"

Tiny made a point of not staring and, in fact, looking away as the Scouser held his lighter under the aluminum foil and, with a tube stuffed up his nostril, chased the smoke and inhaled.

"Fuck me. That stinks really, really fucking bad." I could smell the stench of burning chemicals from the other side of the yard. "What the fuck is that shit?"

Tiny explained the concept: a cocktail of either morphine, oxycodone, opium, yaba, or heroin heated up to inhale the smoke.

"Safer than using needles, apparently. Gets you high as fuck!"

"You tried it?"

"Na, that stuff is fucking lethal. Once yer on it, yer fucking screwed."

We looked over at the Scouser, who had just transformed into a ghost of himself; he was as white as a sheet, his eyes were popping out of his head, and his missing teeth and pocked skin now were even more apparent, as was the reason for them.

"Yer can get anything yer want round here, Willy!"

I knew he was right. The penny dropped. The influx of out-of-towners not only fueled the tourists' desires for those recreational habits but also influenced and fueled the demand among the more sheltered locals, hence the extraordinarily high level of drug abuse and addiction in that otherwise idyllic setting.

*If only my parents knew. Might have been safer to stay in Leeds after all,* I thought to myself. In the big cities, the visibility of the impact of drug addiction was more evident, more clearly on display, and therefore more of a natural deterrent. In smaller towns, it was more closeted, tucked away, and out of sight.

We worked hard and played hard. During the summer months, we worked six days a week, split shifts from ten to two, came back again at five, and usually finished around eleven. In between, we would go play pool at the Stag's

Head or go out on the lake for an afternoon jaunt, and we'd play cards after work, usually drinking, playing for money, sometimes winning but often losing to the more seasoned members of our group, including Mel. I figured he must have been saving up for sailing to Australia, and I was making decent contributions toward his passage.

One such afternoon, we went out on the lake in the middle of summer. The sun was high in the sky, and we decided to go for a swim. The icy-cold waters were renowned for the onset of cramps, which happened to me that day, and as I bobbed up and down, unable to move my limbs, I saw life slipping by as I took in a stomach full of water. Thankfully, Mel came to the rescue and dragged me back onto the boat, where I puked up what felt like a gallon of the ancient waters and remembered the earlier warnings from my swim teacher. *I should have paid more attention in school,* I thought.

Another time, we played pool for money, and I lost close to a week's wages in just one session. Mel cleared me out—another significant contribution toward his Australia fund. But the money was good, and the tips kept me in beer, cigarettes, records, and concerts for another week.

One night, Lilly was there at the bar with us, and we decided to go off to a private club together nearby. She was beautiful in every way, with dark hair and a ski-jump nose. She was an ex–Miss Liverpool, which didn't surprise me at all. She made my heart flutter even more than Becky did, and that was saying something. I sensed she was out of my league, but that didn't stop me from trying.

There was something about her. Again, she was elven-like, and I was beginning to think I had a thing for elven-looking females and wondered if I had taken *The Lord of the Rings* too literally.

I chaperoned Lilly to the local club. Although not strictly a club, it was sort of a private place where restaurant and hotel workers went for an after-hours drink once the customers had gone home.

Lilly and I sat next to three Arabic-looking men. They certainly were not hotel workers; they were just after a late-night drink, among other things, I quickly found out.

As they struck up conversation and plied us with free drinks and even a bonus pack of Benson and Hedges, one of them made an offer for Lilly to sleep with all three of them for a princely sum of £1,000. Now, that was a lot of money back then, like a month's wages or more.

I had never heard of such a thing. Lilly thought about it and asked my advice. I had no clue what to say. The man who'd asked showed her the new, crisp banknotes in fifty-pound denominations, counting it out in front of her. He got to £1,000, paused, and looked at Lilly, seeing that she wasn't saying no but wasn't saying yes either.

He tapped his friend and whispered in his ear in some unrecognizable language, and the other pulled out a huge wad of notes from his expensive-looking, tailor-made suit. "Five thousand pounds. Here you go." He smiled, with his gold tooth shining menacingly in the dark corner of the bar.

She took the wad of notes, and they looked at me, her chaperone, and passed me a whole carton of Benson and

Hedges. The four of them left together, and that was the last time I ever saw Lilly.

Apparently, according to her fellow Liverpudlian Sue, she went home the next day, apparently with a big wad; bought her parents' tenement house in Birkenhead for cash; and moved back to Liverpool, where she purchased a bar of her own, the Cavendish. Apparently, the Arabs were big tippers!

# 12
# BRIGHT SIDE
## WM
### 1980
### A northern town

**THE BUZZCOCKS WERE COMING TO** town. Of all the potential venues, some bands chose to come to our sleepy backwater nestled below the Scottish border. With a county population of fewer people than sheep and a small band of would-be punk rockers, I never understood the appeal to them.

We rocked up in the village hall with an audience of maybe one hundred at most. Strangely, the concert was during the day, which limited the number who could attend, the appeal, and the distance people could and would travel.

Waiting for the band to come on, Tiny and I sat on the dusty wooden floor of the hall, talking bollocks mainly, rambling on about our next trip, our next gig, or something equally unimportant.

We were a generation who had no plans beyond next week. None of us knew what we wanted to do or what might be left of the country once all the crazy people in charge had completely fucked it up.

Some woman called Mary Whitehouse, in horn-rimmed spectacles and prim outfits—a social conservative, whatever that meant—campaigned against punk and the Sex Pistols, getting towns to reject permits for them to play. She even got Monty Python's *Life of Brian* banned from many places, including our local cinema. Tiny and I ended up going to visit his uncle in Portsmouth, way down on the south coast, and watched it there.

I started to hum, and Tiny joined in. Together we sang in a mock cockney accent just like Eric Idle, who sang the original version: "Some things in life are bad; they can really make you mad. Other things just make you swear and curse. When you're chewing on life's gristle, don't grumble; give a whistle, and this'll help things turn out for the best."

A couple of the others came over and joined in for the chorus: "Always look on the bright side of life, de dum, de dum de dum, de dum. Always look on the light side of life, de dum, de dum de dum, de dum."

The song was another defining element of the times. It was a rebirth of the old phrase "Keep calm, and carry on" from World War II. It was a new version of the British stiff upper lip. It sang of hope in dire times and, hilariously, appeared in the film at the point when Brian, who was really an alias for Jesus, was on the cross.

A stray dog appeared from somewhere and started shagging my leg. I stood up and kicked it off, adding to the comedy of the moment we were in.

"If life seems jolly rotten, there's something you've forgotten, and that's to laugh and smile and dance and sing. When you're feeling in the dumps, don't be silly chumps; just purse your lips and whistle. That's the thing."

Then, just like in the film, the tune and the lyrics were contagious, and the entire crowd in the audience sang the familiar and popular tune, complete with the whistled chorus.

"Always look on the bright side of life, de dum, de dum de dum, de dum. Always look on the light side of life, de dum, de dum de dum, de dum."

The whole place was in uproar, with the crowd of spikes, color, leather, chains, and boots singing out the almost silly song of hope in a big "Fuck off" to the establishment for all around to hear.

"For life is quite absurd, and death's the final word. You must always face the curtain with a bow. Forget about your sin; give the audience a grin. Enjoy it; it's your last."

By that time, the band had come out to see what was going on, and even they joined in with the final chorus, accompanied by their instruments and amplification.

"Always look on the bright side of life, de dum, de dum de dum, de dum. Always look on the light side of life, de dum, de dum de dum, de dum."

"Fucking awesome." Tiny grinned and slapped me on the back, making me nearly fall over. "You, Willy, are a fucking legend!"

I smiled back. "I really wish you would stop fucking doing that, Tiny," I said as I recovered my balance.

"What? What are you talking about?" He chased after me as I moved to the front to take in the sounds of the Buzzcocks.

On the stage, the band of four did not look or dress like punk rockers. Pete Shelley, in the lead, was flanked by the bass and another lead guitar, and the drummer was raised on a stage behind. With overgrown mullets, trainers, and ordinary clothes, almost a Perry Boy look, they were from Bolton, near Manchester, and had the cool Mancunian look peppered with the attitude of the industrial city to the south of us.

Almost shyly, Shelley introduced the first song of the set, "Boredom," and the place erupted, pogoing up and down in approximate rhythm to the music and the message resonating across the hall.

It was like being part of a tribe. Our dress and looks were all individual. At the end of the day, punk rock was an interpretation and an opportunity to express yourself how you chose to do so. It was not a uniform; it wasn't rigid. Individuality was the common thread, as was the theme of the song, and of the mood at that time, "No Future."

One of my sister's friends, a couple of years older than I, was a French girl, and over the past few months, I had found she was advanced for her years and a horny French girl at that. Marie flirted with me on her regular visits to our house, and I was flattered and obliged in return. When my sister was out of the room and in the kitchen or bathroom or somewhere, Marie started whispering suggestions at first, then touching, and then kissing, which was quite nice.

One day when she came around the house, my sister was out; my father was in his garage, fixing up his latest pet project; and my mother was out shopping. Marie came to the door, where I greeted her.

"Hey, Willy, is your sister at home?" she said with a coy smile, knowing my sister was out. I let her in, and she suggested we listen to some music.

"Sure. Would you like to come upstairs with me?" I said, knowing her answer and her intent.

Up in my room, with the door locked and music playing, about thirty minutes later, I heard my dad all of a sudden bang on the door. "Willy! You dirty little bastard, what are you doing in there?"

Marie jumped off the bed naked and pulled on her clothes, and I quickly followed. She opened the door and, red-faced, said hello to my dad and scampered down the stairs and out the back door.

My father just stood there shaking his head.

After that, Marie would call me or send me messages to meet at her house while her parents were out. I was like an on-demand toy for her, and over time, she even paid me for my services, following what was the oldest profession of all time. Sometimes, when I was skint, I would instigate a meetup, we'd shag each other's brains out, and she would give me twenty pounds for the pleasure.

It was a good deal. I was happy with our arrangement based on her appetite for more and frequency of requests. I guessed she was happy with it too!

As my exploits matured, I was more and more conscious that I had a crush on Ms. Atkinson—so much so that I signed up for her English literature class. It was the only lesson I attended, and I sat at the front, in full view of that fine figure of a teacher.

She had a buxom bosom framed around her visible choice of French lace underwear; double-cuffed, starched white shirts; and sometimes a chalk-striped suit, never mind her deep brown eyes and wavy brown hair. Although she never directly flirted, I used to imagine she did.

The image of Ms. Atkinson remained vivid over the years, as did my visions of Jessica Rabbit and Betty Boop, both of whom I fancied.

Then there was the Siouxsie and the Banshees concert when, after crashing the stage on her finale, Tiny and I hung around the stage door, and she let us into the backstage party, with drinking and drugs and people making out all over the place.

I hadn't realized that performing onstage was, for some, an aphrodisiac. It obviously was for Siouxsie, and she singled me out as her target. We made out on the sofa with a bottle of vodka between us.

Tiny thought it was pretty cool, but for me, it was pretty scary. I was not experienced enough at that point in my sexual career to do the opportunity justice. In fact, we fell short of any full-blown contact apart from touching, feeling, and kissing. But hey, that was good enough for me!

"You lucky fucker, Willy!" Tiny said.

I looked at him. "What?"

"You just made out with Siouxsie fucking Sioux!" he said, and I guessed he was right. "Wait till I tell the boys, you crazy fucker!"

Tales like those, maybe with a bit of exaggeration on Tiny's part, made both of us into minor celebrities in our little town and fueled the growing number of people in our tribe.

That said, our lifestyle wasn't for everyone; we were seen as a little crazy, and sometimes that made people nervous and happier to sit on the sidelines.

I was in the middle somewhere. I managed to avoid some of the craziness of substance abuse and getting arrested by the police, but at the same time, I was part of the revolution in our little town and bringing glimpses back from the big cities, the concerts, the shopping trips, and the CND marches in London.

It was kinda cool, but not everyone thought so, including my parents and my teachers, who were still harping on about my so-called disruptiveness.

At the Buzzcocks' show, they played their encore performance: "You spurn my natural emotions. You make me feel I'm dirt, and I'm hurt. And if I start a commotion, I run the risk of losing you, and that's worse."

Ever fallen in love with someone you shouldn't have fallen in love with?

# 13
# NIMROD
## WM
## May 5, 1980
## London

**APART FROM TOMMY COOPER DYING** onstage on live TV and Bernard Manning using the f-word and getting banned from the box, that night's news left a real imprint on many that day, including me. The story brought to the limelight a secretive and previously barely heard of arm of the British Army, a group apparently called the SAS.

All week long, there had been developing news about a growing situation at the Iranian embassy in London, a big white building at 16 Princes Gate, South Kensington. A week earlier, six armed men had stormed the embassy and taken twenty-six people hostage, mainly embassy staff but also some visitors and a policeman who had been guarding the building.

The terrorists were from the Democratic Revolutionary Front for the Liberation of Arabistan, who were apparently

131

upset and fighting for Arab national sovereignty in the southern Iranian province of Khuzestan. I had to look it up in my world atlas to even understand where on earth it was. They were demanding the release of Arab prisoners and safe passage back from whence they'd come.

The Iron Lady had already begun her stance against the unions, and now this was her chance to make another stance and earn her reputation as a straight-talking leader who would not bend over and wilt to pressure, as many of her predecessors had done since Churchill.

Britain was on its knees, and at some point, since the sacrifices and victories in Normandy, we had lost the *Great* in *Great Britain*, and the nation needed to get back some self-respect and pride. This was a fight for our future on every front, and we needed to take a united stand as one nation together, not divided and settling for a slow death, which had been the pattern of decline over the past three decades.

Earlier that week, through negotiations and succumbing to minor demands from the terrorists, they'd released five of the hostages but had apparently become increasingly frustrated at the lack of progress of the more material items on demand, including their safe passage home.

The day before, day six, the terrorists had killed one of the hostages and thrown the body out of the embassy and threated to kill a hostage every half hour if their demands were not met. Maggie had called in the SAS, the Special Air Service, to remedy the situation, and the event was unfolding on the news before me, code-named Operation Nimrod.

As the news broadcaster narrated the scene, at the white embassy building in South Kensington, a handful of dark figures dressed in black, with gas masks and guns, stood on the balcony. Explosions rang out, dogs barked, further explosions sounded, and then gunfire rang in the air and from within the depths of the building.

More shadowy figures appeared on the adjacent balconies, shepherding the hostages to safety. In seventeen minutes, they rescued all but one of the remaining hostages, killing five of the six terrorists.

"One of them blokes is a local," Tiny said. "Well, Carlisle," he added to clarify.

I looked at him. "How is Carlisle fucking local, Tiny?"

"Well, it's in fucking Cumbria! Near as dammit," he snapped.

"All right, fair one." I smiled at him, wishing I had not snapped.

"My uncle was tellin' me. Some geezer called Rusty Herman or maybe Dusty Firmin or something like that. Anyway, whatever—near enough. A local boy."

"Good on him," I said. "At least he got out of here and is doing something interesting."

"Diving off balconies and killing fricking terrorists sounds like fun to me." Tiny grinned.

On December 8 that year, news broke from New York of the assassination of John Winston Ono Lennon, MBE.

While leaving his New York residence, the Dakota, Lennon was presented a copy of his album *Double Fantasy* by

Mark David Chapman to sign before leaving for a recording session at Record Plant Studio with his wife, Yoko Ono.

Chapman, a recently unemployed resident of the state of Hawaii, hung around outside the Dakota for Lennon's return later that night, and as John and Yoko walked toward the archway entrance to the building, Chapman fired five hollow-point bullets from his .38 special revolver, four of which hit Lennon in the back.

Chapman remained at the scene, reading a copy of J. D. Salinger's *The Catcher in the Rye*, until he was arrested by police. He later said he was inspired by Salinger's fictional character Holden Caulfield and incensed by Lennon's much-publicized remark that the Beatles were "more popular than Jesus" and the lyrics of his later songs "God" and "Imagine."

Lennon was pronounced dead on arrival at Roosevelt Hospital that night.

*Bang, bang*—you're dead!

Years later, I continued to keep my eye on the press. When I could, I would get a copy of *Le Monde*, which regularly ran the story of an ongoing mystery from the past.

I sat in a pub, the Firkin Up the Back Passage in Plymouth, England. I had done my time in the army. Courtesy of Her Majesty, I was going through resettlement and getting ready for my adjustment back to civilian life.

By that time, I had been to shitholes all around the world. Plymouth was up there alongside Bradford. I fucking hated the place. I didn't like the place or the people, I wasn't really enjoying my course in human resource management—in fact, it sucked. I always had thought that work meant looking after people, but I quickly found out it had fuck all to do with that, apart from just getting out of people what the corporation wanted and needed. It was another form of oppression and leveraging people to make the fat cats even fatter.

Finished with college for the day, I picked up the newspaper from the newsagents on the corner and walked back from the university with my black-box briefcase, distracted by the newspaper headline: *"Mystère de dix ans résolu?"* Having studied French in school, I translated the headline to "Ten-Year Mystery Solved?" I needed to sit down. I had a French-to-English dictionary in my briefcase. As I crossed the road, a black 3 Series BMW almost ran me over as I crossed the pedestrian crossing.

"What the fuck?" I shouted at the driver, who flipped two fingers. "What the fuck is wrong with you, you fucking egit?"

The driver, a man in his midtwenties, full of testosterone, rolled his window down and started to shout back. I turned to walk to the driver's door with my own testosterone and anger levels on overload. As I got closer, he must have seen the red mist in my eyes, as he started to take off. I thrashed my heavy black briefcase at the car and took out the rear passenger window, shattering it, as he sped off.

"Fucker!" I stood in the road, watching the BMW disappear from view, minus a window.

Even years later, I didn't really understand my anger. After leaving the service, I had more of an understanding, but it was far from complete. I felt that familiar postviolence nausea and needed a beer and a quiet space to decipher the newspaper article.

I walked into the Back Passage. I hated the name of the place, but they did serve decent beer, and at that time of day, it would be quiet.

"All right, my lover?" the barman said in greeting.

"What?"

"What can I get you to drink, my lover?"

I theatrically turned to look around and behind me. "Who the fuck are you talking to?" I looked him in the eye, and he looked away. "Just give me a pint of Cold Courage, will yer, and less of the *my lover* shite?"

I had been there long enough to know the term was one of apparent endearment and a common greeting in the town. I despised it as much as I did the city, but I wanted a beer and a cigarette and was keen to read the article.

I sat down in a quiet corner alone.

# 14
# ENEMIES OF THE STATE
WM

**OUR BRAND-NEW FERGUSON 9800 SERIES** color television set was a welcome addition to our home as we watched the procession of Soviet tanks heading into a place called Kabul in a far-off land called Afghanistan.

Apparently, in the days previously, the Russians had persuaded their president, Amin, to leave the People's House palace in the center of the city for a palace retreat outside, therefore isolating him from power.

More than forty thousand Soviet soldiers, tanks, and weapons marched into the capital, largely uncontested, capturing more than twenty thousand Afghan soldiers and, after a midnight trial, executing the president and installing a Moscow-loyal replacement, Babrak Karmal.

The move created concern and instability in the region as the mujahideen pledged to remove the infidels from their lands, and Pakistan was concerned about further Soviet invasions south into their territory. Meanwhile, India aired concerns about Western governments, including the United States, bolstering financial and military support for Pakistan, India's longtime rival neighbor.

"The bloody Ruskies," my father would say.

So it wasn't just the Welsh, the Irish, and the Arabs he had an issue with; it was the Russians too!

He did, however, explain to me that he had a lot of respect for the Russians, as apparently, if not for them, Hitler might have won the war.

"The Battle of Stalingrad diverted the Nazis' attention on the western front, and the Soviets lost over thirteen percent of their population, more than twenty six million souls. And that doesn't include the deaths Stalin ordered himself!"

I figured he sort of was okay with the Russians but not really.

The mujahideen were joined by a young twenty-two-year-old man from Riyadh, straight from university. He acted as the catalyst to funnel money, equipment, and support from the Arab world into Afghanistan and take the fight to the Russian invaders of Arab soil.

Funded by both the Arab world and the United States, the man was called Osama bin Laden and would eventually form Al-Qaeda ten years later.

Earlier that day, I had bought the Boomtown Rats single "I Don't Like Mondays," which apparently was about a school shooting in San Diego. A sixteen-year-old girl, Brenda Spencer, who lived across the street from the elementary school, had shot the principal and a custodian dead and injured a police officer and eight kids.

After the assault, a reporter reached Spencer while she was still in the house and asked her why she had done it. She reportedly answered, "I don't like Mondays. This livens up the day." Hence the inspiration for Bob Geldof and Johnnie Fingers's new release.

"I mean, Willy, I don't like bloody Mondays either, but that's a bit fucking harsh," said Tiny of the story.

Despite our look and our sometimes craziness, Tiny and I had lots of philosophical debates about all sorts of stuff, not only the obvious crap going down at the time with politics, the unions, and strikes but also deeper subjects, trying to make sense of the world we found ourselves in.

Although we were punk rockers of sorts, we shared a love of music in general, especially songs with strong lyrics. One song that often came up for debate was "Imagine" by John Lennon.

Neither of us could really understand the *why*, which was important to us. The *why* was part of the reason for the punk rock movement, because we were sick of being told what to do "just because that's what it is." We wanted to understand the *why* and challenge the status quo, not just conform because we were told to.

We both had grandparents who'd gone through the Great War, some at home, some at the front, and some never to return. There was a local legend of a platoon of riflemen from the local area who had gone off with their tin hats and their guns, and only two of them had returned.

From their trenches, in all the mud and the guts, they were sent over the top to face certain death as victims of

German machine-gun spray mowing them down like a summer's harvest and drenching the fields with blood.

"Fuck that for a game of soldiers," Tiny said. "Why the hell would you do that?" We both shook our heads. "Just because some officer with a bloody handlebar mustache tells you to go over the top. Why the hell would anyone do that?"

It was one of the world's many mysteries, as was another often-discussed subject of debate.

"So I sort of get that mad fucker Hitler and how he justified in his own fucked-up head that what he was doing was right. But what I really don't understand is the guard, the normal guy at Belsen, Auschwitz, or one of them other places. They thought what they were doing was okay as they herded those poor fuckers into the gas chambers?" Tiny said. "Or, as bad, the fuckers driving the tractors that would scoop up the bodies and dump them into the mass graves."

We both shook our heads and often scratched them, trying to get our heads around the tragedy.

It was clearly a topic of confusion for Johnny Rotten and the Sex Pistols too, with their song "Einmal War Belsen Bortrefflich": "Belsen was a gas, I heard the other day. In the open graves where the Jews all lay. 'Life is fun, and I wish you were here,' they wrote on postcards to those held dear."

Our interpretation of the lyrics was as a song of condemnation of the atrocities committed by the Nazis, empathy for all the poor souls lost, and disdain for the evil of the perpetrators.

As a kid growing up in the height of the Yorkshire Ripper rampage, I felt it was just another example of the extraordinarily bleak times of those days, with little future of hope for many. The Yorkshire Ripper captured the headlines, and most everyone followed the gruesome killings in the press with rapt attention. *Why do people love to read about or watch the misery of others?* I often wondered, and I had no answers. Simple human nature, I guessed.

I used to visit my aunt Margaret and uncle Philip in Huddersfield, Yorkshire, with my parents and witness our great country's demise. It was dogged by unemployment and, in Philip's and Margaret's cases, local council employees destined for a life of mediocrity. Cycle-meal menus for the family were cooked up by my grandma—the same meal on the same day every week, sun, rain, or shine.

Going to the local chip shop for our haddock, chips, peas, and scraps was a highlight. We'd eat in the back of the car on the way home. While standing in the line waiting, I looked at the intimidating rendered image of the Yorkshire Ripper on a poster:

## Do you know this man?
### Call the West Yorkshire Police hotline: (01924) RIPPER

Unfortunately, many didn't understand the antiestablishment rhetoric. We were misunderstood, and some, if it suited their agenda, tried to say we were celebrating the atrocities. Quite the opposite was true, in fact. We just did not believe those things should be buried and gathering dust anymore. The same was true for the leaders of the day; their dirty laundry needed to be seen, and they needed to be held accountable for their actions and their sins.

Willy Mitchell

Since the Iranian Revolution that year, the government of Iran had been accused by several countries of training, financing, and providing weapons and safe havens for nonstate militant actors, such as Hezbollah in Lebanon, Hamas in Gaza, the Islamic Jihad, and the Popular Front for the Liberation of Palestine—the subject of fun-poking by Monty Python in *Life of Brian*.

In Europe, Germany, France, Italy, the Netherlands, Belgium, and Luxembourg were all gathering together to create the European Project. The idea was that countries of Europe could band together economically on immigration, trade, other policies, and standardization and rules of engagement to create a united superstate that would hopefully avoid another war in Europe but also be big enough and weighty enough to compete with world superpowers, such as the United States.

Great Britain, led by the Conservative government of the time, joined the European Economic Community in 1973, and in 1975, in a national referendum on the matter, two-thirds of the voters elected to stay in. The last of the right-wing dictatorships in Europe had fizzled with the overthrow of the Salazar regime in Portugal in 1974 and the death of General Franco of Spain in 1975.

By 1979, it was clear voters regretted their decision, as an opinion poll recorded that 60 percent would vote to leave and only 32 percent would stay. Rules on our fishing industry, our currency, bananas, and our beloved sausages fueled the displeasure of the British people.

In one of our debates, Tiny said, "What I don't understand is that Germany started two world wars, we won them both, and now they are calling the shots."

I had to agree; the main gainers in the Euro Project would be ze Germans. "If they couldn't conquer Europe by military might, then doing it through economic warfare might actually work out a lot better for them."

"Exactly, Willy. What do these people not get? What the hell is wrong with them?" He was, of course, referring to our government, Parliament, and all the people supposedly managing our country in a race to the bottom.

"Fucking overpaid, overrated, useless pieces of shit!"

"They couldn't manage their way out of a paper fucking bag."

That sense of disillusion peaked in 1980, when 65 percent wanted to leave, and provided Maggie with the mandate to renegotiate our terms of membership, which she did, and the anti-EU crowd calmed down, at least for a while.

While our own home industries were in steep decline, Germany steadily resurrected its postwar manufacturing sector. Rather than building weapons, guns, tanks, and submarines, some of the most revered engineers in the world were making VWs, Audis, Porsches, BMWs, Mercedes-Benzes, and Siemens and Bosches.

"What the hell is all that about?" Tiny said as I just shook my head in agreement of disbelief.

"And then what about that weird fucker on *Jim'll Fix It*? What a fucking creep he is."

"Why would any of those kids think it's okay to sit on that fucking perverts' knee?"

"Yeh, in his bloody stupid track suit and his medallions and sovereigns."

"Smoking his big, stupid fucking cigar."

Later, came Diego Armando Maradona and his so-called hand of God in the quarterfinal of the World Cup in Mexico against England. He took his revenge on a nation as he scored Argentina's first goal with his hand and his second with pure genius to beat England and knock them out of the tournament.

There was a lot to rant about in those days. It was unimaginable and unbelievable. Was there any wonder the youth of that day were disillusioned and wanted change?

The attitude was "You dirty bastards! The fucking lot of you!"

# 15
# WHITE RIOT
# WM
## 1981
## Great Britain

**FOLLOWING THE WINTERS OF DISCONTENT,** 1981 was the year of fifty riots, a wedding, an arrest, a funeral, and a theme song from the Clash.

Prince Charles and Lady Diana Spencer, an aristocrat kindergarten teacher, married at Saint Paul's Cathedral in London, and the whole nation stopped, with more than thirty million people watching the event on TV, including Tiny, my family, and me, upon the insistence of my mother. Tiny and I wanted to be anywhere else but there.

We all sat in the TV room, around our Ferguson 9800, and watched the proceedings flow with a big pot of Yorkshire tea, sandwiches, cakes, and scones—a perfect and very British way to celebrate the momentous event, my mum thought.

At the time, Tiny and I were more interested in all the craziness going on in the outside world.

Peter Sutcliffe, a lorry driver from Bradford, had just been arrested for murdering thirteen women and brutalizing several others. He had been branded the Yorkshire Ripper, and since rising to infamy over the past several years, he had cast a shadow over the north of England, and his reign of terror had gripped the region.

It was like growing up in the middle of a horror film. Regularly, the news would report on another woman, teacher, doctor, or prostitute brutally attacked, murdered, or seriously injured, often with hammers and often in the dark of night. Their bodies were found like pieces of meat by the roadside.

It was difficult to compute what would lead someone to do that at least twenty times, let alone once. The whole thing set up a disturbing undercurrent in my soul. I found it difficult to comprehend how someone could do such horrific things to other people, yet I somehow understood that we all were capable of committing atrocities simply for the sake of doing it because we enjoyed it. Humanity seemed to me to be a pack of contradictions, which made it almost impossible for me to figure out where I fit in.

Later, Tiny and I would find out the hard way just how far a person was willing to go to simply survive. People killed for a lot less than survival, but when survival was in the equation, all bets were off. People would do anything to stay alive, including killing their own families. However, back in those dark old days of the early 1980s, I was still trying to get my head around what being a human was all about, and I stupidly thought I could trust in the goodness of humanity, when in fact, one could trust only that humanity was inherently fucked up. A person could never trust anyone, not even a spouse, unless he or she was prepared to be hugely disappointed.

The damned IRA were as bad as the Ripper, bombing, kidnapping, killing, and murdering. Tiny said one day during one of our current-affairs sessions, "Look, Willy. They even kidnapped a fucking racehorse." He was right; they had, and it didn't make any fucking sense, at least to us anyway.

But I knew Ireland was far more complicated, and words my father once had said about Africa apparently applied to Ireland: "Anyone who says they understand Africa doesn't truly understand Africa." Despite that, I still tried.

The history was deep and long in the past. I knew from my own roots that the English had raped, pillaged, stolen from, and tried to break the will of the Scots for centuries. The people over the border, including my people, had fought back equally hard. They had fewer resources but made up for it with sheer passion, determination, and the willingness to have a good fight.

"Probably fueled with copious amounts of whisky," Tiny said.

"Why do you have to be always so fucking right, Tiny?"

He answered only with a big grin, a shrug of his shoulders, and his "Ho, ho, ho." We were in the Odana, having a round of Irn-Brus and sharing a plate of chips.

The Irish had been through a similar struggle but not as blatant in defiance as the Scots. The English ruled the Irish with the weapon of economic control, suppressing the Irish to stay in their place. That created a different type of rebellion, a deep hatred, and a more covert fight and retaliation.

"The Irish are similar to the Sicilians in their rebellion against their overlord," Tiny said.

"How so, Tiny?" I was expecting a well-versed and well-researched lecture. "What the fuck do you know about the Sicilians? Or the Irish, for that matter?

"Well, Billy Boy, I'm about to fucking tell yer if yer just shut yer fucking cake hole!"

I enjoyed our sessions. It was the nearest we would ever get to a debating society. Boys like Tiny and me weren't invited to such at school, if a school even had them.

"Well, yer see, there are actually a lot of similarities between Sicily and Ireland."

"Go on."

"Well, as yer know, the English take the mickey out of the Irish, right?"

"I guess so, Tiny!"

"Well, what not many people know is that the Italians do the same to the Sicilians."

"Okay."

"They both look down on their island neighbors."

He went on to explain that the Irish and the Sicilians shared the oppression of the mainlanders' owning the land and renting it back to them at mostly extortionate rates. The Sicilians rebelled by stealing meat, olives, grapes, milk, and fruit from the landlords."

"Yer see, if any of them got fucking caught with a goat, a vine of grapes, or a flagon of olive oil, it meant certain death, hence the formation of the Cosa Nostra!"

"What the fuck? You've been watching too many films, Tiny."

He was now pacing back and forth like a professor at a college, loving every moment. "Yer see, *Cosa Nostra* meant, roughly translated, 'Our Thing' or, in other words, 'the Same Thing,' meaning they were in it together. If one got caught, then everyone was screwed, so that was the foundation of the Honored Society. Ring any bells, young Willy?"

"You fucking know that annoys the fuck out of me." I glared at him. "Did Mr. Stephens ever suggest you should become a lawyer, a barrister, or maybe even a fucking politician, Tiny?"

He blushed and shrugged. "Not sure about that, but he didn't rule out working at the fucking coffee shop!" He recovered, and his big grin came out in full salute. "But seriously, Willy, the formation of the Mafia was really no different from the formation of the IRA. They're fundamentally the same thing. They are built on the exact same foundation."

I had to admit Tiny had a point: the annexation of the northern part of their island, the power entrusted to the Protestants in a predominantly Catholic land, the imbalance of power, and the further suppression of the Irish people, not directly by the English but now by their Irish Protestant proxies.

As my mother always told me, "There's two sides to every story, Willy." That was certainly the case in Ireland, and thanks to Tiny, I now knew that was true in Sicily too.

"It is true, Tiny. Out of suppression comes rebellion. Out of oppression come hatred and violence. What do you think we are seeing right now with all these fucking riots everywhere?"

"No, man, you got it wrong, Billy Boy. That's different. That's rebellion in the face of mediocrity and stupidity. It's totally different."

Again, he was right, but I was not about to admit it to him. It was all part of our friendly banter, our relationship, and how we sparked off each other. It often crossed my mind that we would have made a great double act in the houses of Parliament. But apart from the exceptions of Adams and McGuinness, one needed a clean police record for that. It was too late for Tiny and me!

We had both seen *The Godfather*, and I had been to Sicily on a family road trip, but we also knew about the real and present danger of the IRA.

The shifty Gerry Adams and Martin McGuinness of Sinn Fein fame were former IRA terrorists themselves. On the other side was the equally horrible, if not worse, Reverend Ian Paisley, with his deep, booming voice; his references to the Bible, doom, and gloom; and his encouraging his people to do bad things in the name of the Lord.

Listening to Stiff Little Fingers, I sensed the Irish people had had enough of the troubles and just wanted to get on with their lives. I knew people on my side of the Irish Sea also had had enough of the IRA blowing things up and murdering people. I knew I had.

People in the Maze Prison were on hunger strikes. Bobby Sands somehow became almost a household name as he went through sixty-six days of refusing to eat before his body eventually gave up. Another nine followed, and the world watched.

"Then there's the bloody union bollocks," Tiny said, interrupting my thoughts. "If these fuckers aren't careful, we will have no industry left in this country."

"Yep, close the doors, and turn off the lights." I had heard someone clever on TV say that.

I recalled my father's frequent laments about the UK car industry. We once had made the best cars in the world, but the unions had increased their demands so much that they had taken many long-standing marques out of business, and they would continue to do so if left to their own devices.

"Look at the likes of that fucker Arthur Scargill in his chauffeur-driven Jag, with his big salary, persuading all those poor fuckers to go on strike and fuck up their jobs, their careers, and their livelihoods," Tiny said.

"Their lives." I nodded.

"What a bloody shit show."

He was right; it was a shit show, and no one in power was doing anything about it, although despite a lot of animosity and hatred toward her, Margaret Thatcher was the best chance we had, in my opinion. She made tough decisions. Sometimes they were unpopular, but at least she knew that inaction and sticking with the status quo were not the answer. Now was the time for action, or we'd suffer a long, slow, and painful death.

The youth of the nation had a similar point of view, but the options open to them for action were limited, and rioting spread across the United Kingdom like wildfire, including the riots of Red Lion Square in '74 following a march by the

National Front, Notting Hill in '76, the Battle of Lewisham, the Southall riots of '79, and Brixton in '81, with similar riots reported across the nation. They all appeared as regular occurrences on the ITN *Ten O'Clock News.* Boring suited newsreaders reported on those jolly inconvenient disruptions to society.

The lyrics of the time set the social mood and the commentary on the real state of the union: "White riot. I want a riot. White riot, a riot on my own. White riot, a riot of our own."

Tiny and I boarded the bus. It was early. We had been waiting at the Odana Café since five o'clock. We were heading to London.

Over the course of our recent debates, we had been focusing on the Cold War and the buildup of nuclear armaments as a result.

"If we're not careful, there'll be fuck all left!" Tiny stated his position.

"Yeh, but do you think anyone is stupid enough to press the button?"

"They did in Nagasaki and Hiroshima," he said, making a valid point.

We had seen the videos, which were originally intended as public safety in case of a nuclear strike.

"Have you seen those fucking videos, Willy?"

I nodded, but Tiny already knew I had.

"They're fucking terrifying. What they're really saying is that we wouldn't stand a fucking hope in hell."

I had to admit the notion of lying facedown on the ground with my hands over my head or trying to climb into the refrigerator seemed like grasping at straws.

"It's those fat cats, I tell yer, who'll be all right. In their secret concrete bunkers as they let us all fucking die. Then, Willy, they'll come back out when its safe and be even fucking richer than they already fucking are!"

It was the ultimate conspiracy theory, but like many of those theories, it had good enough grounding and circumstantial evidence that it could feasibly have been true.

We had decided to go support the cause, and we joined fifty other like-minded people on the bus that morning to join the Campaign for Nuclear Disarmament later that afternoon. We boarded the bus, headed toward the back, and found two seats together. I took the window for entertainment on the four-hour or so journey south.

With Tiny's green PVCs and donkey jacket and my leopard-skin pants and blueys, we somewhat stood out from the occupants of the bus.

"What the fuck's this, Willy—a fucking archaeologists' field trip?"

I laughed out loud and looked around the bus at the anoraks, the sandals with socks, and the percentage of people with glasses—half-moon ones at that.

"We just halved the average age of the passengers, Tiny," I said, and we laughed aloud together.

The passengers, who were already paying us a lot of attention, stared at us even more, and like a pair of naughty schoolboys in a library, we suppressed our smirks and sank back into our draylon seats for the ride to London.

"This is going to be a long fucking journey," Tiny said as he fiddled with his Sony Walkman and earbuds and pressed Play, escaping to faraway lands.

"Yeh, thanks for that, Tiny!" I could hear the tinny sound coming from his earbuds to add to my annoyance. I stared out the window as we went round Kendal Bypass and headed toward Kirkby Lonsdale and the M6.

Four hours and twenty-five minutes later, we arrived in London, and I was glad to get off the bus and also see that we weren't the only flamboyantly dressed demonstrators that day, although we still were outnumbered by the archaeologists.

We were on the fancy, lush, and expensive Park Lane in Hyde Park, where the rally would start. We'd head past the Wellington Arch, down Constitution Hill and the Mall, then down Whitehall, and past Downing Street to Parliament Square, just more than two miles.

"Fucking hell, there's a thousand here. How many der yer reckon, Willy?"

I surveyed the crowds; my reference point at that level of magnitude was a United game crowd. "Maybe a hundred thousand?" Later, I would find out that my estimate was under; in fact, there were more than a quarter million protestors that day. We had never seen such a crowd.

We gathered for the speakers. Michael Foot and Tony Benn from the Labor Party seemed to be the biggest political attractions. Speakers were dotted around the park, which made it almost possible to hear what they were saying.

"Told yer we would have seen more watching it on the TV, Tiny," I said.

We squeezed together like sardines in readiness for the speeches.

"President Reagan cannot ignore us, because President Reagan does not own Britain and Europe. This is our continent, and we will shape it for ourselves!" Benn made his play, and the crowd cheered in agreement.

Michael Foot, the Labor Party leader, went on. "In this autumn of 1981, we stand at the most dangerous moment of all, ever since these nuclear weapons have come into operation, and that is why it has been so necessary to reestablish this campaign."

More cheers came from the crowd, but to our left, we could hear some crazy chanting coming from about one hundred yards away, from what looked like a contingent of skinheads. A tide of people got out of their way as they seemed to come in our general direction.

Foot added to his statement. "The people now reject the insanity of nuclear weapons."

We could hear in the distance the crowd roaring, but Tiny and I were distracted by the mob of what must have been more than two hundred skinheads, with all their denim, studs, knuckle dusters, and anger, getting uncomfortably close.

One of them, a big, gangly youth, had probably the biggest boom box I had ever seen on his shoulder, blasting out thrash music like a piper on a battlefield as his army went through the crowd, trashing everything in their way and shouting, "Fuck off home, Commies!"

The archaeologists at the front just turned and ran in the opposite direction as the skinheads got closer, pulling down the speakers, kicking cans on the grass, picking up bottles, and throwing them into the crowd around them.

A nearby concession that was selling tea and bacon sandwiches tipped over and burst into flames as the Calor gas pipe broke loose. With all the archaeologists in full retreat, that left Tiny and me and others of our clan, who were people we didn't know, in the middle of a full-blown riot.

Tiny and I took our positions back to back, ready to fight our way out of the situation. Tiny shouted, "These are a bunch of crazy fuckers!" He was stating the obvious.

"Yeh, thanks for that, Tiny!"

The flames spread to a couple of nearby cars, which not only fueled the fires but also seemed to stoke the level of anger. Now emerged pitched battles, the appearance of clubs, the crunch of knuckle dusters, the flash of razor blades, and police sirens closing in.

"What the fuck?" I yelled.

I was okay with the fists, the clubs, and maybe even the knuckle dusters, but as with my respectful fear of drugs, I was scared of razors, especially in a fight and especially in a situation like that.

"C'mon, Tiny! Let's get the flock out of here."

Evidently, Tiny needed no persuasion. We made our way back toward Park Lane. I was behind Tiny. Some big, fat-necked skinhead tried to take a side swipe to Tiny's temple, but I blocked him and stuffed my knuckle in his eye, and we rushed past and away from him. He was already in a brawl with another. We got to the edge of what looked like a mass battle and came across the police, complete with full riot gear. We were on edge.

"What the fuck now, Willy?"

I looked to the left and saw another concession stand overturned and in flames. "C'mon. I have an idea."

We legged it over, and sure enough, everyone was staying clear of the flames, even the police, until the fire department arrived. Flames roared, and I could feel the heat, but I knew that was a way out: through the flames into relative safety.

A bottle came flying out of the crowd and hit Tiny on the crown of his head, butt first, splitting his head open. Immediately, crimson flowed down his hairline onto his face. "What the fuck?"

I passed him my red Harrington to quell the blood flow. "C'mon, Tiny. Let's get the fuck out of here!"

We ran through the flames around the side of the concession and onto Park Lane. We had made it beyond the cordons and the front line of the police battling with the skinheads a hundred yards back to our right.

"Thank fuck for that, Willy," Tiny said, holding my jacket on the top of his head with blood still running down his face.

"Keep it tight, Tiny. I'll take a look in a minute."

We headed across Park Lane and onto Curzon Street a couple of blocks away, and we were distant enough from the riot to pause so I could take a look at Tiny's head. It was a gash about a half inch. I applied pressure and, after a couple of minutes, quelled the flow. I tore out the pockets of my jacket, made a compress, and wrapped the arms of my jacket round his head, tying a knot on top.

"There you go, mate. You look fucking ridiculous, but that'll stop the bleeding for now."

Tiny grinned back. "You, Willy, are a fucking legend!"

"And you, Tiny, look fucking ridiculous, but hey, what changed there?" It was my turn to slap him on the back.

A double-decker bus pulled up at the stop, and we jumped on and got even farther away from all the madness. Thank fuck for that!

We had no inclination to get back on the archaeologist bus back north. Neither of us wanted to go back to the skinheads. Instead, we headed to Euston Station, got Tiny cleaned up in the toilets, and boarded the next train home.

"Let's get the flock out of here!"

The youth and many others were so frustrated that the mood and the temperature had reached the boiling point. Riots plagued London and were spreading to almost every city across the nation.

The Brixton riots resulted in more than three hundred injured. More than one hundred arrests occurred during clashes with black youths in Finsbury Park, Forest Green, and Ealing, London.

Almost the entire nation was on fire. London was burning!

# 16
# CHARLIE HARPER
## WM
### 1981
## A northern town

**GROWING UP IN THE NORTH** of England at the time had its challenges, especially in a northern tourist town. During the summer months, we had an influx of outsiders from the larger cities and towns, such as Liverpool or Manchester, and all the metropolitanism they would bring, including their fashion, music, attitudes, money, and drugs.

For such a beautiful place nestled in the lakes, it was shocking how many schoolmates fell victim to drugs over the years. I always concluded that it was because we rarely got to see the real horrors of those drugs: the homelessness, prison time, wasting away, loss of family, and squalor associated with the life-draining and life-changing substances.

Thankfully, I was not one who fell into that trap, preferring beer and whisky instead. Thank God something inside me stopped what I suspected would have been a one-way trip to doom if I had developed a love of hard drugs or even weed. I was not the brightest bulb on the Christmas tree, but I did have eyes. I could see what sniffing glue and taking speed and everything else did to some of my friends, and I didn't want to go there. I might have been a bit wiser for my age than I gave myself credit for during that period of my tumultuous life.

Perhaps I owed my relative stability to my family. I was never really all that close to my parents or my sister, but they were a constant. We went on family holidays each year to Portugal. I went to football matches with the hotel's waiter, Miguel, and we would go see the legendary sides, such as Sporting Lisbon or Benfica, play the local team, *Portimão*.

One year, we decided to drive down, and after the ferry to France, we stopped by Paris on our way south, in search of my father's fondest Parisian restaurant, Le Petit Cochon in Montmarte. The old waiters had starched white tunics, napkins over their arms, and mustaches.

I was not sure if it was Paris or me, but I took to people-watching and observation.

Back at home, we had our own fair share of characters and the opportunity to people-watch.

On my daily run to the local newspaper shop, Taskers, I often saw the Old Tramp. In that part of the world at the time, homelessness wasn't really a thing. It didn't really exist, and besides, it was too damn cold and wet to voluntarily sleep under the stars in that part of the world. For weeks, he would hang out and beg in his old tweed woolen three-piece suit, until, I assumed, when he got sick of it, his chauffeur would turn up in his old classic Silver Shadow Rolls-Royce, pick him up, and take him back to the seclusion of his mansion hidden away in the hills and the forest just outside town. Maybe it was that seclusion he was escaping from.

"All the lonely people, where do they all come from?"

Then there was the Bird Lady, who would walk the shore of the lake with a basket full of seeds on her arm, feeding the swans, ducks, and seagulls. She did not speak to anyone apart from the birds, and she would appear as quickly and suddenly as she disappeared, as if she were a ghost. No one knew where she came from or where she ever went.

They both reminded me of that famous Beatles song: "Eleanor Rigby picks up the rice in the church where the wedding has been, lives in a dream."

On those shores, in that vast playground, we would adventure, like *Swallows and Amazons* but in a time of far less innocence.

We would borrow a boat now and again to venture onto the lake, Belle Isle, the smaller islands, and the sunken treasure boat. Once, we headed out to Ambleside, rowing, until a mate passed by in his own borrowed speedboat and towed us to that party. It would have been a lot quicker and far less risky just to get the bus, but it would have been a lot less fun.

Like pirates, we boarded some of the sailboats moored out on the lake and gathered what booty we could. We sold petrol to the tourists on the end of a pier. The old fuel-pump gauge didn't work, so we manually calculated the cost, exaggerating the charge to the customers. They were, for the most part, wealthy tourists and didn't care how much we charged them. The wealthier they looked, the more we charged, and they happily paid.

On one such occasion, an opulent motorboat turned up; the captain wore a captain's hat, fancy watch, and sovereign ring, and the boat was adorned with beautiful young ladies in various stages of undress. Tiny's and my eyes were popping out of their sockets, but we were not distracted too much to charge a double premium on the fuel for their love boat. The captain did not blink as he handed over a fresh, crisp wad of twenty-pound notes.

Tiny and I did get ourselves into some mischief, but it was all pretty innocent, until things unraveled in horrific form on that fateful night in Paris. We broke into one of the local restaurants to steal the tip jar. We climbed in through the half-light window of the women's bathroom and located the disappointingly half-empty jar. Then we saw flashlights through the front windows—the local copper—and made a swift exit from the rear, managing to scoop up a small percentage of the dismal booty in the jar.

Amid the hunting, fishing, and adventuring, girls were becoming of greater interest to us, with Carrie-Ann being my next crush and the focus of our boat trip to Ambleside, which we made to attend her birthday party.

There was little structure, planning, or direction in life; we mostly lived and had fun from one day to the next, from moment to moment. There was little point in planning—planning for what? To grow up and join the post office, marry, have kids, retire, and die?

We discovered an upturned tree on the other side of the lake, and borrowing another rowboat, we would venture across the icy waters, up onto the hill, and into the forest and set up camp in the moss-lined shelter created by the old tree roots.

On our way back across the lake one time, Tiny thought it would be a good idea to pull the plug on the little rowboat, and the vessel gurgled and gushed as it filled with water and sank. Tiny, two of our mates, and I, with our bikes, managed to swim back to the shore, with the local constabulary forming a welcome party and escort back to school and demanding explanations for our absence and the borrowed boat.

Staying local was getting tricky, and we considered expanding our horizons. Manchester's Arndale Center was our first stop, by train, and the opportunity to get some clobber—that was, where we could find customized Doc Marten boots, Sex Pistols ripped T-shirts, tartan bum flaps, and Tiny's infamous green PVC pants.

We purchased and used various arrays of hair paints and then transcended into full-blown skinheads or had Mohicans to match our attire. We started to look more and more like our musical heroes as we matured.

Birmingham was the next stop and the Bull Ring Center. Tiny had heard there were a couple of great shops down there with the latest gear. Then we went on to London a few weeks later, to the now infamous King's Road and Carnaby Street Market, where the legendary store Sex was once located, opened by Vivienne Westwood and Malcom McLaren.

We were all listening to the Sex Pistols by that stage, and Sid Vicious and Johnny Rotten posters hung in our bedrooms at home. *The Great Rock 'n' Roll Swindle* blasted out till late at night, as did *Never Mind the Bollocks* and John Peel on the radio for the latest tunes in the scene.

At King's Cross Station, we bumped into Ms. Atkinson, our infamous English literature teacher, who also apparently was playing hooky from school, with what looked like her boyfriend. Who would have imagined? Of all the stations, in all the cities in the world.

She made us promise secrecy, and we all agreed. Anyway, we all liked Ms. Atkinson and volunteered for her classes, largely because of her French lace underwear and errant top buttons on her blouses. We were, or at least I was, getting more into girls.

Debbie was my next crush and became my first at a party, in her tent, at the bottom of the garden. She was a year older than I was, and I could tell it wasn't her first time. By the time I emerged from the canvas at the crack of dawn the next day after little sleep, the smile on my face was from cheek to cheek, and I confirmed I was officially in love. I was never sure if she felt the same way.

The next trip was my big break. A smaller group of us traveled to Blackburn's Saint George's Hall to see Charlie Harper and the UK Subs.

Thankfully, we had a less eventful evening than our last gig. The UK Subs show was a more pedestrian affair, with the audience consisting almost purely of punk rockers, our own tribe. The absence of other factions made for a much more tranquil show, although it was still filled with fueled anger and attitude.

During the encore of the set, I was at the front, in the mosh pit, pogoing, thrashing, and ranting along with the words. The setup of their most famous tune at the time, "Crash Course," was coming, and I saw my moment. I burst onto the stage beside Charlie Harper and joined him in the lyrics: "Come on; get a crash course. Go where you wanna go. Come and get a crash course."

As it was the finale, I took it upon myself to dive headfirst back into the mosh pit, bouncing around on the heads and shoulders of my chosen tribe, and after the tune ended, the band left the stage, the lights came on, and Tiny Tim, bedecked in his signature green PVCs, stood with arms crossed, shaking his head, and a big smile.

"You're a bloody legend." He let out his signature belly giggle and slapped me so hard on the back that the blow almost winded me.

I looked up at my big brother, proud I had evidently made him proud. He was like a big, gentle giant of a brother I never had. My family was good to me for the most part, but there was always distance between us. I always felt alone and misunderstood. I didn't see much of a future, even though my father was fairly affluent. Hope just didn't exist for me and for most of my friends, so we got angry, and we reveled in that anger. We defied a society that seemed to hold nothing for us, and that was what shaped my life into what it became.

Years later, I saw the UK Subs and Charlie Harper again, in the darkest depths of Gillingham, Kent. They were the same guys, just much older, playing the same tunes and maybe with the same equipment, as it blew up during their set. Thankfully, the technicians managed to get them back on track for the last time I ever heard "Crash Course" amid memories of Saint George's Hall and my big brother, Tiny Tim.

All the lonely people, where do they all belong?

The alarm went off. It was 2:00 a.m. Tiny was sound asleep, snoring.

"Oi, c'mon. Wake up, Tiny. We're off."

"What? What the fuck? What's going on?"

"We're heading up to the Old Tramp's place, remember?"

He wiped his eyes as he kicked back the duvet. "Oh yeh." He stretched.

"Too much of that little-brown-bottle shite, Tiny."

"Aw, whatever, Willy. Can yer give it a fucking rest?"

We pulled on our clothes—dark, with no PVC, tartan, or reflective gear, just jeans, dark T-shirts, black jackets, and black beanies. We were on a night mission, and we looked like a pair of bank robbers.

Tiny and I had been inquisitive about the Old Tramp in the village and discovered his mansion hidden in the forest. We went there regularly and looked through the windows at the grand piano, the antique furniture, the dust covers over the sofas, and the art on the walls. We found the Silver Shadow parked in the quadruple garage. The grounds were well kept and proud, yet there was never any sign of life. We spotted an opportunity for adventure.

We climbed out of the skylight, but instead of climbing up, we climbed down to the left. The sloping roof led down to the lower roof over the annex, and then, after an easy jump down onto the bottom level of the fire escape and into the backyard, we were off.

We had worked out a way to avoid the main road: we headed down Elim Grove, cut through Latimer House onto Biskey Howe Road, and turned left. The streets were dead, with no one around and no lights, just the odd cat and an owl hooting above us.

Tiny and I didn't speak; we were in stealth mode. We had made plans for that night's raid: we'd see what we could pilfer, and then we planned to head up to Scotland, to Edinburgh, to an antiques market to sell our wares. Tiny had done his homework again.

We rushed past the houses, made our way up the hill, and turned off to Biskey Howe itself, an outcrop of stone overlooking the town. We knew it like the back of our hand, and we stopped for a while, sat on the top, had a smoke, and looked down on the twinkling lights of the town below.

"I fucking love it up here," Tiny said.

"Me too," I said. It was hard not to.

"Fucking love you too, Willy. Me and you together, adventuring."

I thought it was time to address Tiny. "Are you okay, Tiny?"

"What der yer mean?"

"Well, the other night."

Tiny paused for a moment. "Aw, don't worry yer mind with that, Willy. Just a touch of cantankeritis."

It was my turn to pause. It was a technique I had learned from my mother.

"Well, I mean, it's kinda difficult, Willy, yer know. You know, we don't have a lot. Not like yous." He looked across at me. "I'd give anything for your life, your family, yer ma, and yer pa. It's not that my mum and dad are not great; they are, but they don't have much time for me. They're just doing their best to survive. And it's fucking tough, Willy."

I nodded slowly, showing my understanding, letting him get it all out. I thought it was time to switch gears. "It is, Tiny. It's fucking hard out there—too fucking hard. It doesn't need to be this hard. That is why we need change. We need to get back on our feet and fight back—win our pride back.

"My dad was lucky. He landed well, but he worked hard too; it's not been easy either. You just get to see us in this moment, but my dad went through a shit load."

It was Tiny's turn for the slow nodding. I got his perspective, but too many people thought, *Woe is me*, and that was part of our problem at the time. We were the only ones who could do something about it. We had choices, and we had the right to exercise those choices or not.

Suddenly, we saw a blue flashing light heading up the narrow road to our intended destination with no siren.

"What the fuck, Tiny?"

We jumped up and made our way across the countryside, across the road, over the stone wall, and into the grounds of the Old Tramp's manor. Under the cover of the dry stone walling, hedge, scrub, and trees, we managed to get within a safe distance of the manor house. Tiny, ever prepared, had binoculars. We had bought them at the bric-a-brac shop next to my house.

With the blue light on the police car still flashing, two officers went inside.

"What the fuck is going on, Tiny?" I asked, although I could get much of the picture without the lenses. The officers escorted two figures out of the house and loaded them unceremoniously into the back of the squad car.

"Who the fuck are they, Tiny?"

He adjusted the focus on the binoculars. "It's fucking Toolan and that fucking Scouser from the Nisi!"

"What the fuck? How do those fuckers know about this place? This night? What the fuck, Tiny?" I could tell by the guilt written all over his face what the situation was. "Come on, Tiny. Let's get the fuck out of here before anything else happens. Who else did yer fucking tell?"

We quickly retreated with our mission aborted. At least that mission.

I would not forget Tiny's indiscretion, and it weighed heavily on my mind, especially for the serious stuff. It had not been intentional; there'd been no malice. It was a mistake, and Tiny knew it as much as I did. I did not blame him, and it wasn't that I didn't trust him afterward, but his indiscretion was sufficient to make me wary for a long time. At the end of the day, loose lips sank ships.

Some people just could not keep secrets, no matter how much you trusted them. I learned that throughout my life, including while serving with the Special Forces and the Det intelligence unit of the British military. Indiscretions cost people's lives. I learned to stack them away; store them out of view, out of sight; and sometimes even forget they were there or choose to forget. That was my way of dealing with secrets.

When it came time to trust Tiny with our own dark secret about what happened in Paris, I found it difficult to believe he would remain silent and guard our secret the same way I would. As it turned out, I had nothing to worry about. Tiny was mum about the terrible incident. He kept his word, and I kept mine. However, my mistrust of all people in their ability to keep a secret partially contributed to the long absence between us. In fact, it almost killed my friendship with Tiny. We became close pals at a distance. The distance was what marked us as the decades passed. It was something I would regret.

# 17
# HE WHO DARES WINS
**WM**
1982

**THEATRE OF HATE RELEASED THEIR** live album recorded at the Leeds Warehouse and reached number one on the UK indie charts, including the tracks "Legion," "Conquistador," "Original Sin," and "West World." Kirk Brandon's unique wailing and signature sound were a more sophisticated transgression for the punk rock movement and a favorite of ours back then.

The press said the Sex Pistols "couldn't play," but they really meant the whole movement. Punk rock was the antithesis of all social norms at that time: unconventional hair, unconventional clothes, tattoos, and piercings for boys and girls and beyond just the ears. It included loud clothes, loud music, and loud antiestablishment statements with no filter and certainly no fear.

But the claim that they could not play was untrue. Granted, the music was not Beethoven. It wasn't in the crooner style of Perry Como, Val Doonican, or Frank Sinatra, which my parents listened to. It was not soft pop like the Monkees or the Beatles. It was not music about love or romance; it was music filled with passion, purpose, and sometimes drugs, with a fair serving of frustration and even violence.

Theatre of Hate was one of those bands. I went to see them as one of my early concerts, in York, at some crappy little bar venue just outside town and out of the old city's historic walls. They played tracks from their latest live album, *He Who Dares Wins*, which would bring a different meaning for me later in my life, but even at that moment, those words really meant something.

Kirk Brandon, with his big, fancy guitar, at the microphone at the front of the stage, shrieked out his high-pitched yet melodic lyrics to "Original Sin," "Nero," and "Incinerator." I stood shoulder to shoulder with Bomber, Kerry, Alec, and, of course, Tiny. We rocked, crashed our heads, and sang to the music with bottles of beer in hand, and when a favorite came on, we would crash the dance floor, thrashing about with our hair, Mohicans, piercings, tattoos, and gear, usually making a mess in the blood and guts and beer.

Bomber was tall and slim and looked like a volleyball player. He had a big pink Mohican and Doc Martens, a smart leopard-skin bum flap, and a leather biker jacket covered in painting and silver studs. "Exploited—Barmy Army" was artistically and lovingly painted on the back of the jacket. Bomber was a little older than I was, old enough to have a driver's license, and was the one most of us looked up to.

Bomber knew Brandon, and after the gig, he and I went to talk to him. We sat at a bar table in a quiet corner, if there was such a thing, and I listened as the blond-coifed icon tried to persuade Bomber to be his roadie. I could not believe Bomber was turning him down. Apparently, neither could Brandon, and he took it out on me by stubbing his cigarette out on the back of my hand!

"Fuck!" I sprang to my feet, staring at Brandon, who, seconds before, had been my idol. I did not have the balls to saying anything and just walked away, nursing my pain. "Fucking bastard," I muttered under my breath as I went back to the boys.

After the gig ended, we got in the minibus. I sat opposite Tiny; we had enough room for two seats each. "What the fuck happened to you?" he asked, watching me nurse my hand and pour beer over it to cool it down.

As I looked up, I saw Tiny snorting his little brown bottle, and within seconds, he was gone, checked out, with glazed eyes and a vacant smile.

"Hello? Hello? Hello? Is there anybody in there? Just nod if you can hear me. Is there anyone at home?"

I looked around in the dark, with the rain on the windows, and the streetlights gave me just enough light to see Ted inflating and deflating a plastic bag full of some sticky and smelly substance. It was the first time I had seen someone sniffing glue. It was one step up from whatever Tiny was on and one step away from even worse concoctions.

"Come on now. I hear you're feeling down. Well, I can ease your pain. Get you on your feet again."

As Bomber got in the driver's seat and we started pulling away, two things terrified me. First, Bomber was driving, though he'd been fucking shit-faced not five minutes ago, and second, I saw the look on Ted's face as the heaving and inhaling of his glue sniffing surrendered him to an alternative state, one I would later liken to that of a zombie or the walking dead. I often wondered if punk rock was responsible for that so-called creativity. After all, there were no rules.

"Relax. I'll need some information first. Just the basic facts. Can you show me where it hurts?"

With no one to talk to, as all my mates were smashed on some sort of hallucinate, I nurtured what was left of my six-pack and looked out the window into the dark, wet northern night, relieved to see Bomber's driving becoming less erratic and more measured. I was surrounded by my friends but lonely as hell.

"There is no pain you are receding. A distant ship smoke on the horizon. You are only coming through in waves. Your lips move, but I can't hear what you're saying."

I knew from an early age that I didn't fit in. I was bullied because I was different, the posh kid. I often reflected on why diversity attracted bullies. It was worse if you were fat or ugly or had spots or buck teeth. It was even worse if you were black, gay, lesbian, or of any foreign descent. I didn't get it. Why couldn't people just get on and accept each other's differences?

I stumbled across the path I found. I wasn't a Goody Two-shoes saying, "Yes, sir. No, sir." I came from a family who were doing okay for ourselves. I didn't fit in with the conformists; I was a rebel inside and therefore wasn't sure if I found punk rock as a release or if punk rock somehow found me.

As I looked around the minibus, I wasn't sure if I even fit in there. I was not the same as any of the other passengers. Tiny probably was the closest, but even Tiny and I were worlds apart in many ways.

As we rumbled through the darkness, I kept glancing over at Ted, Tiny, and the others, contemplating the thin line they trod, the substances they were abusing, and how they were meddling with the most precious things they possessed: their health and maybe even their lives.

In that moment, I was relieved I had not succumbed. I had been tempted, but somehow, a combination of some allergic reaction and my father's teachings always managed to keep me a step away from the edge. I knew what my father had gone through in his life, in World War II, and also knew about our family's eight hundred years of Scottish history. I always felt a responsibility for all those who'd passed before me. I felt a duty, responsibility, and level of respect that life was mine not to throw away but to fight till the end, no matter how hard.

I also remembered my cousin Susan.

"Okay. Just a little pinprick. There'll be no more; ah, but you may feel a little sick. Can you stand up? I do believe it's working. Good."

Unfortunately, there had been no magic pinprick to save her.

Bomber, driving, was listening to his tapes on the stereo in the front—full blast, of course—and I realized what was playing in my mind was "Comfortably Numb": "When I was a child, I had a fever. My hands felt just like two balloons.

Now I've got that feeling once again. I can't explain; you would not understand. This is not how I am."

Bomber and I, him in the front and me in the back with the zombies, broke into the chorus together: "I have become comfortably numb."

# 18
# SCREAMING BABIES
## WM
### 1982
### Egremont

**IT WAS TIME FOR ANOTHER** concert. Tiny, Ted, and I met Bomber outside the Odana as he pulled up in the familiar minibus. We were off to *The Old Grey Whistle Test*, a show that featured alternative, indie, and often off-the-wall bands, usually live, and was on the box late at night.

"What does *The Old Grey Whistle Test* mean?" Tiny asked, though he clearly knew the answer and had done his research.

"I have no fucking idea, Tiny. What does *The Old Grey Whistle Test* mean?" It was like Tiny's and my own version of a pantomime line, such as "It's behind you! Oh no, it's not!" On planes, during the safety briefing, the line "The exit door may be behind you" always cracked me up, as did the whistle and light on the life jacket. I thought, *Can't you just give me a fucking parachute instead?*

Tiny looked excited, as none of us on the bus knew the answer to his random question.

He went on to explain that it was a reference to seasoned music industry executives known as "the old grays" and doormen in grays suits. Any song they listened to just once or twice they could remember and whistle.

"Hence the expression that the song had 'passed the old gray whistle test'!" Tiny declared like a magician doing his grand reveal.

"Tada!" I tried to add to the moment.

There were different subgenres of punk. There was the serious thrash punk, which I did not really understand. One had to be smashed like Ted to understand the words, never mind the music. There was also a political-activist side that was far less about the music than the activism. Every word was a cryptic critique of what the government was doing wrong; a doom-and-gloom prediction of the end of the world; or a story of someone detained, derailed, deranged, or dying somewhere.

We were on our way to *The Old Grey Whistle Test* in Egremont, of all places, a dark, dreary one-horse town with not a lot to do. The live gig would be filmed and shown on TV, which was kind of cool.

"So who's gonna get on the TV tonight?" Bomber shouted from the driver's seat. Tiny was by far the most enthusiastic.

We drove through the main street of the town, which I remembered from a recent cold, wet, windy, and particularly violent rugby game against the unusually hairy and muscular local youth team. There must have been something in the water in Egremont, I thought.

The town had been granted its charter for a market and annual fair by King Henry III in 1266, and it hosted the annual Crab Fair and the World Gurning Championships— another tidbit from our burgeoning resident historian Tiny Tim Timpson.

As we pulled into the car park of our destination, we were at the town's cultural center, on its busiest night in recent memory. Just like *Songs of Praise* on Sundays, *The Old Grey Whistle Test* had the lure of cameras to attract large audiences and, in that night's case, punk rockers from all over the north of England, by the look of it.

"What the fuck is cultural in Egremont?" Tiny asked, speaking maybe a little too loudly. "Egremont, Cumbrian town of culture," he jested. "What is the difference between yogurt and Egremont?"

"I don't know, Tiny. What is the difference between yogurt and Egremont?"

"If you leave yogurt alone for seven hundred years, it develops a culture!" Laughing and guffawing uncontrollably, Tiny slapped me on my shoulder and nearly sent me flying.

"You silly fucker, Tiny. You on that white stuff tonight?"

The headliner that night was a band called Crass, with Steve Ignorant, Eve Libertine, Phil Free, and Joy De Vivre, names I remembered. I also recalled the lyrics from their most famous tracks, such as "Do they owe you a living? Course they do. Course they do!"

Other songs included "Punk Is Dead," "Shaved Ladies," and "Screaming Babies." They were associated with groups like Penis Envy and Poison Sisters, all of which were angry and a bit strange even for those times. Stranger still was the audience, an eclectic mix of individuals who were more like a tribe of zombies than punk concert fans. Politico punk, or anarcho punk, was a new subgenre for Tiny and me. We preferred to call it zombie punk.

"Who the fuck are all these weirdos?" Tiny said under his breath.

I just laughed, kept my head down, produced my ticket at the door, and snuck in my four cans of ale hidden strategically in my leather biker jacket, in a do-it-yourself concealed pocket inside, also thankful for my concealed blackthorn shillelagh, in case that was the start of the zombie apocalypse.

I'd acquired my new leather jacket, which attracted a lot of attention, six months earlier.

I arrived the Odana, my football team's pickup point for away games and, in fact, the pickup point for a lot of my activities. As I walked in, the place was a mess; it looked as if a coach party had stopped by, which often happened. The young girl behind the counter, Lucy, apparently in charge while the owners were out, asked me to keep an eye while she went to the restroom.

"Okay, sure," I said.

I already knew customer service was not my thing, and I got behind the counter, praying no customers would come in. I saw the overflowing tip jar and figured Lucy had not had a chance to clear up the tables, never mind assess her tips haul. I skimmed a big handful or two of coins, taking care to pick out the highest-value ones, and put them in my football sock to stop them from rattling about. Then I stuffed the socks into my hold-all, along with my boots and my shin pads. I heard the familiar pull of the long chain and the flush of the toilet and could imagine Lucy washing her hands, and I stuffed a mysterious leather jacket into my bag too.

As Lucy came out, I saw my team bus pull up outside. "Gotta go, Luce," I said, smiling, and she thanked me. She would never be any wiser about the tip jar or the leather jacket, I thought.

Later that afternoon, the earlier passing visitors returned, and one was looking for a jacket he had left behind at the café. They were not a bus full of blue rinses, tourists, or kids on a field trip to see Beatrix Potter or William Wordsworth; they were a chapter of one of northern England's most dangerous and feared Hell's Angels: the Devil Backs.

I had almost forgotten about the jacket, but as I was going to be on TV that night, I had pulled it out from its hiding place in the eaves cupboard in my bedroom, underneath the skylight. Taking Bomber's lead, earlier in the week, I'd painted it, added some studs, and punkified it with great enthusiasm and creativity, adding it to my growing wardrobe of alternative fashion.

While sprucing it up, I'd discovered the hidden pocket on the inside left and found concealed within what looked like a blackthorn stick. It was hefty, was around eighteen inches in length, and had a gnarly, hard knob on the end. I had seen Gypsies with them and remembered they called them shillelaghs and used them as weapons—ones that could be explained away more easily than other choices of weaponry.

I'd decided to keep it in place. The pocket was also handy to hide my tinnies, and I thought the Shillelagh might come in handy too someday.

In Egremont, the jacket came in good use to shelter me from the bitter wind and sleeting rain outside. We pranced through security and headed to the restrooms at the back. Ted was on his glue, Tiny was sniffing his poppers, and I had a cigarette and a can of beer.

As Tiny was going under and his eyes were making the transformation to the familiar glaze and vacant look, he glared down at my newly revealed leather jacket, grabbed the piping on the lapel, and started laughing manically. "You, my friend, are a fucking legend!" He spluttered all over me. "Look at this, boys! Look at whose fucking jacket he's wearing!"

I looked around, checking to make sure there were no Hell's Angels in sight, as Tiny left the here and now to depart for another world and I headed to the concert.

It was the first and last time I went to see a zombie punk band. They were full of anger, hatred, and opinions about just about everything as far as I could work out. The support band came out, three punkesses took the vocals, and a mosh pit of zombies spit at them all the way through their set. Spit dripped down their faces like a scene too grotesque to make it into even the most horrific C-rated zombie film. I headed to the back of the hall and took comfort in the distance and my cans of beer.

Having escaped the zombie pit, on the bus ride home, I found out that I had in fact picked up the jacket of one of the renowned Devil Backs and that there were certain markings on the jacket that represented the chapter's colors. I knew if I was ever caught wearing it, I would be crucified right there and then or at least taken up to the caves where they partied regularly, and they would do the deed there.

I was careful about if and when I wore the jacket from then on, but over time, as I grew more confident and my "I don't give a fuck" attitude increased, I cared less and less. It was my own form of *He Who Dares Wins*.

That was another aspect of the era that ended up proving invaluable: the "I don't give a fuck" approach. It could be counterintuitive and sometimes was a fine balance.

I learned over time there existed a fine line between (1) not giving a fuck at all and everything falling apart and (2) caring about some fundamental principles and then not giving a hell beyond them. It kinda came back to the principles captured by Kirk Brandon and, unknown to me at that time, derived from the saying of 22 Special Air Service.

In later years, in business, I related the concept to my then boss, a Florida implant in Texas and, I suspected, a Trumpette. She simply did not get the concept, although I'd used it in business and throughout my life, whether knowingly or unknowingly. It was no different from Silicon Valley's mantra of "Fail fast"—it was the same principle.

The journey home was shorter but a reparation of my own set of zombies in the minibus and my own solitude as I looked out the window at the rain and the misery outside.

My thoughts turned to my latest friend of the female kind. I had met her at the county fair, and we had dated for a while. I'd make the bus journey to her hometown of Milnthorpe, and it was difficult for me to get back home, due to the frequency of the buses or lack thereof. As I sat looking out the window, I recalled the week before, when her parents had agreed I could stay the night. I'd sneaked into Beth's bedroom and cuddled up in her bed, too scared for any monkey business, due to the size of her father and his fists and also the screaming and shrieking throughout the night.

"What is that?" I'd asked Beth, who'd been awake next to me.

"It's my sister next door," she'd responded as we heard another wail through the wall.

"What's wrong with her?"

Beth had started sobbing. I'd cuddled her harder. Her sobbing had slowed, her breathing had calmed down, and I'd known that whatever it was, it was not good.

The next morning, I'd left the house and caught my bus home, and an ambulance had been arriving at the house as I left. The mother, the father, and Beth had been in tears as the ambulance crew carried a stretcher into the back of the ambulance. As I'd gotten on the bus, I'd seen the three of them get in the back with the stretcher and had seen the blue lights as the ambulance sped away north toward Kendal with the siren blaring.

Her sister had been only eleven years old and had leukemia. I never saw Beth again. I couldn't handle the sadness of her losing her sister that day; her sister's battle with cancer; and the haunting, tormenting memories of her wails throughout that sleepless night.

About twenty minutes into our journey home, Bomber spotted that I was the only one awake and, rescuing me from my nightmare, invited me up front to sit on the bench seat, and we talked John Peel, music, the best bands, the best places for gigs, and his ambitions. I got to respect Bomber even more on that journey home as he diligently poured his passengers off the bus and sent them back from whence they'd come.

I helped Tiny off the bus, as he was fucked up and completely disoriented. He started getting emotional, crying on my shoulder, feeling guilty for taking that shit, whatever it was.

"I fucking hate myself. I don't want to do that shit no more!" he shouted.

We watched him stumble through the gate of his picket-fence-surrounded house. The windows were all dark, except for the light in his bedroom—a ritual his mum did every night in the hope her son would come home safe and alive that night. She knew of his demons, troubles, and addictions and did everything she could to be patient, support him, and see him through to the other side. It was maybe too late for some of the others destined on a track to harder, more devastating cocktails, but maybe for Tiny, there was still hope. I hoped so too as we watched him eventually get the key into the lock and make it safely inside.

The final track Bomber played as we headed for my drop-off blared. "How the hell can these idiots say we cannot play, eh?" The melodic and haunting tune belted out of the minibus stereo. "Golden-brown texture like sun. Lays me down with my might she runs. Throughout the night, no need to fight, never a frown with golden brown."

"Bloody Stranglers. Classic," Bomber said.

I wholeheartedly agreed, nodding enthusiastically, and although the track always reminded me of a ship sailing somewhere to distant shores, I knew there was a much darker meaning referencing the golden brown of the life-destroying heroin.

As I jumped out at my stop as the last one to get off, Bomber leaned over. "Hey, kid, I'm sorry about that twat in York burning yer hand and all. I told him he was a fucking bastard. He agreed and invited you, me, and the boys to a free gig down in Manchester in a couple of weeks. He said you were a tough little fucker for not wincing and standing up to him." He winked as I shut the door. "I'll be in touch, kiddo!"

Apart from the wind and the ever-present rain, my walk home was uneventful, but I had a spring in my step. "Fuck yes! Brandon thinks I'm a tough little fucker!"

I was proud in the moment, and I remembered my ancestral teachings passed down from my father and the words of my ancestor Jock Half Lugs of the Park and shouted to the wind, the rain, and the houses in darkness around me, "How dare you fucking mess with me?"

# 19
# TIN SOLDIERS
**WM**
## October 13, 1982
## Manchester Apollo

**AFTER MY EGREMONT EXPERIENCE AND** influence from the likes of Kirk Brandon, my fashion style evolved. Sticking with a crew cut and cutting down on the bright, brash colors, I turned to a more understated rebel style, typically a T-shirt with some controversial slogan of the day; a pair of jeans, usually ripped; a studded belt; my Hell's Angels leather jacket, as by that time, I didn't really care who saw me wearing it; and statement footwear. I still loved my oxblood Doc Martens and my blueys, which I had wrestled back from Tiny, and I had a new addition to my wardrobe: a pair of faux leopard-skin crepe shoes, which were cool, I thought.

Stiff Little Fingers was a band from Belfast formed at the height of the troubles, and they provided a different perspective on all the malarkey through their music. "Suspect

Device," "Alternative Ulster," "Straw Dogs," and "Nobody's Hero" all stood out.

The crowd was different; they had matured and evolved in their own ways and, for the most part, also toned down their looks, but as they had grown older and developed, so had the level of violence.

Tiny and I stood there in the concert hall, on the edge of an expectant audience, waiting for SLF to enter the stage. A fight broke out right next to us, sucking us in like a vortex. We were both reasonably sized guys and both knew how to use our fists by that point, and as we got drawn in, we fought back to back, holding our own, until the moment was over. The crowd and the anger subsided, and Tiny and I, unscathed, managed to walk away.

"Come on. Let's go for a fricking beer," said Tiny.

I agreed, so we went to the back of the concert hall and ordered two pints of pissy lager in plastic glasses.

The band opened, but Tiny and I had lost some interest, and we sipped our pints while watching from afar as they cranked out an old familiar tune: "Take a look where you're livin'; you got the army on the street. And the RUC dog of repression is barking at your feet. Is this the kind of place you want to live? Is this where you want to be? Is this the only life we're gonna have? What we need."

"They're right, Willy." He nodded toward the stage. "I know they have it worse than we do across the water, but their message is right."

I nodded in agreement.

"Look at over here. The police are out of control and think they can beat up who the hell they want whenever they want. We have the fricking IRA walking our streets, blowing people up."

"Our politicians are flushing us down the drain. The unions are killing any hope for the future," I added.

"Is there any fucking wonder there is anger on the streets?" he said as he pointed his plastic cup toward the crowd.

He was, of course, right. Tiny and I were not aggressors, although we had learned that if we got dragged into anything, we were finishers and could handle ourselves. We ordered ourselves another couple of beers.

"I don't want to be coming out to these gigs and getting into fistfights," he said.

"And worse, when they drag out a bottle or a knife," I added.

The chorus blasted out, and the occupants of the Apollo chimed in: "It's an alternative Ulster! Grab it, and change it; it's yours. Get an alternative Ulster; ignore the bores and their laws. Get an alternative Ulster; be an antisecurity force. Alter your native Ulster; alter your native land."

"The fight they talk of is nothing different from our own here, Willy. This is the fight and the stance we need to take in our own lands. We need to win our nation back and not through pointless fighting and anger. We have the chance to change things, but that ain't gonna get us anywhere anytime soon." He pointed again with his beer and smiled a smile filled with hope and appeal.

"You're right, Tiny. It's all a load of bollocks! It's all completely fucked up."

As we got on the train that night, heading home, we sat in a carriage with barely anyone in it. I stuck into a six-pack, and Tiny got out his little brown bottle as we both stared in silence out the window as we left Manchester Piccadilly station.

I stared at the chimneys and the seas of redbrick houses through the misery that was Bolton and Preston and wondered how people survived and why. Was this their existence? What this what our fathers and grandfathers had fought for? What was the hope? To work at the steelworks, down the pit, or at the factory? If they were still there for future generations.

As I looked out the window, I thought of the boys and men who had left those towns for the trenches of the First World War, many of them never to return, and, like my own father, of the Second World War and the beaches of Normandy. Others had gone to the opposite side of the world, to remote islands no one had ever heard of, to fight the Argentinians and reclaim the Falklands as our own.

It was another unprecedented story in unprecedented times.

No one had ever heard of the Falklands, and it was unclear why a country like Argentina would want them, but Maggie made the move to declare war and beg, borrow, and steal every available ship, military or otherwise, to mobilize the queen's armed forces and send them nearly eight thousand miles to the Southern Hemisphere to wage war.

We watched from our TV room as the flotilla departed and headed south. The brave soldiers of 3 Para, Royal

Marines, 29 Commando, Scots and Welsh Guards, Gurkhas, SBS, and SAS.

Maggie's war was unfolding before our eyes, albeit in far and distant lands. The Royal Air Force Harrier jump jets dominated the skies, and footage showed them appearing from over the horizon with their deadly raids and bombs. The images showed the troops on the ground donning the Union Jacks and their assorted colors of berets as they marched and swept the islands.

The *General Belgrano* went down, and there was tragic loss of life as the Argentinians sank the *Sir Galahad*, taking fifty-six young Welsh lives, Welsh Guards.

It was difficult for me to get my head around the loss of life and casualties: 255 Brits killed and 775 injured, and 650 Argentinians dead and 1,600 injured. We also managed to capture more than 11,000 Argentinian soldiers.

*What the fuck for?* I wondered. *What was all that about? Was it really necessary?*

I did not understand the *why*, and the *why* was important to us back then. For too long, the powers that be had just handed out instructions, fait accomplis, with no question or accountability for the *why*.

That was what we were doing. We were questioning the leaders of the time everywhere, in politics, business, society, and schools, including our parents and teachers—everyone.

I knew the war had galvanized the country's support behind Maggie, which was a good thing. I knew it had brought back a bit of fighting pride of the British, which was much needed. I also knew from history that bizarrely, wars had the effect of stimulating economies, and that, by hell, we really needed.

But I still had questions in my mind: *Why, and was it really fricking worth all those lives?*

In hindsight, I realized—and maybe those poor servicemen and -women, and their wives, children, families, and friends could take solace—that the Falkland Islands War wasn't just about some islands no one had ever heard of before; it was, in fact, a battle to win back the pride of a nation, the British Bulldog, for the empire, for the people, for the youth, and for our future.

"Rest in peace. I salute you. Respect," I whispered as I stared at my reflection in the window.

The train made its way through the old northern towns one by one and on into the countryside, and we pulled into the dull and soulless city of Lancaster, which, in many respects, was even worse. With little or no industry and little or no excitement, it was dull and boring, a place to be unremarkable, retire, and die.

It was not that I necessarily wanted to be remarkable; I just didn't want the opposite. I didn't want to get to the end of my life, whenever that might be; look back; and think I had wasted my life and never even tried.

I enjoyed the freedom of expression, thinking differently, challenging the status quo, being proud to be an individual, being different, and making my own small contribution to positive change, not just sitting back and waiting for what cards life dealt.

Punk rock was the catalyst. It was a movement that accommodated all those things, but as I looked at my friend

Tiny passed out and snoring, I realized there also had to be some taboos, including tattoos and substances that surely would end up with one's demise in one way or another.

At Lancaster station, a particularly pretty pair of girls got on and joined us in the same carriage. I recognized them; they were from Kendal, a close-by market town. I had seen them at the county fair before, and one of them remembered me too. I smiled, and they smiled back. In particular, Penny's smile was intense. We got to chatting, and she was nice. I liked her, and I thought she liked me.

As we changed trains at Oxenholme and got on the bone shaker, before Penny got off the train, she slipped me a note with her name and home phone number, and I agreed I would call her. I winked at her, and she smiled and fluttered her eyelashes as she left. I watched her through the window as she walked off the platform. With just one look, I knew I was in. As the train pulled away, she turned back, smiled, and waved.

"Yes!" If I'd had any doubt before, I now knew I would definitely call her.

I turned to my reflection and back to my thoughts.

The United Kingdom was still having a tough time of it for the first time since the 1930s: unemployment had reached more than three million; the Welsh miners were on strike; and the Provisional IRA had planted more bombs in London, killing soldiers and horses of the Blues and Royals Household Cavalry in Hyde Park.

The prince and princess of Wales had their first child, William Arthur Philip Louis. The *Mary Rose* was raised from the depths of the Solent, where it had sunk in 1545.

Argentina decided to claim the Falkland Islands as their own and invaded the long-standing territory of Great Britain.

Thankfully, unlike most, I was forearmed with my self-appointed school study of South America, its people, and its countries, so as Argentina invaded the Falkland Islands, I knew better than others of the aggressors, but like most other people at that time, I had never heard of the Falkland Islands or where they were. It was difficult to conceive their relationship to the north of England or the United Kingdom, never mind their precise position on the planet.

From an early age, I had watched the news with my father, trying to make sense of all the austerity, the unions, the strikes, and the feeling of apparent prevailing darkness and misery.

Our prime minister, Maggie, was the first woman in charge, and she was polarizing, but for my parents and me, and probably most of my friends, she was a breath of fresh air against our apparent slide into mediocrity that the other politicians at the time seemed not only content with but driven to use to fuel the decline of our nation.

How dare the Argentinians decide to invade part of our commonwealth without orderly diplomatic discussions and agreement of the empire? It would be another great test of the leadership and a defining moment for our nation.

In many instances in history, war had been used as a stimulus, not only for economic growth and opportunity but also for winning the hearts, minds, and support of a nation united together in defeating a common enemy. What better way to unite a nation than that? That was especially the case with the British people, who had a rich history of fighting among themselves, until they had a common external enemy. Then the wrath of the Brits in their mission focused on their enemy was written into the legends of history.

Maggie's war was a war over a tiny set of islands in the depths of the South Atlantic, almost eight thousand miles away from London, and an attempt by Argentina to win them back and claim the rights to the legendary pot of black gold beneath.

My only reference at that time to those islands was the heroic legend of Sir Ernest Shackleton and his epic and fated 1914 Imperial Trans-Antarctic Expedition, which passed by South Georgia on its way south, as would be told later in the novel *Cold Courage*.

On our televisions in our northern town, we watched how the might of the British Empire, on warships, merchant ships, and cruise liners, made their way across the eight thousand miles to wage war and defend our sovereign land and oil prospects.

It was a heralding moment for us, the resurgence of our might; we were getting off our knees and standing up for something we believed in as a nation. It was less about the Falkland Islands than a galvanizing call to action to wake up, smell the coffee, and not just accept our slide to mediocrity as a nation.

Crackers, really, but until that point, we'd been accepting of our demise.

Tiny was in and out of consciousness. I managed to help him navigate from one train to the next, and soon he was snoring again as my thoughts turned to another great musician, showman, and lyricist—not of the punk rock variety but as creative, alternative, and antiestablishment in his own way as any.

"I will be king. And you, you will be queen. Though nothing will drive them away, we can beat them, just for one day. We can be heroes just for one day."

I could hear the soundtrack in my head. I could see Bowie, cool in his blue suit and tie, onstage with the wind blowing in his hair as he stood before his audience.

"And you, you can be mean. And I, I'll drink all the time. 'Cause we're lovers, and that is a fact. Yes, we're lovers, and that is that. Though nothing will keep us together. We could steal time, just for one day. We can be heroes for ever and ever; what d'you say? We can be heroes, just for one day!'

# 20
# YORKSHIRE
# WM
## 1983
## Down south

**A BUNCH OF US DECIDED** to head down to Wembley for the Charity Shield game, Manchester United versus Liverpool—two titans of the English and world footballing scene and a heap of rivalry between the two.

As the train pulled into Manchester Piccadilly station, the relatively calm and peaceful mix of red shirts from each side of the contest changed as the hordes of Mancunians boarded, singing the tribal songs, making those donning Liverpool shirts nervous as they huddled together in groups of relative safety.

As the train left Manchester, it rocked with the sheer number of passengers and the raucous songs and chants of pending victory against their old rivals.

Farther down the track, as the train was pulling into Crewe, we could see a sea of red Liverpool supporters waiting to board. The train came to a halt, the hordes immediately doubled in size, and the sense of venomous aggravation and pending violence suddenly went off the charts.

The opposing tribes hurled abuse at each other and bantered their songs back and forth all the way down to Euston Station, London, where they spilled off worse for wear after their six-packs of Boddingtons and Special Brew, with scuffles and fights breaking out en masse.

"Fucking hell, Willy, this is a fucking shit show," Tiny rightly said.

"These fuckers are crazy," added Kerry.

"Why can't they just enjoy the game?" I said.

We had seen violence at various gigs, but this was on a completely different scale—two armies of angry opposing supporters full of beer, hatred, and violence.

We managed to keep out of the foray and under the radar. In our various states of punkness, we were not seen as the number-one enemy. We had taken the precaution not to wear our colors, and that was our saving grace. We were just a small pocket of rockers in a sea of nutters.

The tension continued on the train to Wembley Stadium and eventually calmed down as we entered our segregated areas inside, but by that time, we had already heard rumors of fighting in central London and two Manchester United fans getting stabbed on the way.

With the atmosphere electric inside, eighty-two thousand fanatical fans were singing the roof off. It was enough to make the hairs on the back of my neck stand at attention, and they did.

We were awed. Although we had seen a lot in our relatively tender years, this was like being in a war zone, with the tribal Liverpudlians on one side and the Mancunians the other. Our group—impartial, we hoped—were in the middle. We were there for the football.

The scene overwhelmed me, and that was saying something. It took quite a lot to make my head spin. I'd seen violence or the threat of violence at gigs and the riot at the CND march in London, but this was something else—tribal and on a much bigger scale.

With Manchester United in white and Liverpool in red, the game kicked off. The first twenty minutes were tense, with both sides having chances and forcing saves from both Grobbelaar of Liverpool and Bailey of United in goal. Liverpool looked to have the upper hand.

In a passage of play for Liverpool, on the break, Kenny Dalglish made a run from defense on the left side of the pitch and slid the ball into the path of Ian Rush. He passed to Michael Robinson, who ran out of space, and it went out for a corner. It had been the best opportunity so far.

In the twenty-third minute, United's Stapleton picked up a pass from defense in midfield and nicked it to Ray Wilkinson, who slid a perfectly timed pass to Captain Fantastic, Bryan Robson, to beat the offside trap and take on Grobbelaar. He sidestepped the keeper and passed it into the back of the net from the edge of the penalty area.

The game was now 1–0. The Manchester side of Wembley erupted.

"Yes, fucking ripper!" Tiny said, pumping his fist in the air. "That Bryan Robson—what a fucking legend he is!"

Tiny made me smile. I loved the guy, and I thought he loved me too. His putting me in the same legend box was an honor, one I wasn't sure I was worthy of.

The next few minutes saw another chance from Robson with his head, which was saved by the keeper, and then Kenny Dalglish, at the other end, was denied by Bailey. The crowd were on the edge of their seats with roars all around, consumed by the excitement of the moment.

Right at the end of the first half, a Liverpool free kick floated the ball into the box to Ian Rush for an on-line scuffle. The keeper won the decision, and the referee's whistle blew for halftime.

Flags waved and chants roared as the teams left the pitch for their halftime team talks, courtesy of Joe Fagan in the Liverpool changing room and Big Ron Atkinson for United.

Tiny, the boys, and I just watched, in awe of the scene before us: eighty-two thousand people, fanatics on each side, with their songs, chants, and banter and the feeling that extreme violence was a moment away.

"I hope we don't win," said Tiny.

"What do yer mean you hope we don't fucking win?"

"Well, look at them mad fuckers." He pointed to the Liverpool fans. "I am not in the mood to get fucking stabbed today, thank you very much!"

I had to agree with him. Who in his right mind wouldn't have?

Unfortunately, fan violence was at a fever pitch back then. Mobs of fans would meet mobs of fans, and violence would ensue, some erratic and spontaneous and some planned, with mass gangs pitching against each other, sometimes with hundreds on each side. Sometimes there were targeted attacks. Unsuspecting fans isolated from their own side, walking up a back street, through a tunnel, or on the wrong part of the train platform, met knives, specifically the Stanley knife, which packed a razor blade and was capable of quick, easy disfigurement in a matter of seconds. That was the calling card of many of the gangs in those days and, most notoriously, the fans of Liverpool Football Club.

The second half kicked off. Ray Wilkinson took a long-range shot that got tipped over the bar by Grobbelaar. The crowd gasped at how close the ball came. Robson got through the defense again and had another one-to-one with the Liverpool keeper without success.

Wilkins, from the left, sent a deft cross into the box, and Frank Stapleton headed it into the hands of Grobbelaar.

Then a corner for United went into the box; McQueen got a knock toward Stapleton, who headed toward the goal; the goal line scrambled; the ball went back out to Robson; and he bundled the ball into the back of the net. Manchester United led 2–0, and Wembley erupted with the Mancunians roaring and sensing their victory.

Indeed, that was how it ended. Roars of "Glory, glory, Man United!" resounded around the stadium. Tiny, the boys, and I hung back for a while and headed out behind the rivaling throngs, not wanting to get stabbed.

The Liverpool fans were singing their signature "You'll Never Walk Alone."

We heard further reports of more stabbings as we navigated through central London. Tiny and I said goodbye to Kerry and the boys as they headed on the Euston train back north. Given we were all the way down south, Tiny and I decided to head down to Rainham, Kent, one of the Medway towns, to stay with one of his cousins for a few days, going to gigs, playing football, and hanging out for a while.

We got the bus, a red double-decker; headed across town; and jumped off at Whitechapel Station. For our first stop that night, we would stay at my cousin's house. She was a nurse at the Royal London Hospital, and she and her boyfriend were on holiday in Spain, so she let us stay the night.

We headed down Whitechapel Road toward her apartment on Smithy Street. Tiny had done his homework and wanted to call in the infamous Blind Beggar Pub for a few beers.

It was seven thirty, late summer, and balmy in the capital. Cars were still buzzing up and down Whitechapel Road as we walked up the street and came across the pub, a redbrick building trimmed with white stonework. "The Blind Beggar, AD 1894" was emblazoned on its crown, and the pub's name appeared on a sign with gold writing above the door. "Watney Combe & Reid" was etched in the stonework above the windows—the original pub company that had opened the doors.

Tiny stepped back to the edge of the pavement by the street, more like an artist than a tourist. "Look at that fricking beauty, Willy," he said, and I looked at what, to me, seemed like a pretty normal-looking London pub. "She's like a bloody rock star, a beauty, a fricking legend." He turned and smiled at me. "Fucking awesome to be here. Let's go for a beer." He slapped me on my shoulder, a signature show of affection I somewhat had gotten used to and didn't even bother to say anything about anymore.

On the way from Euston, Tiny had gone through the history of the Blind Beggar. The current building had been built in 1894 on the site of the original pub of the same name and named after the legend of Henry de Montfort. De Montfort at one point had been landed gentry but had lost his sight in battle and become a regular feature of Bethnal Green, begging on the streets.

On that site, William Booth had given his first sermon, which had led to the creation of the Salvation Army back in 1865.

But its most recent claim to fame was its notorious connection to the East End gangsters and the Kray twins, and just seventeen years earlier, on March 9, 1966, Ronnie Kray had shot and killed George Cornell, a member of the rival Richardson gang.

"Come on. Let's go inside and sit where Cornell met his maker." Tiny opened the door and stepped inside, and I followed behind as he headed to the saloon bar.

The place was pretty quiet. We found a place at the bar and ordered a couple of pints of London Pride, taking in our surroundings and eyeing the patrons, trying to work out if any of them were gangsters. We made no reference to the Krays, just in case anyone was listening. Instead, we drank beer and whisky and had one of our regular philosophical debates about the state of our world.

All of a sudden, it was eleven o'clock, and we staggered to my cousin's two-bedroom apartment on Smithy Street. Feeling too awkward to sleep in her bed and a little worse for wear, I took her boyfriend's office floor, and Tiny slept on the couch.

The next morning, we headed to Victoria Station and on to Rainham. We quickly realized that in the Medway towns, although they had many of the same problems we had up north, the people were as mad as ships' cats.

We went out to a caravan site on the Isle of Sheppey one night, as there was a local band playing. Apparently, it was a haven for former London and southeastern bank robbers, as the patrons had gold watches, rings and sovereigns, and looks of suspicion toward outsiders and looked as hard as nails.

Tiny and I ended up at a late-night kebab shop on Rainham High Street, where an altercation spilled out onto the street. The locals were savage and vicious in their attacks. Tiny and I stepped in.

In the Working Man's Club the next evening, big Mal, a local thug with gold, tattoos, and "Cut here" etched around his throat, picked up on my distant Yorkshire accent and wanted to know what had gone down in the kebab shop the night before. His nephew apparently had been there and gotten out worse for wear, thanks to Tiny's and my help.

"So, Yorkshire"—he looked down at me, and I guessed he must have been six foot six and at least twenty stone—"what the fuck went down at the kebab shop last night?" He stared menacingly, making it clear he was looking for the right answer; otherwise, the situation might not end well.

Playing pool, I had my cue in my right hand, and I knew exactly what I would do with it should he kick off. I also had the comfort of my secret stash inside my leather jacket.

It was small enough to conceal, hard enough to do serious damage, and long enough to serve as a neat extension to my reach, even for a big fucker like the one before me. The art was to keep adversaries at a distance so they couldn't inflict damage on you, while being quick and nimble enough to do significant damage in return, especially on key targets around the temples, jaw, nose, and eyes.

"Looked to me like your nephew probably deserved what he got," I said.

He looked down at me, puzzled. "Why's that then, Yorkshire?"

I looked right back up at him. "Because they were calling the guys at the shop a bunch of fucking Pakis."

He grabbed his chin and stroked it with his big sovereign ring sticking out from his big, fat hand.

"You see, those boys are, in fact, from Turkey, nowhere near fucking Pakistan," I said. I could feel Tiny right next to me, keeping a watchful eye, but I could also see the big cockney wasn't on his own either. "You see, all they are trying to do is earn a living, and your nephew was hurling abuse at them, off his fucking head on something."

The big man started nodding in agreement, and I knew my explanation was working.

"Like I say, he probably deserved a few bruises and a sore head this morning. Hopefully teach 'im a lesson to leave people alone and let them live in peace. After all, we all like a fucking kebab, right?" I slapped his shoulder.

He shrugged as if to say, "Fair enough."

"I think you're fucking all right, Yorkshire. You know that."

It wasn't a question. He returned the slap on my back, and the situation was defused.

He then said his Football Association ban was being lifted that week, and he was going to be allowed back onto the grounds. "First time for three fucking years." He smiled.

"What the fuck did you get banned for?"

"I fucking stabbed a couple of fuckers at a game." He smiled again, in a friendly yet menacing sort of way.

He went on to invite Tiny and me to the Gillingham game that Saturday; they were playing Millwall in some cup game.

Tiny and I looked at each other, and I responded for both of us. I knew his look and what it meant. "Yeah, that's really good of you to ask, but we are heading back north in the morning."

I thought, *Let's make like shepherds!*

# 21
# NO FUTURE

**WM**

1983

Up north

**AS THE YEARS TICKED BY,** either my awareness of the outside world was increasing, or things were getting worse. Strike action and riots spread across the country, factories were closing, whole industries were shutting down, the coal miners were on strike, and Scargill rode around in a chauffeur-driven Jaguar while the miners gave up their wages and food on their family tables.

Coal mines were closing across the country, never to return, losing out to less expensive and certainly less complex Russian and Canadian supplies. Unemployment was increasing, and there was less and less hope for decent, qualified, and experienced job seekers, never mind a bunch of tattooed, pierced freaks with Mohicans, who were not prime material at the front of the unemployment line.

Was there any future? Did we really give a fuck? Was there any point?

Although by that time I was drinking, mainly beer, and smoking tobacco, I hadn't succumbed to tattoos. I had pierced one ear, but I knew that was reversible, unlike some of the other things I was witnessing.

I did not do drinks stronger than beer, thanks to the Cinzano Bianco incident, when I'd puked the contents of a whole bottle over the pavement and over myself. I never touched the stuff again, and it brought back the memory if I even smelled the stuff.

Similarly, I had dabbled with marijuana, Moroccan black, weed, speed, LSD, and magic mushrooms. I'd stopped short of sniffing glue, snorting cocaine, and certainly injecting anything. Each of those vices gave me a reaction, a rejection of the alien substance in my body, and each experiment was a one-time-only event, thank God.

Tiny turned up at the house one day and didn't want to come in, which was weird. As we walked out of the gate and headed down Lake Road, he showed me his stash of LSD.

"Lucy in the Sky with Diamonds." He winked at me with his big grin.

"Where the fuck did yer get that from?"

He tapped his nose, indicating he wasn't prepared to say. I knew Tiny, and I knew I would get it out of him later. He was not great at keeping secrets. At the time, that aspect of Tiny's personality didn't pose any sort of liability. In fact, his loose lips were an asset if I wanted to pump him for information he was at first reluctant to give. Later, after the Paris incident, I often wondered if he would reveal to anyone else what we had done. My mistrust of him pushed me away out of fear of what might happen if he shared our secret with the wrong person.

We got down to Steeley's parents' jewelers and went into the arcade by the side. All the shops were closed. The arcade wound around, and we sat on the floor at the end, in the doorway of a hat shop. The floor was tiled in black and white checkers. Tiny pulled out his stash: little stamp-like pieces with pictures of cherries printed on them.

"What the fuck is this? What the fuck do you do with it?"

Tiny popped a stamp into his mouth, placed it on his tongue, and grinned.

I followed suit. "Fuck it. Why not?"

I could feel the stamp melting in my mouth and slowly lapsed from the real world. Five minutes later, we were both proper fucked. The walls of the arcade started closing in, the checkered floor started moving like a kaleidoscope, and we both tried to stand up. I struggled to find my footing on the moving floor, feeling the need to get out of the house of mirrors.

We stumbled out onto the street, relieved to escape, and stumbled and rolled our way down toward Saint Martin's, past the Stag's, and down to the lake. We sat on a bench, mesmerized, in total silence, just staring out at the lake, ducks, swans, seagulls, steamers, and boats. Like a scene from Pink Floyd, everything turned into psychedelic versions of reality. The swans turned into gondolas, the ducks became soldiers, and the seagulls became warbirds above. The tourists were enemies marching around like nutcrackers with tall heads like hats.

Tiny started getting all paranoid on me, and I couldn't move. We just sat there for what seemed like minutes, but as the sun set and the stars came out, when the sensation started to wane, we realized it had been hours. We had lost five hours like the blink of an eye.

We went back to my house; raided the pantry, as we had the munchies; and went straight to bed to sleep it off. *Never again,* I thought.

I was in relatively good shape compared to many of the others around me as I watched their deterioration into drugs, glue bags, syringes, and pipes. Some even injected straight alcohol into their veins.

Despite my aversion, I had another good reason not to dabble, as I was now dating the girl from the train, Penny, and I was smitten.

The next stop with the boys was Manchester, to go to the infamous Hacienda Club to see the Angelic Upstarts. Bomber had managed to get enough interest to hire a bus to take us down the M6 and into the heart of Manchester.

After driving for a couple of hours, we neared the venue and sensed the electricity and volatility of the audience. Violence was never too far away in those days, especially with the new punk rock movement.

Perry Boys, with their skinheads, red Perry jackets, and Doc Martens, marched in crowds with purpose to the Hacienda. Bikers wore black leather jackets, steel-toed boots, and chains. Then came the influx of punks, with their bright-colored Mohicans, piercings, chains, tartan, and PVC.

Inside, the Angelic Upstarts were loud and angry, with plenty of attitude, singing, "I'm an upstart, oi. What yer gonna do? I'm an upstart, oi. I'm talking to you."

Members of the audience sat on the front of the stage, smashing Newcastle Brown Ale bottles and slashing their forearms. A punk at the bar, showing his drinking skills, was downing pints and then biting a chunk out of his pint glass, crunching it with his teeth, and swallowing it, with blood oozing out the side of his mouth with a big, manic red-toothed smile.

It wasn't my thing, but I kind of liked the sense of danger and the adrenaline of being around such lunatics. Years later, in Sydney, I walked King's Cross all night, experiencing similar yet different sets of horrors and extremes and the same sense of violence at any moment. It was my version of thrill seeking. The need for an adrenaline rush first emerged in those days, and that need only grew stronger as I moved into adulthood. It was interesting how things early on could shape a person for the rest of his or her life.

In San Francisco, I was befriended by two local Polynesian drug dealers and hung out with them all night, witnessing the life of a drug dealer and pimp. In Northern Ireland, I nearly was blown up, chasing known terrorists through the streets, my lonely transportation of marked cars from the province back to some secret hangar on the mainland.

It was behavior I couldn't explain to myself; nevertheless, it was a pattern that existed in my life.

In the Hacienda, although the night threatened extreme violence throughout, it wasn't until the final song and encore finished, the lights came on, and the audience, full of anger, hatred, and alcohol, spilled onto the street outside that all hell broke loose among the Perrys, the skinheads, the leather, and the Mohicans, with fists, batons, bottles, and motorbike chains flying. People were knocked to the ground, kicked, stamped on, and brutalized.

"Come on, Tiny. Let's make like shepherds," I said.

"Yep, let's get the flock out of here."

We legged it to the bus and were the first ones there as the fight raged on. Within five minutes, the rest of the crew were on board in various states of survival or injury. Ted had a sliced scalp and the imprint of a motorcycle chain on his bald scalp on either side of his bright red Mohican.

As the driver pulled way, I could hear various projectiles hitting the side of the bus, and then, just as we thought we had gotten away, I heard the smash of glass as one projectile, on target with the right amount of weight and force, managed to make its way through the rear side window and penetrate the bus.

It was a long and miserable ride back, with people nursing their wounds. Ted grabbed the first-aid kit and wrapped gauze around his head, stemming the blood flow. We heard the sound of the wind and the rain, the motorway, and the rush of cars coming through the broken window, and the occupants, in their various states, numbed their pain and their attitudes and anger with their go-to substances of choice, escaping on their own personal trips into oblivion.

Thankfully, because all my dabbling had made me ill, I figured I would stick with beer. Football, boxing, and rugby all helped me stay just on the right side of the track, and my father's teachings too managed to keep me mostly on the straight and narrow.

He had forced me to smoke cigars in an attempt to make me sick, although that didn't work. He had also drummed into me from an early age the importance of self-discipline and pride, and even through those days, including a good stint in the army, I proudly never succumbed to marking my skin with any indelible tattoos, unlike some of my friends over the years: madcap Geordie had a *W* tattooed on each cheek of his arse, Will had "Press here for sex" around his belly button, and Pete had a list of girls' names down his arm of all his conquests. He crossed out each name as he moved from one to another.

Ted and Monkey were in the worst shape of the lot. Ted spent most of his day and night with his head in a Walter Willson's plastic shopping bag full of glue, inflating the plastic on the exhalation and taking in the hallucinogenic fumes of the glue on the inhalation and repeating for as long as he could before he passed out. He would just stare into nowhere like a zombie. I noticed he started getting boils on his skin, including his face. It was not acne; it was some sort of poisoning over time. Large, pus-filled bright yellow spots appeared on his face, and his moments of lucidness became fewer.

Monkey had been hanging out with some of the Scousers and apparently had discovered heroin, meth, and crack. His weight was deteriorating quickly, along with his self-esteem, looks, hygiene, and teeth, which started to rot and fall out of his face. Barely out of his teens, he had the look of a grandfather.

I was witnessing firsthand what addiction was doing to these people I had known as friends only months ago. So quickly, they had changed, and it made me sad. *No future!*

One of Dave Senior's friends turned up to a family affair and sat at the bar. He was six foot six, with hands the size of dustbin lids. He wore a maroon beret, a blazer, a Parachute Regiment tie and lapel badge, and another enamel badge of a pair of golden gloves.

His connections to his military past were obvious, and the golden-gloves badge spoke of his transition from milling to the fine art of pugilism. He apparently was an Olympic amateur champion at light heavyweight. Judging by the look of him, that must have been at least half a century before.

Big Ron was clearly an interesting character, and he was also, through his connection to Dave Senior, connected to the boxing fraternity.

"Who's that big fucker sat at the bar?" Tiny pointed.

"Dunno, but I won't be messing with him tonight," I responded.

"Do you see the size of his bloody hands?"

"Aye, and his feet. They must be like size fifteens."

"Away, they dunnay even make shoes that big, do they?"

"C'mon. Let's go find out."

Big Ron was the kind of interesting character I was drawn to and wanted to learn more about, and in Big Ron's case, the *more* was even more interesting than I had imagined.

It turned out Big Ron was a bodyguard and bouncer for the infamous Kray twins of the London gangster infamy. I bought him a pint of Jennings, paid my respects, and bid him farewell.

"Fricking hell. Do yer think he was straight up?" Tiny said.

We remembered our trip to London and the Blind Beggar, and by that time, Tiny and I considered ourselves aficionados on the subject. An abundance of Londoners made similar claims, basking in the limelight of borrowed or stolen valor of the Krays.

"If Big Dave vouches for him, that'll do for me," I said.

Tiny nodded in agreement.

"C'mon. Let's head to the Wheely."

As we left and walked on the shoreline, Tiny asked, "Did yer ever hear that joke?"

"Which one's that, Tiny?" I asked, expecting the worst.

"The wheelie bin one," he said with his big grin, and I turned my eyes to the skies.

"Yer mean the dustbin man and the Chinaman one? The latter responds to 'Where's yer been?' by saying, 'Hong Kong.'"

"And the dustbin man says, 'Na, mate, where's yer wheelie bin?'" Tiny laughed his signature belly laugh and slapped me on the back with his own dustbin lids, temporarily winding me.

Just short of our destination, we could hear the music reverberating across the still waters of the lake. Tiny and I pulled over to sit on a park bench and have a smoke. I wore my oxblood Doc Martens with yellow laces; ripped, bleached skinny jeans; and my favorite *Never Mind the Bollocks* T-shirt, and Tiny wore his green PVCs and a pair of blue suede shoes I had lent him.

"Don't go messing up those blueys tonight, Tiny." I looked over at him in the dark through the cloud of smoke now surrounding us. He returned the look of innocence of an altar boy. "Fuck off, Tiny. I mean it. Them babies came all the way from King's Road. I don't want them covered in puke like them others I leant yer." I was beginning to regret lending him probably one of my top three pairs of footwear.

Although the punk era was fueled by political and social dissatisfaction and a new style of music, the popular commentary was that we had no dress sense, when the reality was quite the opposite. We treasured not only our footwear but all our garments. I especially treasured my Doc Martens; I had new ones, old ones, painted ones, polished ones, and even steel-toed ones. In addition to my blueys, I had a pair of black suede winklepickers I was proud of too.

Tiny and I traveled to Leeds, York, Blackburn, Liverpool, Preston, Manchester, Birmingham, Leicester, and London not only for concerts but also for shopping trips to get the latest gear. We went to jumble sales, wore our uncles' old Teddy Boy gear, or made our own.

It was a bit like our music, really: if we didn't hear it on John Peel or buy it from the local record store, we would just make it up.

Those were not only austere and often violent times but also times for an unprecedented level of creativity. Unlike the trends and movements previously, with their loose rules of conformity, punk had no rules.

Tiny took a snort from his little brown bottle, sticking the rubber teat up each nostril and taking a big snort. Seconds later, with eyes glazed, he was buzzed, gone. A vacant smile crossed his face as we tramped up the stairs to the Wheelhouse, passing Big Bertha, a friend and the bouncer, at the door.

"Evening, boys! No trouble tonight, der yer hear?"

It wasn't a question; it was a warning that he had his eye on us and would throw us one by one down the long flight of stairs and buy us a pint in his local, the Queen's Head, up the dale.

"Aye, all right, Bertha!" Tiny shouted back with a knowing smile.

Bertha, in his monkey suit, just shook his head.

The north of England had a handful of celebrities, including a couple of recognized chefs, a soap actor, and a couple of musicians and artists, but since Wordsworth and Potter, the next-best level was a pro snooker player on the circuit, who was on the TV and a proud owner of a new bar in town. Tall, slim, and handsome, like the Bryan Ferry of snooker, he attracted a lot of attention, no less so from Gorgeous Jane, a serious and serial divorcée.

One evening, following one of Tiny's and my pool sessions at the Stag's, a bunch of Evertonians with too much ale, whisky, and energy in them got louder and more obnoxious and joined the pool deck on a small mezzanine above the bar.

Tiny and I took the challenge: ten pounds a corner and ten pounds each person. We took the wager confidently and probably a bit too arrogantly for the Liverpudlians' liking.

We won the coin toss.

The Scousers, of the blue affinity, with their tattoos, unfathomable accents, bad teeth, and cheeky-chappy "We will stab you" smiles, watched as Tiny smashed the balls, threatening to launch the white through the patio sliding windows in front of the three tables up above. Tiny's dustbin-lid grip on the cue, rugby forearms, and boxers' shoulders had such power that the white hit the target ball at the head of the diamond and threatened to smash it to smithereens, whatever it was made of. Miraculously, the white stayed on the table and bobbled up and down under the immense pressure of the shot, scattering the fifteen-ball pack across the table and sinking three stripes in one shot.

Tiny wasted no time. The two Scousers looked at each other, then me, and then back to Tiny as he took a difficult cut into the center pocket, which left him right on for a slide into the right corner and a straight into the middle.

The last remaining stripe was snookered behind a wall of Evertonian spots, but as quickly as our Liverpool friends' hopes rose, Tiny sank them down again with a round-the-table shot that pocketed our last ball and allowed Tiny to nudge the black into the far corner pocket, ending the game in one visit and winning the stake. We'd won twenty pounds, and the score was 1–0.

The Stag's was our home turf. We knew the lay of the land, the speed of the cloth, the divots, the slants, and the awkward pockets. When they doubled up, although we took the bet gladly, Tiny and I suspected the situation might not end well.

In frame two, I took the table after their break and three ball visits to clear the table in one visit: 2–0.

Game three was closer but a long shot. Tiny sank the black against all odds, and I saw the jaws and the attitudes of our guests drop.

In the fourth game, Tiny and I were at 100 percent, and now the stakes were eighty pounds a man—a lot of money in those days, the equivalent of about a week's wages.

Tiny and I knew instinctively that the situation wasn't good. While we enjoyed cleaning up and winning £160 between us, we could hear the rising volume and banter in the bar, and by that time, we knew each other well enough to communicate our intentions without words.

The crowd of Scousers grew for the fourth game, and I knew it wasn't good. They were trying to put us under pressure, and as Tiny sank the black in his final fling of pool genius, I saw the lift of pool cues and balls from the other tables. I didn't see any Stanley knives, but I was pretty sure they were present. I grabbed the £160; Tiny smacked Robbie over the head with the blunt end of his pool cue; and in synchrony, we legged it to the patio and balcony and jumped off, landing on the street below with our cash and our lives intact.

"C'mon. To hell with it. Let's head to Vinegar Joe's for some fish 'n' chips." Tiny grinned his big "I don't give a fuck" smile.

*Onwards, always a little further.*

# 22
# (THE) WILLIAM SHAKESPEARE
**W**M
1984
Bootle, Liverpool

**LYRICS ALWAYS HAD BEEN AS** important to me as the music—in some ways, more so. As with Shakespeare, the Bard of Avon, the words on the page meant everything. Some of the great lyricists and lyrics included the Dead Kennedys' "Holiday in Cambodia"; Adam and the Ants' "Kings of the Wild Frontier"; the Stranglers' "Golden Brown"; David Bowie's "Heroes"; and many more, including the Smiths. I felt Morrissey was likely the greatest lyricist and poet of our time, without the recognition and fame he was worthy of and deserved.

A pub called the William Shakespeare was situated at 403 Stanley Road, Bootle, Liverpool, and it was the location of one of my most memorable shit-house pub experiences ever, although there were many.

The Shakey was conveniently close to Marsh Lane Police Station and a stroll to the docks. It was a Victorian affair with three stories, six windowed floors, and a gallery that looked like the rear of an old oceangoing pirate ship.

But now it was the transient home of dockworkers, sailors, stowaways, and, by the time of my visit, a bunch of punk rockers gathered from across the north of England, as well as steadfast locals stuck in the misery of declining Britain and the seaports that once upon a time had been the backbone of the empire's trade and naval prowess—days long past.

A distant cousin from California was in a band playing there one night. The lead singer Waldo's thing was to crawl out of a bag on the stage at the start of their signature tune and crawl back in at the end, like a chrysalis, a worm, or maybe a mole—I was not sure which he was trying to represent.

Tiny and I walked into the pub early, at only six o'clock; the band didn't start till nine. We were greeted by stares reserved for out-of-towners arriving at a place where welcomes were scarce, strangers were treated with suspicion, and you had to prove you were safe before anyone, including the bar staff, would even talk to you, let alone serve you a drink.

I was dressed in my favorite leopard-skin trousers, Hell's Angels jacket, tartan bum flap, and *Never Mind the Bollocks* T-shirt. Tiny wore his green PVCs, my fricking blueys, and his furry T-fleece with chain and padlock around his neck.

We were too far-fetched in our outfits to be considered anything undercover; Tiny and I were the real deal.

That got us a beer at least. Tiny got a Snake Bite.

"What the fuck is this shithole you bought me to?" he asked with his usual smile.

I went off to the toilets, where a couple of locals were snorting white powder—I assumed cocaine.

"Hey, la, do you want some of this?" one asked with bulging eyes.

I knew from experience that cocaine did not agree with me, and I gracefully declined.

Back in the bar, Tiny was playing pool with some local scallies hoping to fleece him, but they soon found out the boot was on the other foot, as he thrashed the first contender in a clean sweep and five-pound winning. They challenged us to doubles game with a similar outcome before I advised that we pass on further games to avoid any unnecessary conflict.

With the matlows long gone, the Shakey had a small collection of locals, alcoholics, druggies, and folks who didn't necessarily have a bright future in front of them, if any at all.

Tiny and I went off to play the fruit machine, and after fifteen minutes, we had won a double jackpot, just to piss off the locals even more.

At that point, the band arrived, and I spotted my cousin Louis.

"Hey, Cuz, how's it goin'?" He greeted me with his Buddy Holly glasses and neatly trimmed beard. He had a wonky eye and partial paralysis to his jaw due to a car accident with his dad when he was a kid. "What the fuck are you doing here all the way in sunny Bootle?"

"Came to see you, yer silly fucker. What do you think?"

We gave each other hugs and back slaps as Tiny waited patiently.

"Ah yes, Louis, this is Tiny. Tiny Tim," I said.

Louis looked down at his PVCs. "Of course you fucking are. Tiny fucking Tim, any friend of my cuz is a friend of mine." They hugged like old brothers, family.

With the awkward moment over, Louis went to set up their four-piece band, and Tiny and I had a smoke and a shot of whisky. There was a game of three-card brag in the corner, but we decided not to get engaged, as we didn't want to get stabbed, and that was the capital of stabbings in the country.

Some posh friends of Louis arrived from their downtown nosh-up in their brand-new Audi and parked in the car park next door. The only other vehicle in the lot was on bricks, with all its alloys long gone. No other vehicle owners dared even consider the risk.

Seeing an opportunity, Tiny and I offered to keep an eye on the car for the small sum of fifty pounds and go out to the car park every five minutes or so to check on the owner's precious pride and joy. He agreed and paid the money, and we obliged.

The bar was filling up. Waifs and strays from across the north were coming to see my cuz's band; it was kinda cool. I saw Bomber arrive, went over to catch up, and realized that none other than Kirk Brandon had joined him.

"Now, that's fucking supercool. They'll never take me alive." Tiny grinned at him.

Brandon, as cool as ever, just shrugged off the comment.

The band started. The Shakey erupted, now full to the brim.

Throughout the sets, Tiny and I took turns checking on the Audi, me with a smoke and Tiny with his little brown bottle. Fuck knew what he could see after sniffing that shit.

The Audi remained safe, and the posh stockbroker, Richard, and his equally posh and hot wife, Emily, left just before the end and returned to whatever fancy hotel they were staying in that night.

As far as Tiny's and my sleeping arrangements, things looked up as the local police decided to raid the place around one o'clock, but the lack of criminality on our behalf didn't secure us a bed courtesy of the bizzies for the night, despite my protestations to one of the officers and my allegations of abuse of people's basic rights to have a drink and have fun. To be fair, the copper was understanding, calm, and courteous, and unlike most of his type, I kinda liked him. That said, he wasn't playing to give Tiny and me free lodging for the night.

As our only alternative to sleeping on the streets, Tiny and I settled to sleep in the bar of the Shakey instead, thanks to the landlord.

Nigel was in his thirties, was white but had dreadlocks, and had attempted to resurrect the fortunes of the William Shakespeare. Six months later, I saw a newspaper clipping saying he'd gotten shot with two barrels and fallen down the stairs of the pub, breaking his neck. *Brown bread, proper fucking dead. Rest in peace.*

I fucking hated Pikeys, specifically the non-Gypsy version of the race—the tinkers, thieves, and downright fuckers who, for whatever reason, believed they were beyond the law. The police feared treading on their temporary camps, where the Pikeys would burn, destroy, and wreak havoc until they had raped all they could before moving on to the next unsuspecting community.

If you messed with a Pikey, you had another hundred to answer to. I knew one, Gypsy Rob, a despicable, horrible son of a twat who deserved nothing more than being buried on the moors or next to Myra Hindley or Peter Sutcliffe, the modern-day Ripper. He was responsible for fueling a good friend's habit that eventually ended with him stringing himself up on a rope in his front room and taking his own life.

At the local county fair, the Pikeys abounded. They came into town with their caravans and a wave of crime. With their dealer boots, knives, and sheer numbers, it was better to stay away than get engaged.

There were consequences to getting engaged in general, and we didn't plan our engagements well back then.

Once, Tiny met the father of a girlfriend at her birthday party. He was a priest, so we were on our best behavior as we consumed egg and smoked salmon sandwiches with the crusts cut off and homemade lemonade we laced with alcohol.

"So what's your belief in the Lord, young man?" asked the priest of Tiny.

"Well, sir, it's simple: *God* is just *dog* spelled backward."

The room went dead silent as all heard his profound response. The priest did not know how to answer, and the listeners giggled together.

"Very interesting take on it, young man" was the only response he could muster.

At another party on another night, Kerry, Tiny, and I climbed out onto the window ledge of Carrie-Ann's four-story house and were mistakenly misconstrued as potential suicides, when there was nothing further from our minds. We were young, arrogant, and invincible, so why the hell not?

Above the town hall lived a priest. He was one of the youth leaders at our local youth club and creeped me out. He often invited me, Tiny, and others to go to his apartment for beers and more. Tiny and I always declined politely, unlike others, who took up his offer, and he plied them with drinks and who knew what else as the silence of their drunken exploits resounded.

At that same town hall, Tiny, Blez, Conrad, and I were to be the opening set for the Southern Death Cult, who were famous for their "She Sells Sanctuary" sound.

Though the media misrepresented some of the other bands of that time, they were right about our band, Contraband. We truly couldn't play or, in my case, sing.

Conrad and I were the lyricists of our main and, in fact, only song of notoriety, "Fucking Bastard," which we wrote in a haze of magic mushrooms: "There was this kid lived down our street, and the clothes he wore were pretty neat. Then he started messing with my girl; now I think he's a fucking turd."

Then came the highly creative chorus: "The fucking bastard ..."

Well, that was it—our two minutes of fame. We opened for the Southern Death Cult, playing our single signature tune, and just about got kicked off the stage to let the professionals do their thing.

Appleby Horse Fair was always an interesting affair. It was an annual homage to that otherwise sleepy town in the middle of the country, above the Pennines and on the borders of Cumbria and North Yorkshire.

The fair had been held in Appleby-in-Westmorland since 1685, and caravans ancient and new, including horses and more than thirty thousand Gypsies, travelers, and tinkers, would converge from across the United Kingdom and Ireland and descend for a week or two of mainly drunken misdemeanors, horse trials, gambling, and bare-knuckle boxing.

Tiny, the boys, and I went one year in all our garb, stayed for a couple of hours, and then jumped onto the next red double-decker to take us back to the safety of our hometown—a wise move, as we learned two lads from the next-door town ended up in an altercation, lost out to the bottles and the blades, and ended up in hospital for a couple of weeks, alive but just.

I concluded that birds of a feather flocked together, but sometimes birds of a different feather, when mixed together, could be toxic. "I fucking hate Pikeys!"

# 23
# THE QUEEN'S SHILLING
## WM
### 1985
### Carlisle

MY MOTHER ANNOUNCED WE WERE going to Carlisle on a shopping trip for my long-wanted Patrick football boots. I had been nagging her about them for months. Why would I have suspected an ulterior motive? How could even the greatest imagination of conspiracy theory have conjured up any possible alternative to what seemed such an innocent and ordinary announcement?

The Patrick boots were something special at that time. They were not the molded stud type or the ubiquitous Adidas and other brands but a special pair of boots with lime-green stripes and bright-colored laces, an individual set of footwear, as were my Doc Martens, winklepickers, and blueys.

Later that week, my mother and I headed up to the largest and most dismal city in our county, just below the Scottish border, forty-six miles north up the M6 into the city of granite. My favorites played on the stereo, and my mind was in London and "Down in the Tube Station at Midnight": "The distant echo of faraway voices boarding faraway trains. To take them home to the ones that they love and who love them forever."

On the way, we chatted about school, what was next, work, my two counts of being expelled from school, and my disruptive behavior. We talked about college, prospects, travel, and my obsession with the song "Moon River," which might have indicated a potential wanderlust.

"It's true. I think there is something else out there for me," I said, and she noodled as she drove. I got the sense her silence meant she wanted more. "Thing is, Mum, I don't know what that means or even is."

I looked across for her encouragement, and she glanced over. My mother had not been outside the county of Yorkshire since the family moved down from Glasgow, until she met my father, so I was not talking to the best traveled or most ambitious person in the world, but I knew she had my best interest at heart.

"You see, the thing is, I am not bad; I'm just different, and they don't know how to handle it." I was referring to the teachers at school mainly. I could tell she was about to impart some wisdom.

"You see, Willy, your grandfather always used to tell me, 'Those who can, do, and those who can't, teach.'" She turned and smiled at me. I returned her smile and appreciated her understanding and support.

My mother wasn't a prolific driver; in fact, she barely drove at all, usually relying on my dad to be at the wheel and the captain of the ship, a role he took willingly. She concentrated on her driving as I looked out the window of my dad's silver BMW 630 CSi, which had red leather upholstery. I gazed at the dreary M6, the rain, and the cars heading north, surely to bypass Carlisle, as most people did, straight to the infinitely more interesting Scotland instead.

"The glazed, dirty steps repeat my own and reflect my thoughts. Cold and uninviting, partially naked, except for toffee wrappers and this morning's papers."

I thought some more about what she had said as I stared out the window, dressed in my posh Mother's Day outfit: a pair of jeans, my Doc Marten eight-hole boots, my smart but seemingly controversial red Harrington jacket, and my now staple crew cut.

I remembered the time I had come home with noughts and crosses etched in my grade-one haircut, and she had made me wear a bobble hat in the house. Sick of hearing my music full blast in the middle of the night, she had moved me outside to the caravan on the grounds of our house, where I'd had a sense of having my own pad. I'd electrocuted myself while trying to fix my stereo and spent a night on magic mushrooms, exploring my own version of Middle-earth in my bed.

"What do you think the future holds, Mum?" I tested her, as was my way.

She turned to me and did a double take. "What do you mean?"

I knew she was stalling to gather her thoughts. "Well, what's next? Where do we go from here? What's the best next step?"

"For you, Willy?"

"Maybe, but what about the country, you, dad, and the world?"

"Gosh, I don't know."

I was testing her for sure. My mum had a way of avoiding questions, and our arrival in the metropolis of Carlisle was sufficient distraction to change the conversation.

The lyrics on the stereo continued: "Behind me, whispers in the shadows. Gruff, blazing voices, hating, waiting."

Neither of us had been there before. I saw lots of underwhelming buildings and scenery, and people were all around. I wondered why we had not gone somewhere more exciting, such as Manchester.

I listened to the song playing: "'Hey, boy!' they shout. 'Have you got any money?' And I said, 'I've a little money and a takeaway curry. I'm on my way home to my wife; she'll be lining up the cutlery. You know, she's expecting me, polishing the glasses and pulling out the cork.'"

We parked the car. It was mid to late morning, and we made a stop at tea shop for sandwiches, cake, tea, and, in my case, a glass of lemonade. My mum liked cake; it was one of her treats. A stacked cake stand came out, carried by a pretty waitress with a cute apron, white shirt, and nervous smile. I smiled at her, and she smiled back. I started to kinda like Carlisle all of a sudden.

My mum poured her tea, I supped on my lemonade, and we both tucked into the sandwiches and cake before us. We talked about the latest family updates, including Grandma; Grandad; uncles Arthur, Tommy, and, the youngest, Billy;

Margaret and May; and all the cousins. She then moved the subject on.

"Are you still enjoying the air cadets?" she asked.

I looked at her. The question had come out of the blue, I thought. "Yeah, sure, it's fine. Sort of."

Although the camps had been fun, including flying gliders, shooting Lee Enfield 303s and elephant guns, and flying Chipmunks, the uniforms were itchy and uncomfortable; the place was dark and dingy and smelled of stale sweat; and the routine was mundane and boring. It was a pursuit of conformists and not individuality.

"I love the Seabrook crisps, especially the Worcestershire sauce flavor," I said.

She rolled her eyes.

"Come on. Let's go get those boots." I pushed the agenda as she finished her last morsels and took her last sips of tea. The song continued to play in my head: "I first felt a fist and then a kick. I could now smell their breath. They smelt of pubs and wormwood scrubs and too many right-wing meetings. My life swam around me; it took a look and drowned me in its own existence."

We left the café and walked a short distance to the shoe shop. After going through the selection of my favored boots, debating screw-in studs versus molded soles again, and making the transaction, I was the proud owner of brand-new Patricks. At that point, I would have probably done most anything my mum asked me. As we walked back to the car, we passed an army careers office, and she stopped, looking through the window at the displays of all the wonderful things one could do in the British Armed Forces.

"But Dad always said if I were ever to join, then I should take his advice and join the Royal Navy," I said.

My mother ushered us inside, and surprisingly, we were expected. We apparently had an appointment. After an initial introduction to the merits of joining, I was invited to watch a video on the proud British Army and take a type of psychometric test, and then, shortly after, came the sales pitch.

"Listen, son, you are impressive. Clearly bright and intelligent, and from your scores and preferences, we have a couple of options that might really suit you down to the ground."

"Okay." That was all I could muster. I was a little nervous now.

"We think from your scores that the Parachute Regiment, the REME, or the Blues and Royals might suit you down to the ground."

"Okay." I looked at my mother, not quite knowing what was going on.

I went into a back room and watched three more videos on the merits of the three areas I had being selected for as ideal.

My father had been in the REME, and despite the many advantages, including meaningful work and qualifications, I was put off by his counsel. The reputation of the Parachute Regiment also put me off; I considered myself more of a thinking man's individual than a mindless monkey. Then I remembered going to London, to Horse Guards Parade, and seeing the Blues and Royals years earlier with my father.

*Hold on a minute. What the hell is this? I came to Carlisle to buy a pair of long-overdue football boots, not to join the fucking army!* I said to myself. I did not want to upset my mother, though.

Song lyrics played in my mind: "The last thing that I saw as I lay there on the floor was 'Jesus saves' painted by an atheist nutter, and a British rail poster read, 'Have an away day, a cheap holiday; do it today.'"

After I finished watching the military propaganda, I exited the back room. I said I'd have to think things through, as I wasn't really interested in joining the British military, regardless of which branch. I noted the distinctly disappointed look on my mum's face but dismissed it as simple nerves. My mum thanked the staff sergeant, I shook his hand and nodded, and we left. We journeyed back home in silence. I looked out the window at the rain that glimmered and shone in the sunlight as we drove back to the land of Beatrix Potter and William Wordsworth.

"I fumble for change and pull out the queen, smiling, beguiling. I put in the money and pull out a plum."

I moved on quickly in the happiness of my Patricks over the next few weeks, realizing that form over matter wasn't always the best plan as I witnessed the shoes slowly disintegrate after each practice and each hard-fought match, notwithstanding the test of time, never mind the season.

I kept my Carlisle experience quiet. I didn't even tell Tiny, but to be fair, I hadn't really computed it and connected the dots myself to understand what the hell it was all about.

A few weeks later, on a Sunday, after my weekly game, I got back home for the usual scrub-down and the family meal—a roast, of course, the usual—and *The Black and White Minstrel Show* on the radio, with their signature kickoff tune: "Sing Something Simple."

Before dinner, my mother produced some documents from the "nice man at the army careers office" and said how well I had done in being provisionally accepted and given the honor to be invited to initial selection at their training depot in Sutton Coldfield, just outside Birmingham.

How stupid was I? I still had not worked out the ploy, and I signed on the dotted line.

"What do you mean you're off to army selection?" Tiny said when I told him the news. It was hard to explain, mainly because I did not understand it myself.

*Fuck that for a game of soldiers!*

# 24
## END OF AN ERA
**WM**
### 1985
### Great Britain

**IT HAD BEEN A WHIRLWIND,** with much turmoil and change in a short space of time, an explosion in the blink of an eye in the bigger scheme of the universe and of world history—a forgotten decade that many chose to forget.

The catalyst on the rise was the melting of the elements of trust among the government; the unions; the people; the youth; and the shameful, apathetic middle class who, for whatever reason, would not and did not get engaged. The breakdown in the social contract of continued evolution and progress was clear.

Britain once had been a proud and victorious nation, an empire on which the sun never set. But all empires in the history of the world faded and eventually died. Back then, Great Britain seemed to be in its death throes. In the view of some, that was acceptable, and in the view of many, it was far too premature.

But we were not necessarily focused on that at the time; the mood of the nation was more about a reaction, like the body rejecting poison. It was a rebellion, a revolt, a revolution.

The various horrors playing out at the time included international and domestic terrorism, kidnapping, bombs, murder, fear of the future, fear of AIDS, unhinged serial killers, assassins, and a feeling of mediocrity.

Music was the scripture of evolution and the buildup to the era. There were groups, bands, and individuals who stood out. There were the challenging lyrics of John Lennon: "Imagine there's no heaven and no religion too." What did he really mean? Bob Dylan wrote songs of rebellion, as did Iggy Pop, Johnny Cash, Pink Floyd, and the Who.

The difference was that the punk rock era made music, as the message, accessible to not just musicians but also people who couldn't play. The platform for creative expression opened to the masses, just like when the grand masters of art, with their big canvases, oil, and commissions, were challenged by upstarts with more creative and more accessible methods.

The mood had softened, with the edge taken off the rawness of the late 1970s. Tiny, the boys, and I had also moved on from the fever pitch. Our ideology had evolved in what seemed a relatively fleeting period of time; it was like an epoch in which stands were taken, choices were made, and the popular survived.

The Egremont incident had swayed us significantly and pushed us back the other way. Even Johnny Rotten,

John Lydon, the Godfather of Punk Rock, had transformed from his raw, in-your-face "Fuck you at all costs" to a more, frankly, entertaining and tuneful approach. That said, his truthfulness lived on, and maybe the nation needed his commitment to telling it how it was and telling the brutal, honest truth.

Too many people and families, including mine, pretended the troubles weren't happening and eventually would just go away, a strategy as effective as an ostrich burying its head in the sand and hoping its predator would go away or a child closing his eyes out of fear.

We needed Lydon's and others' brutal honesty and observations in those times. I felt that like Winston Churchill and Margaret Thatcher, John Lydon should be credited for his contribution to making the nation sit up, listen, and do something about it.

The rise of Band Aid's "Feed the World," although undoubtedly a great and worthy cause, was a deflection from the issues we faced at home, though maybe it was a healthy distraction, as things did calm down, and the Maggie effect started to take hold. Maybe the distraction was a good thing, turning our attention to how our great nation could return to the world stage and perhaps, in different ways, be a global leader.

Things for me were moving too, at what felt like an out-of-control pace—things not planned by me, but then again, I didn't have plans beyond the next day. I suspected my mother had more to do with it than I realized or cared to admit at the time.

"How did you get on in Sutton Coldfield?" Tiny asked me out of the blue.

"Okay, I think. Must have been okay, because they offered me a place."

"What the hell, Willy? Really? What does that bloody mean?"

I could not answer him, as I didn't really know yet. I knew only that I had passed all the physical, mental, and psychometric tests, and the recruiting sergeant major and officer in charge had interviewed me at the end of the three days' selection and seemed positive and keen to have me on board.

"What else am I gonna fucking do, Tiny?"

He shook his head in his hands. "I have no bloody idea, but what about me, you fucker?"

I did feel bad, as if I would be deserting Tiny and the rest of the crew, and I did feel somewhat manipulated into the situation and the opportunity, but I relished the opportunity to get the fuck out of Dodge.

"Why don't you come and join me? That would be fun. We could have a crack together. Why the hell not?"

He continued to shake his head.

"What's wrong, Tiny?"

"I can't."

"What do you mean you can't?" It was clear he was upset. "What do you mean?"

"I already tried last year."

"What?"

"Failed the fucking medical, didn't I?" It was not a question. "Maybe too much of that popper shit," he said, and he lifted his head with tears in his eyes.

"What the fuck, Tiny?"

"Apparently, it fucked up my heart." He stared blankly. "I want to get the fuck out of here too, Willy."

Now was not the time to say, "I told you so."

"Good on yer, Willy. Yer right to get the fuck out of here."

I silently agreed, nodding with concern. That moment sealed the deal. I needed to get out. I needed to explore, and that was my route out of town and my escape to the future, maybe one day as far as Moon River.

The moment was gone. I knew it was time to move on.

*Bring me my bow of burning gold!*

Many had been given the title, but in my mind, there was only one Godfather of Punk. As with any godfather in life, there were multiple contributors to such an honor, including grandparents, parents, siblings, and children, and that was how I saw the evolution of the punk rock era.

Iggy Pop, bashing out his tunes in the late 1960s and the 1970s, was a controversial and larger-than-life character. A friend of mine told me that while growing up as a kid in Australia, he had seen Iggy Pop perform live on a kids' TV show, thrashing around and jumping into the crowd, and the show's presenter had not known how to deal with him.

Johnny Cash, the man in black, had a bad-boy image and straight-talking lyrics, even performing in front of prisoners at San Quentin Prison.

The New York Dolls; the Ramones; the Damned, who released the first UK punk rock single; the Clash; the Stranglers; Stiff Little Fingers; the Dead Kennedys; Crass; and Killing Joke all had significant contributions and parts to play in the revolution.

Then there were the nonpunk influencers who also contributed to the story, such as David Bowie, with his myriad personas, and Pink Floyd, who took us to far-off lands and dark places. Another godfather in his own right was Paul Weller of the Jam and, later, Style Council. Also significant were the Specials and their iconic "Ghost Town," the Boomtown Rats, Chrissie Hynde and the Pretenders, the Smiths, Morrissey, and Madness, to name but a few. The foundations laid back then would form a lasting foundation for music forever.

But beyond just the music, the biggest and probably the most influential person of that time set the tone for our attitudes toward bucking the trend and challenging the status quo in favor of individual thought, truth, and honesty—often mistaken for brash or rude behavior. The true Godfather of the time believed in the saying "The truth will set you free" to the extreme.

Sometimes awkward and sometimes taken with offense, his interpretation was in phrases like "Anger is an energy." He was misconstrued as an advocate for violence, but in fact, he was far from it. He advocated turning that powerful emotion into a positive and truthful energy to effect positive change through nonviolent, passionate resistance. That was what he did for the youth of a nation who were in the straits of desperation.

With many revolutionaries, it took time—a generation, decades, or maybe even centuries—to recognize how the brave individuals fearlessly went beyond the bounds of the status quo to challenge it, rip up the rule book, stand in the face of the establishment of the time, and fight for their beliefs, such as William Wallace in Scotland, Emmeline Pankhurst for women's rights, Winston Churchill as the country considered cowering to Hitler's Nazi ways, Martin Luther King Jr. in his fight for the rights of blacks, Mahatma Gandhi, and Nelson Mandela.

While growing up in a two-room apartment next door to Arsenal Stadium in Highbury, North London, he contracted spinal meningitis at the age of seven, which resulted in periods of coma and memory loss that lasted four years of his early life.

At that point, he was probably an unlikely choice to lead a historic and era-changing movement, but that changed when he met with Malcolm McLaren and auditioned in front of a band called the Sex Pistols. John Joseph Lydon, known as Johnny Rotten, became an iconic front man, a progressive and sometimes brutally honest leader of a revolution, and, in my mind, the rightful and deserved Godfather of Punk Rock.

*Anger is an energy!*

# 25

# GRACE

WM

1986

Paris, France

**LIKE LYDON, I AGREED THAT** anger was an energy and believed in nonviolence; however, back in those days, sometimes violence came looking for me.

I was young and fit and kept off drugs, and boxing and rugby had taught me well how to look after myself. From a young age, I had learned to detest bullying and bullies of any shape or form, no matter how big.

I had also connected with my Scottish history and connected the dots to my sometimes Highlander traits of never backing down or giving up. I had an ancestor nicknamed Jock Half Lugs, named so because he had his ears half bitten off in fights. His war cry was "How dare you fucking mess wi' me!"

Since I'd started at high school, there had been one challenger after another in what felt like a never-ending line of people who wanted to prove themselves. I always felt I had nothing to prove to anyone else; I just wanted to tread my own path, mind my own business, and put one sure foot in front of the other boldly and rightly, bravely and truly. Those were the teachings passed on to me by my father and his father before him and many generations going back eight hundred years, all the way back to the Scottish Highlands.

The thought of conflict made me nervous. In moments of violence, I was razor sharp and focused on nothing but the victory, and afterward, I had feelings of loneliness, physical sickness, and deep sadness, if not some state of depression, similar to the symptoms of post-traumatic stress disorder, which I would become more familiar with later in my life.

The offer to join the army had arrived a couple of weeks earlier, and I was not sure what I wanted to do. I had been offered a place in the local community college and vocational training, which surely was a path to mediocrity; nevertheless, going away to the army was a gigantic leap from the relative safety of my little northern town I called home, where I had a roof over my head, my friends, my girlfriends, and the countryside around, which all afforded me comforts of sort.

Tiny and I decided we would head to Paris to see the Parisian punk rock band Bérurier Noir and sneak a glimpse of the phenomenon Grace Jones.

Our tastes were evolving quickly. We were both lyricists, and we were interested in the message of the revolution, the evolution of the message, and the broadening delivery of the message. It was no longer a message just for angry punk rockers, misfits, and outliers but a rhetoric existent in all genres of music and arts at the time.

Bérurier Noir was a new breed of punk from France. They had a similar message but a unique style and language of delivery. Grace Jones, on the other hand, was just unique. She was a black woman from Jamaica, a New Yorker living in Paris, a model, a singer, bold, muscular, and intimidating.

The two of us wore toned-down, grown-up outfits, but somehow, miraculously, Tiny's green PVC pants had survived. We borrowed Dave's Volkswagen Beetle and headed down the M6, across the M62, and then down the M1 to London and then on down to Dover and to our ferry. After a hop across the channel, we headed into Paris.

We had both been to Paris before—many times, in fact, including with the school rugby team—but this was our first time going on our own. We were free, all grown up, and independent, and the world was at our feet.

The feeling of disenfranchisement was gradually lifting and being slowly replaced with a level of optimism for the first time in my living memory.

We motored south, only stopping for petrol when we needed it and loading up with more delightful snacks from the service station. We had a ferry to catch, where we would have a few beers and some semidecent food. Then we'd get to Calais and crack on to Paris.

We planned to stay for a few days, intending to look around the French capital and see what trouble we could get up to, cranking out tunes on the VW cassette player. Tiny and I had many compilations we had recorded over the years of our favorite music.

"So, Tiny, most influential people of our time?"

Tiny looked at me. "What?"

"Who have been the most influential people in our time?"

He paused, looking out the side window as I steered the Beetle south. "Well, Maggie for sure. Lennon, McCartney, the Pistols, the Clash, Brandon, Weller, and maybe Chrissie Hynde for the sexiest voice in music." He looked back over at me. "Why?"

"Just something I've been thinking about."

"You do a hell of a lot of thinking, Willy."

I could see his big grin out of the corner of my eye. He lit up two Marlboro Lights and passed me one.

"What about Churchill? Does he still have an influence today?"

"Damned right he does, the old boy: 'Never, never, never give up.'" We chorused the familiar catchphrase we had grown up with that had pulled the nation through the war.

"Then there's Bowie, McLaren, Geldof, and what about Pink Floyd?"

My memory went back to watching *The Wall* at Tiny's house, on his sofa in the middle of the day. With his parents out and the curtains closed, we watched the film, and I had my first ever joint.

"Oh yeh, good one, Tiny. But not just the positive. The negative too."

"What—like Harold bloody Wilson, that meddling fricking toss pot? Mary?"

"You mean Whitehouse?"

"Yeh, that fucker. What was her bloody problem anyway?"

"No idea. As mad as a ship's cat if you ask me."

"What about old Sutcliffe the Ripper?"

"Well, that fucker deserves a place in hell right next to Hitler."

"And that IRA fucker Gerry Adams."

I nodded as we took the slip road heading deeper south. "What about our boy Johnny?"

"I'd say so. He's a bloody legend!"

I turned to him and smiled. I realized I truly loved my friend Tiny. *Legend* was one of his favorite words, and I was proud he had called me that several times during our friendship.

He moved the conversation on to my decision to join the army. "You still looking forward to getting out of Dodge?"

I paused for a moment. "I think so. Although things have improved, there's still not too much to make me stay." I could sense the sadness in my friend. "Apart from you, Tiny, my old mucker."

He slapped me on the back with his usual bearlike force, making me swerve across lanes and causing a big articulated lorry to blurt its horn at us. Tiny wound his window down. "Fuck off!" he yelled, sticking two fingers in the air, causing the lorry driver to repeat the horn honk and flash his lights at us, right up our tailpipe.

"On the subject of France, you know the origins of the two fingers, right?"

"Enlighten me, Tiny!"

He went on to tell me the tale of the Battle of Agincourt. The French told the English that once they won, they would cut off the bow fingers of all the English archers so they could not use their bows again. After the English won the battle, the English archers walked off the battlefield while sticking their two fingers up in defiance and victory at the French prisoners.

I liked that Tiny always needed to understand the *why* and always did his homework.

We pulled into the line on the dock with our ferry in front of us, waiting to board. We got out of the Beetle to stretch our legs and take the sweet, salty air into our lungs, working up an appetite.

On board, we parked the car on the deck, scampered up into the ferry seating areas, and headed straight to the cafeteria for our pie, chips, and mushy peas with gravy and two bottles of Kronenbourg each. We clinked our bottles, dug in, and ate in silence.

The ride from Calais down to Paris was uneventful. We had a concert to get to, and as we reached the outskirts of the city and drove toward the center, the smells, sights, and sounds of Paris came at us as we cruised with the windows of the Beetle down and made our way slowly through the Parisian traffic.

We were heading to Le Caveau de la Huchette, a small jazz club on the Rue de la Huchette, where Grace Jones was playing a one-off gig that night.

Grace Jones was unconventional and unexpected, an international yet mysterious superstar of fascination to many and shrouded with intrigue. With deep connections to Paris, including the place, the people, and the music scene, she had stayed loyal to the city where she had found herself and flourished.

We managed to find a parking spot on the Rue Saint-Severin, just a couple of blocks away from the venue; got out of the Beetle; stretched our legs; and headed toward the club. It was early evening, and I was tired from the drive.

"Fancy a sherbet or two, Tiny, my old boy?"

"Damn right I do, my old mucker." He slapped me on the back.

We walked across to the Boulevard Saint-Michel and down to the River Seine on our left, with Notre Dame on the opposite bank. We stopped at the railing overlooking the river, and I reached into my leather jacket, pulled out two bottles of Kronenbourg, and popped the caps while Tiny lit two smokes, one for me and the other for him.

We leaned on the railing.

"She's a thing of fine beauty, yer know, Willy."

"Aye, she sure is, Tiny," I said as I looked at the scene before us. "I've always liked Paris. Maybe one day I might want to live here."

Tiny looked at me sideways. "I don't mean Paris, you fucking blockhead. I meant Grace Jones!" He slapped me again, nearly bowling me over the top into the river.

"She's kinda scary," I said as I caught my breath.

"Fuck off, man. She's a fricking stunner." Tiny went on to wax lyrical about her uniqueness and what set her apart from the rest of the potential targets of his admiration.

"Anyway, Tiny, looks like you lost out. She's dating that Dolph Lundgren geezer. Seems you might be too late, old boy." I smiled and slapped him on the back, getting my own back on him.

"Who? That big fucker from *Rocky*?"

"That would be the one." I smiled. "Come on. Let's go."

We finished our beers and our smokes and headed toward Le Caveau de la Huchette. Tiny trailed behind me, swearing and cursing under his breath at my recent news. We turned right at the Jardin Notre Dame and continued on to the tiny little frontage that was our destination that evening.

"This place is tiny." Tiny was right.

We walked through the front door; pulled the insulating curtain, a Parisian tradition, to one side; and stepped inside. The big Parisian bouncer looked us up and down and, given our dressed-down look, let us in after an exchange of franc notes.

Beyond the bouncer was the long, crowded bar. We made our way through the throng; ordered a double order of Pelforth beer; and headed downstairs to the cavern, where we could hear the warm-up music for the main event; and found ourselves a perch.

The place was dark, with mysterious bright red leather seating, benches, and stools, and was crowded to the hilt. The lights dimmed even further, and the lights of the stage brightened, adding to the atmosphere. The small but packed crowd erupted into screams and shouts as the distinctive bass rang out, and the tall, sleek, distinctive black figure walked out. There was an introduction in English, not French: "Ladies and gentlemen, introducing the one and only Miss Grace Jones." She strutted up to the front of the stage and broke into her latest tune, "Nightclubbing," menacingly staring around at her audience.

Avoiding eye contact with the singer, I glanced over at my friend. Tiny's smile was as big as the Cheshire Cat's as he made every effort to make eye contact, and that sight made me happy.

*Hinky-dinky parlez-vous!*

# 26
# BORIS
**WM**
## 1986
## Paris, France

**AFTER GRACE, WE HEADED BACK** to the Beetle and to the campsite Tiny had heard about close to the concert hall for the next night. In the Twelfth Arrondissement district of Paris, it was a temporary site in a hidden-away corner of a park filled with the homeless, hippies, and punk rockers there to see Bérurier Noir the following day.

We rolled in around eleven o'clock, pulled the two-man tent out of the back of the car, pitched it, got out the Calor gas stove we had borrowed from a boat on the lake back home, opened a can of beans and sausages, cracked a couple of beers from our provisions, and took in our surroundings.

There were various versions of shelter on display, from shopping trolleys with homeless folks' worldly possessions stacked high to groups of people in sleeping bags on the grass to makeshift shelters made from sticks, tarpaulin, and rope.

It was dark, but I could see maybe one hundred souls in all, with probably half of them identifiable as concertgoers like Tiny and me, as was evident by their dress, demeanor, and self-made fire pits, where they were drinking, shooting, or smoking, whatever their preference. Close by was an area sheltered by trees, and in the middle was an upturned oil drum, like a campsite community fire.

We could hear one group who were particularly loud, brash, and, by the sound of it, wasted. They looked proper hard core, wherever they came from.

"What is that accent?" asked Tiny.

"I have no idea. It's not French or German," I said.

Next to us was a makeshift shelter where a lone man and his dog sat quietly staring out into the dark vacantly. He seemingly was a long-term occupant of the place.

When the beans and sausages were ready, we served them up in our tin trays and started to eat.

"Looks like we're living the high life compared to some of these fuckers."

"Pretty bloody sad, really."

Apart from the old tramp back home and what we had seen on our travels, mainly in London, we didn't know or understand what homelessness really meant.

"It makes you realize how fricking lucky we are really." Tiny looked up from his feast.

"It's too bloody cold and wet to live rough where we are."

"Yeh, it's grim up north," Tiny said with his usual sense of humor.

The man next to us sat in his tent, and the dog, on a leash, licked its chops. I reached into our store, grabbed another tin of beans and sausages, and put it on the stove. A couple of minutes later, I served it up with a spoon, a couple of slices of bread, and a tin of beer and took it over to the man with the staring eyes. I realized as I got up to him that he was blind; his eyes were glazed over with what I assumed were cataracts, probably too much abuse in his time, and likely a lack of access to medication.

I left the plate with him, he thanked me in French, and I watched as he and his dog shared the meal together, and he supped the beer as if it were the first one he'd had in a month. Maybe it was.

"Did you know that nearly twenty percent of homeless are ex-squaddies?" I asked.

"Yep, I heard that. Bloody sad, isn't it?"

"Look at them poor fuckers in the Falklands. What do they have when they get out?"

"A tin hat and a fucking gun no more. What next?"

The dog licked the plate clean.

"Thank fuck we've got spares!" Tiny cracked.

"Come on. Let's get our heads down. I am bloody cream-crackered."

We washed down our plates, packed away the stove and other kit back in the Beetle, and settled down for the night in our two-man tent, huddling in our sleeping bags like maggots, and within just a few minutes, we drifted off to sleep.

It had been a long day, and I was ready for a good old kip.

It must have been around two in the morning when I woke up and heard what I thought was the Beetle's engine trying to spring to life. I looked over, and Tiny was sparko in his sleeping bag next to me. I shook him. "Tiny, what the fuck? Some fuck's trying to steal the Beetle!" I grabbed my leather jacket and jumped out of the tent and ran toward the car.

A big fucking skinhead sat in the driver's seat.

I went to the open door. "What the fuck are you doing?"

He turned and looked at me with his big, angry, cracked-up eyes.

"What the fuck are you doing?" I repeated. By that time, Tiny was at my shoulder.

"Fuck you. I take car," the big youth said in what Tiny and I both recognized as a Russian accent. He probably was from the group we had overheard a couple of hours earlier.

He sat in the driver's seat, had pulled out the wires from the Beetle's dashboard, and was trying to hot-wire the car. I could feel the red mist descending upon me. In its midst, I lost control of all sense and sensibility, and my adrenaline-infused bloodstream made me capable of just about anything.

"Get the fuck out of the car, Boris!" I shouted at him, and he turned and glared like a madman as he removed his bulk from the car and squared up before us. He was probably six foot six and about twenty stone, had tattoos covering his arms, and wore a swastika T-shirt.

"You talk to me, English boy?" he said in his obvious Russian accent, and he started to walk toward me, pulling out a big, fat blade that sparkled in the light of the moon above. The entire campsite was in silence, with all long since stupefied, crashed out, and asleep.

I saw the flash of the blade coming toward me, and using my boxer's instincts, I managed to flip back my head and evade the slice and the disfigurement. I was paranoid of knives of all shapes and sizes, and his was a big fucker of a blade.

Boris wreaked of alcohol and body odor. He was a big man, angry, and probably off his head and had what must have been at least a twelve-inch blade in his hand, and he was trying to steal my fucking car I'd borrowed from my mate.

"What the fuck?" I yelled.

"I take car back to Russia, English boy."

"Like fuck you do, Boris!"

At that, he took another swing with the blade in his right hand and connected a punch that landed on my temple with the left.

"You dirty fucker!" I yelled.

Boris grabbed Tiny, and I saw him lift the blade and point it down toward Tiny's back, flopping over the front of the Beetle. This was really fucking serious. Old Boris was off his fucking rocker, big, and violent.

Leaping over, I was relieved as I felt the hard, polished wood handle in my inside pocket. I grabbed the blackthorn shillelagh and, in one motion, knocked the knife out of his hand, kicking him with my size-nine Doc Martens in the bollocks. Thank fuck we had decided to sleep with our kit on just in case.

Boris turned back toward me with his big fists, the size of cannonballs, clenched. I saw some Russian shit tattooed on his knuckles. While coming toward me, he paused to pick up his blade.

Now in full red-mist mode, I swung the shillelagh as Boris was picking up his blade. I swung the rod of blackthorn, with its gnarly head, with all my might, connecting on the right side of his head, hitting his temple and, at the same time, crushing his ear, disorienting him. Almost simultaneously, from behind on the other side, Tiny, who had found two stone pebbles on the ground, hit Boris around the head in a mirror fashion, sending the twenty-something-stone Russian giant down to the ground, poleaxed. His head hit the front side bumper of the Beetle hard, and it was driven into Boris's left eye socket as he went down with all his weight behind him.

There was someone behind us holding what looked like a truncheon and wearing a military-style jacket—we assumed another Russian. The shillelagh went back to work and caught the man in the shadows right on the temple. A pincer movement from Tiny followed with the two rocks on each side of his head. The man fell to the ground unconscious, crumpled. I quickly sat astride his body, beating his head with the blackthorn, with sheer adrenaline driving me in hit after hit. Tiny stood by me with his hands on his hips, looking down at the focus of my attack. There was something wrong with Tiny's expression, and I gradually slowed to a stop. The man's face was pummeled and unrecognizable as a human face.

"What the fuck?" gasped Tiny.

I looked down at the limp body, and slow realization dawned on me. "Oh fuck!" I went into an immediate state of shock and felt more postviolence nausea than I ever had before. "Fuck, fuck, fuck!" I looked up at Tiny, and he looked back down at me.

It was quick, fast, and furious, a nanosecond of time. Tiny and I looked at each other, gasping for air, with adrenaline seeping through our veins.

"What the fuck just happened?" Tiny asked.

"I have no fucking idea," I said as I looked down at the lifeless Parisian police officer in front of me. This was no neo-Nazi punk from the shadows. This was a bona fide, real-deal fucking Parisian gendarme. "What the fuck? Fuck, fuck, and fuck!" The policeman was dead.

I got up slowly and looked over at Boris. His head was half impaled on the bumper of the Beetle, his eyes were almost popping out, and blood was draining from his ear. We didn't need to check his pulse; he was clearly proper fucked, brown bread, fucking proper dead.

Tiny and I just stood there for what seemed an age, motionless, frozen in the headlight of the moon above. The blind man's dog barked. It was the only sound.

"Give the dog a fucking sausage or something to shut him the fuck up," I barked at Tiny, watching him carefully to see how he was reacting to the situation.

Tiny stood next to me now. "They're both fucking dead."

"For fuck's sake." I could see the fear in Tiny's face.

Without much of a plan, almost instinctively, the pair of us grabbed Boris's body and lifted him like a dead weight to a dumpster on the edge of the park. We doubled back, grabbed the much lighter body of the gendarme, and threw him in next to Boris, burying both bodies as deep beneath the trash as we could. When we were satisfied they were sufficiently concealed, we closed the lid and headed back to the car.

Apart from the moon, there was no light, and the dog was now silent, just as it was all around—just me, Tiny, the Beetle, and the blind man staring blankly from the darkness of his shelter.

"Come on. Let's get the flock out of here!" I said, deliberately not using Tiny's name for the benefit of our silent witness.

As Tiny packed up the tent, I put the wires back into the dashboard as best as I could. I used our jerry can of water to wash down the Beetle's bumper and used the soil around as a cleaning agent to mop up the blood from the ground. I surveyed our work; we had done a pretty good job of hiding any obvious clues. Looking first at Tiny and then at myself, I realized we were both covered in blood.

"Come on. Get your fucking clothes off, and get changed," I said, and I did the same. We used the remaining contents of the water can to scrub ourselves down, doing the best we could, employing the buddy system to check each other's appearance, touching up here or there in an attempt to get rid of all traces of blood, which I knew was impossible, but at least we could make sure none was visible.

We piled our clothes, including Tiny's green PVCs and my favorite Doc Martens, into a black dustbin sack and stuffed it into the makeshift community campfire a few yards away in the trees. With an added douse of petrol, we watched the bag take light, until we were satisfied that the contents would be fully consumed.

While we waited, using a wet towel, we made sure one last time that there was no blood evident on our faces, arms, or hands. Satisfied, I threw the towel into the fire, and the fire roared in response to the additional offering.

It was now three thirty in the morning and silent everywhere around, with no movement and just the moon providing light, as I jumped into the driver's seat of the Beetle, cranked her up, and reversed to do a U-turn. As we swung by, the blind man waved. "Good travels, boys. Your secret's safe with me," he said, and he winked.

Tiny and I looked at each other. "What the fuck!" I said.

We paused for a second, not knowing how to react. I didn't want a triple murder on my hands, so I put my foot down, and we sped away.

The ride out of Paris was eerie. The normally packed streets and boulevards were empty at that time of day. If we were lucky, we would be well out of Paris by the first glimmer of rush-hour traffic and sunrise.

We were silent, apart from Tiny occasionally hitting the dashboard and repeating, "What the fuck?"

Although we didn't say so, we were both nervous. We passed a few police cars as we headed out of the city, and at one point, I spotted one right behind us. I didn't let Tiny know, because I didn't want to stimulate the natural reaction associated with "Don't look now, but ..." Thankfully, the police were behind us for only a couple of blocks and had no interest in us; they were probably heading back to the station after a busy Parisian night and ready to have a cup of coffee and a Gitanes and wait for the end of their shift in a couple of hours.

Thank fuck we were soon out of the city and headed toward Calais. Tiny had the timetable, and there was a ferry at 8:00 a.m., which would be okay. We both wanted to get home as we never had before. We at least wanted to get off French soil and onto British soil, where we would stand half a chance in the judicial system. I looked in the rearview mirror; my eyes were bloodshot, and I looked pale, but Tiny was as white as a fucking sheet.

"Was they really fucking dead, Willy?"

"Yep, as dead as fucking doornails."

"Are you sure?"

"As eggs is eggs, Tiny."

"Was that really a fucking copper?"

"Yep, true blue. He had it written in big fuck-off letters across his back. Pity I didn't see 'em or that he didn't declare himself," I said, thinking out loud, still feeling the nausea and for a second almost vomiting. I wound down the window just in case and to get the fresh early morning air into my lungs.

"Then we'd both be in a prison cell now, charged with murder, Willy." It was a sound observation from Tiny.

I looked across at him. I was deeply concerned. I remembered the loose-lips incident, and that worried me. I kept glancing over to see if I could get a read on where his mind was. The last thing I intended to do was go to any fucking jail, never mind a pair of Brits in the French prison system.

"What the fuck we gonna do?"

"Nothing, Tiny. Absolutely fucking nothing," I said. He was looking at me. "What?" I asked.

"Nothing."

We were silent all the way to the port, deep in our own thoughts. *What the fuck just happened? What happens when they find the bodies? Will they find the bodies, or will the bodies just get lost in some huge Parisian waste dump? What about the blind man? Was he really fucking blind? What did he hear? What did he mean "Your secret's safe with me"? Will Tiny keep his mouth shut? Can he?*

My mind envisaged a future Tiny sitting at a bar somewhere, full of booze and poppers, spilling the beans to one of the boys. Then, in turn, the Parisian incident would become legend, and then the knock on the door would come.

I shook my head to get rid of the thought and breathed in the salty sea air, which made my nausea worse, trying to hold it together to get through the port security, onto the ferry, and back to the white cliffs of Dover.

"When we go through security and customs, Tiny, not a fucking word," I said, and he nodded in compliance. "Have you got any shit on yer?"

His faced changed to a look of alarm. "Oh fuck!" he reached into the back to grab his bag.

"Get rid of it, Tiny; we don't want to give these fuckers any excuse to stop us from getting on that boat." I pulled over into a supermarket car park and had a smoke as Tiny got rid of his shit.

"Sorry, mate. Sorry, Willy." Tiny was all of a sudden being subservient, and that worried the hell out of me. Getting into the realm of victim mode would do neither of us any good.

Our silence continued as we boarded the ferry and went past customs, showing our passports and facing the usual questions, including "Why have you been in France?" The normal level of nervousness was, that morning, on fucking steroids. I was nearly shitting myself, and by the look of Tiny, he was at least twice as bad.

"C'mon, Tiny. Get a grip on yerself. Be strong, my friend." I was doing and saying what I could to get him through the shitty situation. After all, we were in it together, and my liberty depended on Tiny's staying strong, not breaking down, not spilling the beans, and keeping his fucking mouth shut.

Once on the ferry, we went to the lorry drivers' showers, showered, and changed into another set of new clothing, and as a precaution, we bagged up the clothes in Tiny's hold-all and would burn them when we got home.

We needed food, but we had no appetite. We stared into space in silence into Dover and on the long road back to our northern town, nervous at every sight of police on the way.

A song kept playing in my head constantly on repeat, haunting me: "Mother, I killed someone. It wasn't that I hated him. You see, he was trying to stop me, but he found out I'd go the whole way."

*What the fuck?*

Neither of us was sure which of our blows had killed Boris. It was clear to us who was responsible for the death of the policeman, but we never discussed it. As each nervous day went by, my level of paranoia was through the roof. I couldn't concentrate on anything. I panicked at every ring of the doorbell or the phone; I anxiously waited to scan the daily newspaper for any news; and innocent looks from strangers, in my mind, turned into the gaze of undercover police. I had nightmares, and the shift in Tiny's and my hanging out or his coming round the house was noticeable. We barely saw each other in the days and weeks after.

My parents noticed the change, especially my mother.

Thankfully, my military papers had come through for me, and I had my dates. My departure couldn't come quickly enough; I had to get the fuck out of that place, and I felt I might have some protection once in Her Majesty's service. *A damn sight better than being a guest of Her Majesty's Prison Service*, I thought to myself with no hint of humor intended.

The day eventually came, and I couldn't fucking wait.

The night before, I had no big party or send-off. Tiny and I went for a beer together, just the two of us, and sat in a quiet corner of the Royal Oak.

We hadn't discussed the incident much, but that night, we vowed to keep our secret buried forever and never tell a soul. We would both have to internalize it, lock it away, and live with it.

"I fucking hate Russians anyway," Tiny whispered, making an effort at his former big signature grin.

"Tiny, you can never utter a fucking word of this to anyone." I looked him in the eye. I could see he was hurt, and he probably knew I was referring to the Old Tramp incident and his indiscretion.

"I fucking promise, brother. I will never say a single word to anyone."

We were both dealing with guilt and also the specter of paranoia that our crime would catch up with us on some unsuspecting day in the future, but we knew that as each day, month, and year passed, the prospect of it coming back to haunt us would diminish; however, the guilt and our oath of silence never would. As the years went by, I would drift and be ever more reluctant for the reminder, the memories, or the danger of it to come out.

The next day, my father drove his BMW 630 CSi, my mother sat in the passenger seat, and I sat in the back with my backpack, ready to go off to new lands and new adventures and get the flock out of there for the last time.

We parked the car and walked to the station platform together. The army had sent me a travel warrant. I handed it in to the ticket counter in exchange for my rail ticket: "Windermere to Aldershot, changing at London Euston Station. One way."

The last two words on the ticket gave the sound of permanence to the moment, of no going back, of the end of one chapter and the start of a new one.

I was surprised at the lack of emotion from my mother on the platform as we said our farewell; maybe she was happy to see me go, maybe this had been her plan all along, or maybe she knew this was my shot at getting to my own Moon River.

In contrast, I was touched by the look of pride etched on my father's face as I sat in the carriage. As the train pulled away from the station, my parents waved at me until I was out of view. As I headed out on my journey, a familiar song haunted me: "I'm leaving on the fast train. Don't ask me when I'm coming back again."

# AFTERWORD

Soon after my last meeting with Tiny at the Royal Oak, our boat ride, his revelation of cancer, and my return to Glasgow, I headed to the Americas on the next leg of my pursuit for Moon River. Finally, after all those years, I was heading to Hotel California, apparently such a lovely place.

I had finally had enough of the United Kingdom. I had tolerated her for so long, but on my travels around the world, I had seen so much, including many alternatives better than the dark, wet, cold, and misery. Although things had gotten better with time, the underwhelming elements I remembered remained.

I never heard from Tiny again after my trip back to my hometown, and perhaps as some sort of self-protection, I did not reach out either. I knew things were bad. I had used the ostrich approach in the past when my own father was dying and when my first marriage was falling apart, and I used it now when my boyhood best friend was departing the world.

On June 25, I sat in my new writing studio, my posh name for a rented two-bedroom apartment in Cabos San Jose, Baja California, overlooking the Sea of Cortez, and saw an alert pop up on my iPad, on Facebook: "Tiny Tim, Rest in Peace." I slowly and reluctantly opened the app and read the announcement:

> Tiny Timpson, the gentle giant, gave up his fight earlier today. Tiny, the man, a father, a son, a brother, a friend, will be sorely missed by so many who loved him in life, but he will be remembered in our hearts until we meet him once more. He has gone to see Saint Peter and will be sure to rock those pearly gates. Join us in sending best wishes to the family and seeing Tiny Timpson on the other side someday.

As I sat there thinking about my friend, my brother, being laid to rest, I poured myself a Liddesdale with ice, searched my iPhone playlist, and came across the ideal tune to think about the man, the legend, the one and only Tiny Tim: "I'll sing it one last time for you. Then we really have to go. You've been the only thing that's right in all I've done."

On Facebook was a photograph of Tiny and a little girl playing by the lakeside. He had his big signature smile on his face. I could almost hear his belly laugh as I sat there on the other side of the world, a reminder of the kind and humorous nature of the gentle giant known as Tiny Timpson.

"Light up, light up, as if you have a choice. Even if you cannot hear my voice, I'll be right beside you, dear."

I turned back to my laptop and looked at the screen: "*Northern Echo*. A novel by Willy Mitchell." That was as far as I had gotten.

"To think I might not see those eyes; it makes it so hard not to cry, and as we say our long goodbyes, I nearly do."

I took a sip of my whisky and started to type, starting with my most recent encounter with him in the Lake District and my promise to him that I would one day write his story, our story, the story of our time.

With the whisky and my tears blurring my words on the screen, I paused for a while, looking out my window, out across the ocean. Somewhere a long way away, Tiny was being laid to rest.

"Louder, louder, and we'll run for our lives. I can hardly speak. I understand why you can't raise your voice."

Our lives and our story came flooding back to me, and I remembered the last time we'd met and his immortal words as he left in the taxi the last time I ever saw him: "They'll never take me alive!"

*I hope I did you justice, my friend, and I look forward to our next adventure together one day in Valhalla.*

# AUTHOR'S NOTES

## DARK DAYS

As should be obvious by now, the punk rock period in the United Kingdom represented a distinctly turbulent time for the nation across numerous fronts. The cultural changes among the youth arose from a desire to effect change that did not seem to be possible if political policymaking remained in the hands of the establishment. Of course, shifting power on a national level takes time, and we punkers were only capable of nudging things along at a faster pace than otherwise would have been possible.

I wanted to streamline the story, focusing most on the coming-of-age narrative featuring Willy and Tiny. I didn't want to bog down the novel with too much news reporting. However, the big-picture context of the times is important, in my view. Many people don't know just how bad things were in the United Kingdom during the punk period, and I thought it would be helpful to sum up some of the key events that occurred as the story unfolds. Below, you will find short write-ups for each year. Collectively, the news items will give you a good view of what was happening as Willy came of age with Tiny in a dark period in the United Kingdom's long and storied history.

# 1976

The year kicked off with hurricane-force winds of up to 105 miles per hour, which killed twenty-two people and caused millions of pounds of damage. Ten Protestant men were killed in the Kingsmill massacre in Northern Ireland. In the Cod War, British and Icelandic fishing boats clashed at sea, and Iceland broke off diplomatic relations with the United Kingdom. Twelve IRA bombs exploded in London's West End.

Harold Wilson announced his resignation as prime minister, and James Callaghan took over. Carry On star Sid James died onstage at the Sunderland Empire. Liverpool clinched their ninth Football League title. Southampton won their first major trophy in ninety-one years, beating Manchester United in the FA Cup final.

In Angola, four mercenaries, three British and one American, were shot by firing squad. Ford Motor Company launched the first hot hatch, the Ford Fiesta, and a fire destroyed the head of Southend Pier. Riots at the Notting Hill Carnival resulted in one hundred police officers and sixty carnival-goers being injured.

Later in the year, the Damned released the first single marketed as punk rock in the United Kingdom. The seven perpetrators of an £8 million van robbery in Mayfair were sentenced to a total of one hundred years in prison. Chancellor Denis Healey announced he had secured a £2.3 billion loan from the International Monetary Fund on the condition that Britain cut £2.5 billion in public expenditure.

Inflation reached a peak of 24 percent and then leveled at 16.5 percent, one of the highest records since records began in 1750.

# 1977

The Sex Pistols, after releasing only one single with record label EMI had their contract terminated for so-called disruptive behavior. Clive Sinclair introduced a new two-inch television set. Seven more IRA bombs exploded in London's West End. Police discovered an IRA bomb factory in Liverpool.

A twenty-eight-year-old homeless woman, Irene Richardson, was murdered in Leeds, at almost the exact location where prostitute Marcella Clayton had been badly injured nine months earlier. This added to the murders of Wilma McCann and Emily Jackson and at least three other attempted murders of women in the region.

Prime Minister Jim Callaghan threatened to end state assistance to vehicle manufacturer British Leyland unless union strike action ceased. The government revealed that inflation had pushed up prices by almost 70 percent in the last three years.

Red Rum won the Grand National for the third time. The Clash released their debut album, *The Clash*, through CBS Records. National Front marchers clashed with anti-Nazi supporters in London.

Prostitute Patricia Atkinson was murdered in Bradford, thought to be another victim of the glowingly infamous Yorkshire Ripper. Liverpool was the English League champion for the tenth time, and Manchester United won the FA Cup, defeating Liverpool 2–1. Sixteen-year-old shop assistant Jayne McDonald was found battered and stabbed to death in Chapeltown, Leeds. Later, Bradford woman Maureen Long, forty-two, was injured in another brutal attack.

Kenny Dalglish, a twenty-six-year-old Scotsman, became Britain's most expensive footballer with a £440,000 transfer from Glasgow Celtic to Liverpool. Meanwhile, legendary Yorkshireman and cricketer Geoff Boycott notched up his one hundredth career century.

In the Battle of Lewisham, a National Front march resulted in violent clashes in the capital. Car industry futures revealed that foreign cars were outselling British cars for the first time in British history. Marc Bolan, a musician, died in a car crash in Barnes, London.

Missing twenty-year-old prostitute Jean Jordan was found dead in Charlton, Manchester. Fourteen people were injured in an explosion in a London pub. The Sex Pistols released *Never Mind the Bollocks* on the Virgin Records label. Another prostitute, twenty-five-year-old Marilyn Moore, was injured in an attack in Leeds.

# 1978

An eighteen-year-old prostitute, Helen Rytka, was murdered in Huddersfield. Gordon McQueen, a twenty-five-year-old Scotsman, became the first £500,000 footballer, signing for Manchester United from Leeds United. *The Hitchhiker's Guide to the Galaxy* was broadcast for the first time, and the body of a twenty-one-year-old prostitute, Yvonne Pearson, a mother of two, was found in Leeds.

Ipswich Town beat Arsenal 1–0 in the FA Cup final, Brian Clough's Nottingham Forrest won the league, and Liverpool retained the European Cup with a 1–0 win over Club Bruges. Cricketer Ian Botham became the first man in history to score a century and take eight wickets in the same test match.

A forty-year-old prostitute, Vera Millward, was found stabbed to death on the grounds of Manchester Royal Infirmary. Gunmen opened fire in an Israeli El Al airline bus in London. Bulgarian dissident Georgi Markov was stabbed with a poison-tipped umbrella as he walked across Waterloo Bridge, London.

Twenty-three Ford Motor Company plants closed across Britain due to the strike action. Rioters sacked the British embassy in Tehran. The British Broadcasting Company was hit by a series of union strikes and taken off air over pay claims.

Unemployment hit a postwar high of 1.5 million. Norton Villiers Triumph went into liquidation, and the Concrete Cows were erected in new town Milton Keynes.

# 1979

Lorry drivers went on strike, causing new shortages of heating oil and fresh food. Rail workers began a twenty-four-hour strike. Tens of thousands of public workers went on strike too. Even gravediggers were out on strike, causing burials of the dead to be held out at sea.

Sid Vicious was found dead in New York after apparently suffocating on his own vomit as a result of a heroin overdose. Trevor Francis signed as the first £1 million footballer as he moved to Nottingham Forrest. One thousand schools closed due to the heating fuel shortage.

National Health Service workers threatened to go on strike under demands of a 9 percent pay increase. The British economy shrank by 0.8 percent in the first quarter. A nineteen-year-old bank worker, Josephine Whitaker, was murdered in Halifax. The Anti-Nazi League's Blair Peach was fatally injured by a member of the Met's Special Patrol Group.

The Conservatives won the general election with a forty-three-seat majority, and Margaret Thatcher became the first female prime minster of the United Kingdom.

Liverpool won the football league for the twelfth time. Arsenal defeated Manchester United 3–2 in the FA Cup final. Lord Mountbatten was assassinated by the IRA, and eighteen British soldiers were killed in the Warrenpoint ambush in Northern Ireland.

Another woman's body was discovered in an alleyway in Bradford city center. Barbara Leach was just twenty years old.

Statistics showed a whopping 2.3 percent contraction in the British economy for the third quarter of the year. The government announced a £3.5 billion cut in public spending and an increase in prescription charges. The Clash released the album *London's Calling*.

Workers at British Steel Corporation went on a nationwide strike over pay in a bid to get a 20 percent raise. The UK indie chart was published for the first time. Margaret Thatcher announced that state benefits to strikers would be halved. Alton Towers theme park opened in Staffordshire.

Liverpool won the football first division for the twelfth time. West Ham United won the FA Cup, beating Arsenal 1–0. Nottingham Forrest retained the European Cup in a 1–0 win over Hamburger SV. By May, inflation was at 21.8 percent. Gunmen attacked the British embassy in Iraq. Unemployment hit 1.9 million.

Miners threatened to strike, demanding a 37 percent increase in pay. Thirty-seven people died as a result of an arson attack in adjacent nightclubs in Denmark Place, London. Thirty-four-year-old Singapore-born doctor Upadhya Bandara was attacked in Headingly, Leeds.

The great British MG car production ended after fifty-six years and more than 1.1 million cars made as the plant in Abingdon, Oxfordshire, closed. The Iron Lady said she would not give in to seven jailed IRA terrorists on hunger strike in Maze Prison; they were trying to claim prisoner-of-war status.

A sixteen-year-old girl, the mother to a young baby, was stabbed and wounded near her home in Huddersfield.

University student Jacqueline Hill, twenty years old, was murdered in Headingly, Leeds.

John Lennon was shot in New York.

# 1981

The Yorkshire Ripper was arrested and charged with thirteen counts of murder. A parcel bomb addressed to the prime minister was intercepted. A bomb attack occurred on an RAF base in Uxbridge. Two soldiers were found guilty of murder in Northern Ireland. Civil rights campaigner Bernadette McAliskey was shot at her home. Sir Norman Stronge and his son, both former Stormont MPs, were killed by the IRA.

Thirty thousand marched in an unemployment protest in Glasgow. Margaret Thatcher flew to Washington, DC, to meet US President Ronald Reagan. Unemployment passed the 2.6 million mark.

Peugeot closed its Talbot car plant in Scotland. Bobby Sands, a twenty-seven-year-old Irish Republican, was the first to die in Maze Prison after a sixty-six-day hunger strike.

The one hundredth FA Cup final ended in a 1–1 draw between Tottenham Hotspur and Manchester City. Tottenham won 3–2 in the replay. Liverpool won the European Cup for the third time, beating Real Madrid 1–0. Bryan Robson became the most expensive footballer at £1.5 million in a move from West Bromwich Albion to Manchester United.

Racehorse Shergar won the Epsom Derby. Chelsea Barracks was bombed by the IRA.

More than one hundred thousand marched to Trafalgar Square, London, in protest of unemployment levels.

Prince Charles and Lady Diana Spencer married at Saint Paul's Cathedral with more than thirty million viewers on TV.

A Campaign for Nuclear Disarmament march in London attracted a crowd of more than 250,000 people. British Leyland's fifty-eight-thousand-person workforce went on strike over pay.

The first case of AIDS was diagnosed. Severe snowstorms hit the United Kingdom with the lowest temperatures recorded since 1874. Riots spread across the nation.

# 1982

Unemployment reached three million in the United Kingdom. The Welsh Army of Workers claimed responsibility for a bomb explosion at the headquarters of utility Severn Trent Water, Birmingham. The prime minister's son, Mark Thatcher, was found six days after going missing in the Sahara Desert during the Paris-Dakar Rally.

Korean cars were imported into the United Kingdom for the first time: the Hyundai Pony. Laker Airways collapsed, leaving six thousand passengers stranded and a £270 million debt. The Glasgow-registered coal ship *St. Bedan* was bombed and sunk by the IRA in Lough Foyle.

The European Court of Justice banned corporal punishment in British schools. Argentines landed on British territory, South Georgia, and then invaded the Falkland Islands, precipitating war.

Tottenham Hotspur won the FA Cup final in a replay with Queens Park Rangers in the absence of star players Argentinians Ossie Ardiles and Ricardo Villa, due to the war between the two countries.

The Smiths were formed in Manchester by Johnny Marr and Morrissey. Israeli Ambassador Shlomo Argov was shot in London, triggering the 1982 Lebanon War. Welsh miners went on strike in support of health workers, demanding a 12 percent pay raise.

The IRA detonated two bombs in Hyde Park and Regents Park, killing eight soldiers, wounding forty-seven, and killing seven horses of the Household Cavalry. Seventeen people were killed by the Irish National Liberation Army in a bombing at the Droppin' Well Inn, Ballykelly, County Londonderry. Margaret Thatcher rejected calls for the return of the death penalty for murder by terrorism.

The government announced that more than four hundred thousand council homes had been sold off in the right-to-buy program. More than thirty thousand women held hands to form a human chain around the perimeter of Greenham Common in protest of the government's decision to allow the storage of nuclear-capable cruise missiles.

# 1983

Stephen Waldorf was mistakenly shot by an armed policeman who thought he was escaped prisoner David Martin. Two policemen were charged with attempted murder. Unemployment reached 3.2 million.

Thirty-seven-year-old Pat Jennings, goalkeeper for Arsenal, became the first player ever to appear in one thousand senior football matches. The compact disc went on sale in the United Kingdom for the first time.

Liverpool won the Football League Cup, beating rivals Manchester United 2–1. Liverpool went on to win the league for a record fourteenth time. Thousands of protesters formed a fourteen-mile human chain around British military bases housing American nuclear weapons.

The biggest robbery in British history occurred: a £7 million heist of a Security Express van in London. The one-pound coin was introduced into circulation. Manchester United beat Brighton and Hove Albion 4–0 in the replay, with Captain Bryan Robson scoring twice and Arnold Muhren and Norman Whiteside scoring the other two.

Margaret Thatcher won a landslide victory in the election, with a majority of 144 seats in the houses of Parliament.

Thirty-eight IRA prisoners escaped from Maze Prison, County Antrim, Northern Ireland. Richard Noble, driving *Thrust 2*, broke the world land-speed record, notching up 634.051 miles per hour at Black Rock Desert, USA.

More than one million people demonstrated at a Campaign for Nuclear Disarmament march in London. Serial killer Denis Nilsen went on trial, confessing to murdering "fifteen or sixteen men." US forces invaded Grenada. Gerry Adams took office as the elected leader of Sinn Fein, the political arm of the IRA.

An IRA car bomb exploded outside department store Harrods in London, killing three police officers and three civilians and injuring ninety. On Christmas Day, a bomb exploded on London's Oxford Street. An SAS undercover operation ended in the shooting and killing of two IRA gunmen and injuring of a third.

Famous racehorse Shergar was stolen in County Kildare, and the thieves demanded a ransom of £2 million. In the Brink's-Mat bullion robbery, 6,800 gold bars were stolen from a vault at Heathrow Airport, a value of nearly £26 million.

# 1984

Japanese car manufacturer Nissan signed a deal to build a car factory in Washington, Sunderland. Austin Rover announced that the Triumph marque would be discontinued after sixty-three years of production. Sinn Fein's Gerry Adams and three others were seriously injured in a gun attack by the Ulster Volunteer Force.

Led by Arthur Scargill, the National Union of Miners called a strike, and more than one hundred picketers were arrested in violent clashes at Creswell Colliery, Derbyshire, and Babbington Colliery, Nottinghamshire. Only 46 of the 176 coal mines in the United Kingdom remained active, and the government planned to close down 20 more, due to the effects of previous strike action, the expense of mining, and increasingly cheaper imports of coal.

Comedian Tommy Cooper collapsed and died on live TV, on the show *Live from Her Majesty's*. Female police constable Yvonne Fletcher was shot dead during a siege outside the Libyan embassy. Eleven other people were shot and injured.

Liverpool secured a third consecutive league title and the fifteenth in the club's history. Everton won the FA Cup, beating Watford 2–0. Fighting at Orgreave Colliery between police and striking miners left sixty-four injured. Arthur Scargill was arrested and charged with obstruction. Liverpool won their fourth European Cup, beating AS Roman in a penalty shoot-out after a 1–1 draw.

The IRA attempted to assassinate the Conservative cabinet at a Brighton hotel, killing five and seriously injuring others. Margaret Thatcher escaped unharmed.

Thirty-six of the United Kingdom's top recording artists gathered at a Notting Hill studio to record Band Aid's "Do They Know It's Christmas?" to raise money for famine relief in Ethiopia.

Unemployment reached 3.26 million.

# 1985

The first mobile phone calls were made in the United Kingdom, and British Telecom announced it would phase out the iconic red British telephone boxes.

The IRA launched a mortar attack on a police station in Newry, Northern Ireland, killing nine officers. The miners' strike eventually ended. At its height, it had included more than 140,000 miners.

Fifty-six people died in the Bradford City FC stadium fire. Everton won the Football League and then won the European Cup Winners' Cup, their first silverware in fifteen years. Manchester United won the FA Cup for the sixth time, defeating Everton 1–0.

In the European Cup final, Juventus beat Liverpool 1–0, but thirty-nine fans died and hundreds were injured in what would be called the Heysel Stadium disaster.

Police arrested thirteen suspects in connection with the Brighton hotel bombing. Patrick Magee was charged with murder.

Live Aid raised more than £50 million for famine relief. Rising racial tension in Birmingham was blamed for riots in the Handsworth area of the city that left two dead and several injured. A riot in Brixton resulted in one dead, fifty injured, and two hundred arrests. The Broadwater Farm riots broke out after Cynthia Jarret, a forty-nine-year-old black woman, died after falling during a police search of her home. PC Keith Blakelock was fatally stabbed during the riot, with many others injured.

Production of the Peugeot 309 began at the Ryton car factory near Coventry. Phil Lynott of Thin Lizzy died of a heroin overdose at his home in Berkshire.

# Ten Most Influential People of Those Times

Below, I have taken a stab at listing the individuals who, in my view, were among the most influential people, for better or for worse, during those unprecedented times.

1. Margaret Thatcher, UK prime minister from 1979 to 1990
2. John Lydon, singer and songwriter
3. Diana, princess of Wales
4. Harold Wilson, UK prime minister from 1964 to 1970 and 1974 to 1976
5. Malcolm McLaren, musician, songwriter, band manager, and entrepreneur
6. Arthur Scargill, leader of the National Union of Miners
7. David Bowie, singer, musician, and songwriter
8. Bob Paisley, manager of Liverpool Football Club
9. Pink Floyd
10. John Lennon, singer, musician, and songwriter

I cannot condone the IRA as an entity, but undoubtedly, they also had a big effect on the mood of the times, as did Sinn Fein under the leadership of Gerry Adams and his sidekick Martin McGuiness.

Although I refuse to rank such an evil, brutal excuse for a human being or credit this monster with any fame, Peter Sutcliffe, the Yorkshire Ripper, presented a great dark shadow over our land during those unprecedented times.

# Best Punk Albums of All Time (Pre-1985)

## *Rolling Stone* magazine

1. Ramones: *Ramones* (1976)
2. The Clash: *The Clash* (1977)
3. The Sex Pistols: *Never Mind the Bollocks, Here's the Sex Pistols* (1977)
4. The Stooges: *Fun House* (1970)
5. Gang of Four: *Entertainment* (1979)
6. Wire: *Pink Flag* (1977)
7. Minutemen: *Nickels on the Dime* (1984)
8. Black Flag: *Damaged* (1981)
9. X: *Los Angeles* (1980)
10. The Buzzcocks: *Singles Going Steady* (1979)
11. Patti Smith: *Horses* (1975)
12. Husker Du: *Zen Arcade* (1984)
13. New York Dolls: *New York Dolls* (1973)
14. Descendants: *Milo Goes to College* (1982)
15. Television: *Marquee Moon* (1977)
16. Bad Brains: *Bad Brains* (1982)
17. X-Ray Spex: *Germfree Adolescents* (1978)
18. Richard Hell and the Voidoids: *Blank Generation* (1977)
19. Pere Ubu: *Terminal Tower* (1985)
20. The Jam: *All Mod Cons* (1978)
21. Mission of Burma: *Vs.* (1982)
22. Flipper: *Generic* (1982)
23. The Germs: *(GI)* (1979)
24. The Replacements: *Sorry Ma, Forgot to Take Out the Trash* (1981)

25. The Misfits: *Walk among Us* (1982)

26. The Slits: *Cut* (1979)

27. Joy Division: *Unknown Pleasures* (1979)

28. Crass: *Penis Envy* (1981)

29. Devo: *Q: Are We Not Men? A: We Are Devo!* (1978)

30. Dead Kennedys: *Fresh Fruit for Rotting Vegetables* (1980)

# Best Punk Singles

## OpenCulture.com

The following are as voted by the readers of *Sounds* music paper in 1981 (top fifty only).

1. "Anarchy in the UK," Sex Pistols
2. "New Rose," Damned
3. "No Government," Anti Pasti
4. "White Riot," Clash
5. "God Save the Queen," Sex Pistols
6. "Last Rockers," Vice Squad
7. "Holidays in Cambodia," Dead Kennedys
8. "Suspect Device," Stiff Little Fingers
9. "Alternative Ulster," Stiff Little Fingers
10. "Decontrol," Discharge
11. "Punk's Not Dead," Exploited
12. "Army Life," Exploited
13. "Pretty Vacant," Sex Pistols
14. "Warhead," UK Subs
15. "I'm an Upstart," Angelic Upstarts
16. "California Uber Alles," Dead Kennedys
17. "Bodies," Sex Pistols
18. "Public Image," Public Image Limited
19. "SPG," Exploited
20. "Ain't No Feeble Bastard," Discharge
21. "Love Song," Damned
22. "Hong Kong Garden," Siouxsie and the Banshees
23. "Murder of Liddle Towers," Angelic Upstarts

24. "Holidays in the Sun," Sex Pistols
25. "Chaos," 4-Skins
26. "Big A, Little A," Crass
27. "Stranglehold," UK Subs
28. "Too Drunk to Fuck," Dead Kennedys
29. "Banned from the Roxy," Crass
30. "Days of War," Exploited
31. "Smash It Up," Damned
32. "Neat, Neat, Neat," Damned
33. "Wardance," Killing Joke
34. "Resurrection," Vice Squad
35. "Complete Control," Clash
36. "CID," UK Subs
37. "Babylon's Burning," Ruts
38. "Bloody Revolutions," Crass
39. "Requiem," Killing Joke
40. "Wasted Life," Stiff Little Fingers
41. "Nasty, Nasty," 999
42. "My Way," Sid Vicious
43. "Fight Back," Discharge
44. "Where Have All the Boot Boys Gone?", Slaughter and the Dogs
45. "Fuck a Mod," Exploited
46. "No More Heroes," Stranglers
47. "Borstal Breakout," Sham 69
48. "I Believe in Anarchy," Exploited
49. "Party in Paris," UK Subs
50. "Police Oppression," Angelic Upstarts

# DEFINITIONS AND CLARIFICATIONS

**100 Club:** Music venue located at 100 Oxford Street, London, that has been hosting live music since 1942. Bands who've played at this iconic club include the Sex Pistols, Siouxsie and the Banshees, the Clash, the Buzzcocks, the Stranglers, and the Jam. Under the promotion of Ron Watts, the venue booked punk bands Angelic Upstarts, UK Subs, Discharge, GBH, and Crass, to name just a handful.

**999:** Active from 1977 to 1982, 1983 to 1987, and 1993 to the present. Formed in London in 1976 with Nick Cash on vocals and guitar, Guy Days on lead guitar, Jon Watson on bass, and Pablo LaBrittain on drums. Known as one of the longest-lived groups of the punk era.

**Adam and the Ants:** Active from 1977 to 1982. Fronted by Adam Ant, it has continued on in various incarnations to today. Albums include *Dirk Wears White Sox* (1979), *Kings of the Wild Frontier* (1980), and *Prince Charming* (1981).

**Alternative Music Foundation:** Opened in 1986 in Berkley, California, at 924 Gilman Street, on the corner of Eighth and Gilman, and is regarded as the springboard for the 1990s punk revival led by bands such as Green Day, Operation Ivy, Rancid, and the Offspring.

**"Anarchy in the UK":** Iconic 1976 track from the Sex Pistols calling for social and political change in those times.

**Angelic Upstarts:** Active from 1977 to the present. Their original debut single, "The Murder of Liddle Towers," made it to *Mojo* magazine's list of the best punk rock singles of all time.

**Anti-Nowhere League:** Active from 1979 to 1989 and 1992 to the present. Founded in Royal Tunbridge Wells, England, in 1979 by founding members Animal, Tommy H, Carnage, and Shady. The band has appeared in various iterations in their journey to date.

**Anti Pasti:** Active in 1978 to 1984, 1995, and 2012 to present. Founded by vocalist Martin Roper and Dugi Bell in Derby in 1978, with Kev Nixon on drums and Will Hoon on bass guitar. They later were joined by second guitarist Ollie Hoon.

**Billy Idol:** Born in Middlesex, England, in 1955 as William Michael Albert Broad. Emerged on the punk rock scene as part of the bands Chelsea and Generation X and went on to a career as a solo glam punk rocker with signature tracks, such as "White Wedding."

**Black Flag:** Formed in 1976. American punk rock band formed in Hermosa Beach, California.

**Blondie:** Born in Miami in 1945, Angela Trimble launched her career as the iconic lead singer of the cult band Blondie, known for their brand of new wave, a precursor to the punk era, with tracks such as "Call on Me."

**Boomtown Rats:** Active from 1975 to 1986 and 2013 to the present. An Irish rock band originally formed in Dublin and led by vocalist Bob Geldof and original band members Garry Roberts (lead guitar), Johnnie Fingers (keyboard), Pete Briquette (bass), Gerry Cott (rhythm guitar), and Simon Crowe (drums). They famously released the album *The Fine Art of Surfacing*, which included the iconic track "I Don't Like Mondays," in 1979.

**bum flap:** A piece of cloth, typically a half-moon shape, worn by punk rockers, attached to a person's belt or belt loops and hanging to the rear. Often in bright patterns or colors, such as Scottish tartan, leopard skin, zebra skin, or PVC.

**Buzzcocks:** Active from 1976 to 1981 and 1989 to the present. Originally formed in Bolton, Manchester, England. In 1977, Pete Shelley became the principal singer-songwriter. The song often regarded as their signature track is "Ever Fallen in Love (with Someone You Shouldn't Have Fallen in Love With)?"

**CBGB:** A New York music club opened in 1973 in Manhattan's East Village. It became a famed punk rock venue for bands such as the Ramones, Television, Blondie, and Talking Heads. The club closed its doors in 2006.

**Chaos UK:** Active from 1979 to the present. Aggressive, hardcore punk band formed in Portishead, near Bristol, England. The original lineup featured Simon Greenham on vocals, Andy on guitar, Chaos on bass, and Potts on drums. Current members include Chaos, Mower, Gabba, and Chuck.

**Charlie Harper:** Born in Hackney, London, in 1944. Lead singer of UK punk band the UK Subs, whose signature tracks include "Crash Course." In addition to vocals, he also plays the harmonica, guitar, and bass guitar.

**CND (Campaign for Nuclear Disarmament):** An organization that advocates unilateral nuclear disarmament by the United Kingdom, international nuclear disarmament, and tighter international arms regulations. It was prominent especially during the 1980s, as the threat of nuclear hostility was a real fear in those times.

**Cockney Rejects:** Active from 1978 to the present. Formed by the original members in the East End of London. Band members are loyal West Ham FC supporters and released a hit cover version of "I'm Forever Blowing Bubbles," an anthem the London club's supporters traditionally sing on match days.

**Crass:** Active from 1977 to 1994. A British art collective and punk rock band who promoted anarchism as a political ideology, a way of life, and a resistance movement during the often highly charged political climate of those times.

**David Bowie** (1947–2016): Born in Brixton, London. A legendary, iconic singer, songwriter, lyricist, and actor. A forerunner and parallel to the punk rock movement but a legendary influencer of modern music of all genres. "Space Oddity," "Hunky Dory," "The Rise and Fall of Ziggy Stardust and the Spiders from Mars," "Aladdin Sane," "Heroes," "Scary Monsters," "Let's Dance," and "Blackstar" are just a few examples of his musical and poetic genius.

**Dead Kennedys:** Active from 1978 to 1986 and 2001 to the present. Politically satirical punk rock band originally from San Francisco. Albums include *Fresh Fruit for Rotting Vegetables* (1980), *Plastic Surgery Disasters* (1982), and *Frankenchrist* (1985), and a notable track is "Holidays in Cambodia."

**Discharge:** Active from 1977 to 1987, 1991 to 1999, and 2001 to the present. Hard-core punk and thrash-metal band formed in Stoke-on-Trent, England. They have a catalog of existing members and ex-members of the band.

**Doc Martens:** In existence from 1947 to the present. English footwear and clothing brand headquartered in Wollaston, Wellingborough, Northamptonshire, England. Their footwear, especially their boots, became a fashion icon. Sometimes with steel toe caps and often with bright laces, they were fixtures of both the skinhead and the punk rock movements.

**F-Club:** Known as Fan Club. A punk rock nightclub in Leeds, Northern England, that was open between 1977 and 1982. F-Club was held at various venues across the city.

**ferreting:** The ancient method of catching rabbits with the use of ferrets or polecats. The method involves pegging the escape holes of a warren with nets and then sending the hunter down the main hole to flush the rabbits out of their nest. The rabbits run into the nets to make for easy pickings.

**Flux of Pink Indians:** Active from 1980 to 1986. Anarchy punk band founded in Bishop's Stortford, England. The group signed to the Crass Records label in 1981, and hits include the indie "Tube Disaster."

**gaffing:** The ancient method of catching or poaching salmon using an oar-like implement with a split at the end. The hunter, while wading in the stream, piles down the gaff on top of the fish and wedges it between the staggered tines, making escape unlikely, though not always impossible.

**Gang of Four:** Active from 1976 to 1984, 1987 to 1997, and 2004 to the present. Originated in Leeds, England. The band plays a stripped-down version of punk rock, funk, and dub, with a lyrical emphasis on social and political issues. Their album *Entertainment!* (1979) reached number forty-five in the United Kingdom.

**GBH:** Active from 1978 to the present. Charged GBH, commonly known as GBH, is an English punk rock band formed in Birmingham, England, by vocalist Colin Abraham, guitarist Colin "Jock" Blyth, bassist Sean McCarthy, and drummer Andy "Wilf" Williams.

**"God Save the Queen":** The national anthem of the United Kingdom and Commonwealth. Also the name of an antiestablishment track by the Sex Pistols, released in 1977, the year of Queen Elizabeth II's Silver Jubilee.

**Grace Jones:** Active from 1973 to the present. Iconic Jamaican-born American model, singer, musician, and actor. Her hometown is Syracuse, New York, but she spent several years in Paris, disrupting the modeling scene and breaking into music in her distinctive style and into acting. Her movies include James Bond's *A View to a Kill.*

**Green Day:** Active from 1986 to the present. An American self-proclaimed punk-pop band formed in the East Bay of the San Francisco Bay Area by lead vocalist and guitarist Billie Joe Armstrong, bassist Mark Dirnt, and drummer John Kiffmeyer, who was replaced by Tré Cool in 1990.

**gurning:** A gurn, or chuck, is a British tradition wherein competitors put on an extremely distorted facial expression. *Gurn* can also be used as a verb to describe the action. A typical gurn involves projecting the lower jaw as far forward and up as possible and covering the upper lip with the lower lip.

**Hacienda Club:** In existence from 1982 to 1997. An iconic club and venue in Manchester, England, conceived by Rob Gretton and largely financed by the record label Factory

Records, the band New Order, and label boss Tony Wilson. A long list of bands performed at the Hacienda, including Angelic Upstarts, the Smiths, Morrissey, Happy Mondays, and even Madonna.

**Happy Mondays:** Active from 1980 to 1993, 1999 to 2001, 2004 to 2010, and 2012 to the present. British rock band formed in Salford, Manchester, England, with an original lineup of Shaun Ryder on vocals, his brother Paul Ryder on bass, Mark Day on guitar, Paul Davis on keyboard, and Gary Whelan on drums. Mark "Bez" Berry later joined as dancer and percussionist.

**Hazel O'Connor:** Active from 1975 to the present. British actor, singer, and songwriter born in Coventry. She left home at sixteen; sold clothes in Amsterdam; picked grapes in France; joined a dance troupe in Tokyo; went to Beirut, West Africa; crossed the Sahara; and performed for troops in Germany. She starred in the film *Breaking Glass* and wrote all the songs for the film.

**Ian Drury** (1942–2000): Born Ian Robbins Dury in Harrow, England. British singer-songwriter and actor who rose to fame during the punk era. He was lead singer of Ian Dury and the Blockheads, whose tracks included "Reasons to Be Cheerful." At the age of seven, Dury contracted polio, possibly from a swimming pool, and his illness resulted in debilitating paralysis on his left side. He famously wore a black leather glove on his left hand.

**Iggy Pop:** Born in 1947 as James Newell Osterberg Jr. in Muskegon, Michigan. He is known as the Godfather of Punk Rock, with a career of outstanding contributions to the genre, and is one of rock's most iconic performers. He is a singer, songwriter, musician, producer, and actor with associated acts including the Stooges, the Trolls, the Iguanas, David Bowie, Slash, Debbie Harry, and Underworld.

**ITN:** In existence from 1955 to the present. Independent Television News is a producer of news programs on the British television network ITV, an alternative to the BBC, otherwise known as Beeb or Auntie.

**Joe Strummer** (1952–2002)**:** Born in Ankara, Turkey. A British musician, singer, composer, actor, songwriter, and cofounder of arguably one of the greatest rock and punk bands of all time, the Clash.

**John Lydon:** Born in 1956 in Holloway, London. Known as Johnny Rotten, he is a singer, songwriter, musician, and actor and was the lead singer of the Sex Pistols and founder of Public Image Limited. He created the archetype of the outspoken, rebellious, and antifashion icon of the punk movement and is considered one of the founding fathers of punk rock.

**John Peel** (1939–2004)**:** Born John Robert Parker Ravenscroft, he was a British disc jockey and radio presenter of the Peel sessions from 1967 until his death in 2004. Peel's radio show was a showcase for the latest up-and-coming artists in a multitude of genres, including punk rock. He died on a working holiday of a heart attack in the Inca city of Cusco, Peru.

**Joy Division:** Active from 1976 to 1980. Founded in Salford, Manchester, England, by vocalist Ian Curtis, guitar and keyboard player Bernard Summer, bassist Peter Hook, and drummer Stephen Morris. Curtis suffered from depression and epilepsy and occasionally experienced seizures onstage. He killed himself on the eve of the band's first US tour in May 1980 at age twenty-three. The remaining members of the band went on under the name New Order.

**Killing Joke:** Active from 1978 to 1996 and 2002 to the present. Originally formed in Notting Hill, London, by Jaz Coleman on vocals and keyboard, Paul Ferguson on drums, Geordie Walker on guitar, and Youth on bass. Killing Joke was a key influence on industrial rock, "dancing to a tune of doom and gloom."

**Kirk Brandon:** Born in 1956 in Westminster, London. Founder, front man, vocalist, songwriter, and guitarist for the Theatre of Hate and Spear of Destiny. Tracks included the classics "Do You Believe in the Westworld?" and "They'll Never Take Me Alive."

**Madness:** Active from 1976 to 1986 and 1992 to the present. From Camden Town, London, one of the most popular two-tone ska bands of that era, with Graham "Suggs" McPherson as the lead, who joined the founding members in 1977: Mike Barson (Monsieur Barso) on keyboard and vocals, Chris Foreman (Chrissy Boy) on guitar, Lee Thompson (Kix) on saxophone and vocals, John Hagler on drums, Cathay Smyth (Chas Smash) on bass, and Dikron Tulane as lead vocalist. Madness smashed out a number of hits, including "One Step Beyond," "Baggy Trousers," "It Must Be Love," "House of Fun," "Our House," and "Night Boat to Cairo."

**Malcolm (Robert Andrew) McLaren:** Controversial and colorful character born on January 22, 1946. He was an English impresario, visual artist, performer, and clothes designer and was accredited with the foundation of the punk rock movement, managing bands such as the New York Dolls and the Sex Pistols in addition to partnering with Vivienne Westwood and the boutique Sex on King's Road in London. McLaren died in Switzerland of peritoneal mesothelioma in October 2009. At his funeral, which was attended by many of his former acquaintances and stars, on his coffin was sprayed, "Too Fast to Live, Too Young to Die." He was buried to his masterminded version of "My Way" by Sid Vicious.

**Margaret Thatcher (1925–2013):** Born Margaret Hilda Roberts in Grantham, Lincolnshire, England. Became the first female prime minster of the United Kingdom in 1979 (and served until 1990). She often was characterized as a divisive symbol between the left-wing socialists and the Labor Party and the right-wing nationalists of the Conservative Party. She led the nation to war and rebutted Argentina's attempt to invade the Falkland Islands, she took on and defeated the unions, and she is credited by many for getting the United Kingdom back on its feet during the depressed years at the beginning of her term. She was also fondly known as the Iron Lady.

**Misfits:** Active from 1977 to 1983 and 1995 to the present. Founded in Lodi, New Jersey, the Misfits were an American punk band recognized as the founders of the horror punk subgenre. Vocalist, songwriter, and keyboardist Glenn Danzig; drummer Manny Martinez; bassist Jerry Only; and several other members have come in and out of the band over time, including Marky Ramona and Marc Rizzo.

**Mohican:** A hairstyle, also referred to as a Mohawk, in which both sides of the head are shaved and a strip of hair is left down the middle of the head. Taken from the Mohawk nation, an indigenous people of North America, the style was adapted through history as a symbol of the warrior and widely adopted during the punk Rock era. Punk rockers often wore Mohicans spiked high and brightly colored.

**New York:** The founding city of the punk rock movement in the mid-1970s with bands like the Ramones, Blondie, Talking Heads, and the lesser known Wayne County and Johnny Thunders and the Heartbreakers. As the movement spread across the Atlantic to London, punk rock started to morph into a sound different from those original bands at the start of the musical and expressive phenomenon.

**New York Dolls:** Active from 1971 to 1976 and 2004 to 2011. Founded in New York, along with the Velvet Underground and the Stooges, they were one of the first bands on the punk rock scene, featuring vocalist David Johansen, guitarist

Johnny Thunders, bassist Arthur Kane, and guitarist and pianist Sylvain Sylvain. Onstage, they donned a unique look of high heels, eccentric hats, satin, makeup, spandex, and women's dresses. They influenced many of the punk and other genres and glam rock bands to come, including the Sex Pistols, Kiss, the Ramones, Guns N' Roses, the Damned, and the Smiths.

*Never Mind the Bollocks:* Released in October 1977, it was the only studio album by the Sex Pistols on Virgin Records and includes tracks such as "Holidays in the Sun," "God Save the Queen," "Anarchy in the UK," and "Pretty Vacant."

**Nirvana:** Active from 1987 to 1994. Formed in Aberdeen, Washington, Nirvana was an America rock band founded by lead singer Kurt Cobain and bassist Krist Novoselic. They played with a long list of drummers, but the most long-lived was Dave Grohl, who joined the band in 1990. The band dissolved after Cobain's death in 1994, a suspected suicide.

**Paul Weller:** Born in 1958 in Woking, England. It's difficult to write about the punk era without incorporating some nonpunk influencers, including Paul Weller, the founder of the new-wave mod band the Jam. Weller is recognized as one of the leading artists of his time. He went on to form and lead the Style Council and launch a solo career, with greatest hits including "Down in the Tube Station at Midnight," "Elton Rifles," "You're the Best Thing," and "Wild Wood."

**Pink Floyd:** Active in 1965 to 1995, 2005, and 2012 to 2014. One of the most commercially successful and influential bands in the history of popular music. Formed in London in 1965 with an original lineup of Syd Barrett on guitar and lead vocals, Nick Mason on the drums, Roger Waters as bassist and vocals, and Richard Wright on keyboard. Guitarist and vocalist David Gilmour joined the band at the end of 1967. They released albums including *The Dark Side of the Moon* (1973), *Wish You Were Here* (1975), *Animals* (1977), *The Wall* (1979), and *The Final Cut* (1983). Personal tensions saw the departure of Roger Waters and reported long-term rivalry and animosity, including claims to performing rights of *The Wall*.

**posh:** Originating in the colonial days, the term related to passenger ships traveling from Great Britain to the subcontinent of India. *Posh* stands for "port out, starboard home," referring to the ships' most expensive cabins with the best views and most pleasant temperatures.

**Plasmatics:** Active from 1977 to 1983 and 1987 to 1988. Formed in New York by Rod Swenson and Wendy O. Williams, the Plasmatics were known for their chaotic, destructive, and controversial theatrics, including chainsaw guitars, speakers blown up onstage, sledgehammered TV sets, and blown-up cars. Williams was arrested in Milwaukee and charged with public indecency.

**Public Image Limited (PiL):** Active from 1978 to 1992 and 2009 to the present. A British postpunk band formed by singer-songwriter John Lydon, former front man of the Sex Pistols; guitarist Keith Levene; bassist Jay Wobble; and drummer Jim Walker. The band's lineup has been a revolving door over the years, with the only constant being Lydon.

**Pussy Riot:** Active from 2011 to the present. Although a much later addition to the punk rock scene, Pussy Riot is worthy of note as a Russian feminist protest punk rock band based in Moscow, Russia. The group has staged various unauthorized guerrilla performances, much to the ire of the Russian government and in opposition to President Vladimir Putin, whom the group consider to be a tyrant and a dictator.

**Queen:** Active from 1970 to the present. Founded in London by Freddie Mercury on lead vocals and piano, Brian May on guitar and vocals, John Deacon on bass, and Roger Taylor on drums, Queen is one of the most iconic and influential bands of modern popular music and a forerunner and then parallel to many of the key features of the punk rock scene.

**Ramones:** Active from 1974 to 1996. Formed in Queens, New York, and often cited as the world's first punk rock band. All the band members adopted the last name of Ramone, although none of them were biologically related. Johnny, Dee Dee, Joey, Tommy, Marky, Richie, Elvis, and C. J. were all past members of the band.

**Sex Pistols:** Active in 1975 to 1978, 1996, 2002 to 2003, and 2007 to 2008. Formed in London and coordinated by the impresario Malcolm McLaren, with Johnny Rotten as lead singer, Steve Jones on guitar, Paul Cook on drums, and Glen Matlock on bass. Matlock was replaced by Sid Vicious in early 1977. The band attracted controversies that both captivated and appalled Britain, with many venues canceling their tour dates in protest of their profanities and antiestablishment, anti-Christ, and anarchist rhetoric.

**Sham 69:** Active from 1975 to 1979 and 1987 to the present. Also known as the Hersham Boys, as the band was formed in Hersham, England. Popular hits include "If the Kids Are United" and "Hurry Up, Harry." The original group broke up in 1979, with front man Jimmy Pursey moving on to pursue a solo career.

**Sid Vicious** (1957–1979): Born in Lewisham, London, as John Simon Ritchie. Bassist, drummer, and singer of the Sex Pistols after replacing Glen Matlock. Controversy surrounded Vicious right to the end with the death of his girlfriend, Nancy Spungeon, in New York. Under suspicion of murder, he died after overdosing on heroin.

**Siouxsie and the Banshees:** Active in 1976 to 1996 and 2002. Formed in London by vocalist Siouxsie Sioux and bass guitarist Steven Severin, the band is credited with a high degree of musical influence and their own version of postpunk, alternative, and gothic rock, with eleven studio albums spanning twenty years.

**Slaughter and the Dogs:** Active from 1975 to 1979, 1979 to 1981, and 1996 to the present. Formed in Wythenshawe, Manchester, England, and one of the first British punk bands to sign with a major record label. The original lineup included vocalist Wayne Barrett, guitarist Michigan Rossi, drummer

Brian "Mad Muffet" Grantham, and bassist Howard "Zip" Bates.

**snaring:** The method of using carefully placed wire in various positions—loops, slings, straight lines, and nooses—to catch prey. Varying forms are designed to catch everything from rabbits to bears. It is not the most humane means of catching food, due to the potential longevity of suffering of a snared animal.

**Spear of Destiny:** Active from 1982 to the present. Originating in London, the band was created by former Theatre of Hate front man Kirk Brandon and bassist Stan Stammers. Spear of Destiny has had an ever-changing lineup over the years.

**Stiff Little Fingers:** Active from 1977 to 1982 and 1987 to the present. From Belfast, Northern Ireland, SLF was formed in the height of the troubles in Ireland. They started as a schoolboy band called Highway Star, doing rock covers, until they discovered punk rock. Jake Burns was the founder, lead vocalist, and guitarist.

**Talking Heads:** Active in 1975 to 1991, 1996, and 2002. One of the most iconic American popular music bands of the age, formed by David Byrne on lead vocals and guitar, Chris Frantz on drums, Tina Weymouth on bass, and Jerry Harrison on keyboards and guitar. Classic tracks included "Psycho Killer" and "Once in a Lifetime," which were both included on the list "500 Songs That Shaped Rock and Roll." Talking Heads were number sixty-four on VH1's list of the "100 Greatest Artists of All Time."

**TCP:** A mild antiseptic produced in France by Laboratoires Chemineau in Vouvray. TCP was introduced in 1918, taking its name from its original chemical name, trichlorophenylmethyliodosalicyl, and was used to resolve almost all ailments, rashes, irritations, and infections. It had a distinctive odor that many still identify with antiseptic.

**Television:** Active from 1973 to 1978, 1991 to 1993, and 2001 to the present. From New York City, Television was formed by Tom Verlaine, Richard Lloyd, Billy Ficca, and Richard Hell. Television's music was based on a stripped-down guitar and, compared to the music of other punk bands at the time, was clean, improvisational, and technically proficient. Their debut album, *Marquee Moon*, is often considered one of the defining recordings of the time.

**Theatre of Hate:** Active in 1980 to 1983, 1991, 1993 to 1996, and 2005 to the present. Postpunk band founded in London by lead singer and guitarist Kirk Brandon, guitarist Simon Werner (deceased in 2010), bassist Jonathan Werner, drummer Rab Fale Beith (later of the UK Subs), saxophonist John "Boy" Lenard, and drummer Luke Randle. They released the live album *He Who Dares Wins* in 1981 in Berlin. *Westworld*, the band's first recording studio album (1982), reached number seventeen on the UK album charts and featured the top-forty single "Do You Believe in the Westworld?"

**The B-52s:** Active from 1976 to the present. Formed in Athens, Georgia, America. The B-52s' original lineup included Fred Schneider on vocals and percussion, Kate Pierson on vocals and keyboard, Cindy Wilson on vocals and percussion, Ricky Wilson on guitar, and Keith Strickland on drums, guitar, and keyboard. They created what was termed the "thrift shop aesthetic" and went on to release hits such as "Rock Lobster," "Love Shack," and "Roam."

**The Clash:** Active from 1976 to 1985. A key player in the original wave of punk rock. Out of London, they were originally formed by lead vocalist and rhythm guitarist Joe Strummer, lead vocalist Mick Jones, bassist Paul Simonon, and drummer Nicky "Topper" Headon. For many, they were the most influential rock band of their era, with albums such as *London Calling* (1979) and single tracks such as "London's Burning," "Daddy Was a Bank Robber," and "Rock the Casbah." Their legacy lives on today.

**The Cramps:** Active from 1976 to 2009. Psychobilly, garage-punk band formed in Sacramento, California, by members Lux Interior (deceased in 2009) and Poison Ivy, his wife, and then the addition of guitarist Bryan Gregory and drummer Pam Balam in 1976 to complete the lineup.

**The Damned:** Active from 1976 to the present. The first British punk rock band to release a single, "New Rose," in 1976. Created in London by lead vocalist Dave Vanian, guitarist Brian James, bassist Captain Sensible, and drummer Rat Scabies. The Damned have nine singles that charged on the UK singles charts, and they were one of the more commercially successful punk rock bands of that era.

**The Exploited:** Active from 1979 to the present. Formed in Edinburgh, Scotland, by Stevie Ross and Terry Buchan. When Buchan's brother, Wattie Buchan, joined later, the band's notoriety increased significantly. They signed with Secret Records, and their debut album, *Punk's Not Dead*, was released the same year, in 1981. They built up a cult audience of both punk rockers and skinheads.

**The Fall:** Active from 1976 to 2018. A postpunk alternative rock band formed in Pres twitch, Manchester, England, by founder and vocalist Mark Smith, who was the only constant member of the band. The Fall's long-standing members included drummers Paul Hanley and Karl Burns; guitarists Marc Riley, Craig Scanion, and Brit Smith; and bassist Steve Hanley. The Fall has been described as the most prolific band of the punk era, with more than thirty studio albums spanning more than forty years.

*The Great Rock 'N' Roll Swindle:* A 1980 British mockumentary centering on the Sex Pistols. Written and directed by Julien Temple and narrated by Malcolm McLaren. Apart from Johnny Rotten, who refused to get involved, it starred the band members of the Sex Pistols, adult film star Mary Millington, and Rene Handl and featured a cameo by convicted on-the-run bank robber Ronnie Biggs. Many movie theaters banned the film in a boycott of the Sex Pistols and the anarchic and poor-taste content of the film.

**The Jam:** Active from 1972 to 1982. Formed by lead vocalist Paul Weller in Woking, England, with band members Steve

Brookes, Rick Buckler, Dave Waller, and Bruce Foxton. They created a spin-off of punk rock, and although they still had the look of angry young men, they were more poetic in their lyrics and tuneful in their performances. The Jam cranked out six studio albums in five years, and when they split in 1982, their first fifteen singles were rereleased, and all made it onto the top-hundred charts.

**The Pogues:** Active from 1982 to 1996 and 2001 to 2014. Originating in London, the Pogues created their own brand of Celtic punk, reaching international notoriety and recording several hit albums and singles, including "Dirty Old Town" and "The Fairytale of New York City," possibly one of the most successful punk rock tunes of all time and one remembered for its annual homage in New Year's Eve celebrations around the world. Lead singer Shane MacGowan left the band due to a drinking problem in 1991, and Joe Strummer stepped in for a while before the band broke up in 1996. They re-formed in 2001, playing gigs in the United Kingdom, Ireland, and the United States, but did not release any new material.

**The Pretenders:** Active from 1978 to 1987, 1990 to 2012, and 2016 to the present. Originated in Hereford, England. The founder was an American, Chrissie Hynde, who was lead vocalist and played rhythm guitar. Hynde was often credited with having the sexiest voice in punk rock and even on the charts. In addition to nearly marrying two of the Sex Pistols (Johnny Rotten and Sid Vicious) to extend her UK visa, she was also credited with teaching Sid Vicious how to play the guitar. The Pretenders had a string of memorable hits, including "Brass in Pocket" (1979), "Talk of the Town" (1980), "Back on the Chain Gang" (1982), "200 Miles" (1983), "Don't Get Me Wrong" (1986), and "I'll Stand By You" (1994), and were inducted into the Rock and Roll Hall of Fame in 2005.

**The Roxy:** A fashionable nightclub located at 41-43 Neal Street in London's Covent Garden. Credited with the nurturing and flourishing of British punk rock in its infancy and beyond.

**The Ruts:** Active from 1977 to 1983 and 2007 to the present. A punk rock, reggae-rock, ska-punk band founded in London. They had a 1979 UK top-ten hit with "Babylon's Burning." Founding members of the band were singer Malcolm Owen, guitarist Paul Fox, bassist John "Segs" Jennings, and drummer Dave Ruffy.

**The Slits:** Active from 1976 to 1982 and 2005 to 2010. London-based postpunk dub band formed from members of the bands the Flowers of Romance and the Castrators. The early lineup consisted of Ariane Forster (Ari Up), Palmolive (Paloma Romero), Viv Albertine, and Tessa Pollitt. Their 1979 album *Cut* has been credited as one of the defining albums of the postpunk era.

**The Specials:** Active in 1977 to 1984, 1993, 1996 to 2001, and 2008 to the present. Iconic two-tone ska band of the era, formed in Coventry, England, at the heart of the UK depression. Vocals were led by Terry Hall, and hits such as "Too Much Too Young" and "Ghost Town" defined the mood of those times.

**The Stooges:** Active from 1967 to 1971, 1972 to 1974, and 2003 to 2016. Also known as Iggy and the Stooges. An American band formed in Ann Arbor, Michigan, by singer Iggy Pop, guitarist Ron Ashton, drummer Scott Ashton, and bassist Dave Alexander.

**The Stranglers:** Active from 1974 to the present. Founded in Guildford, England, by guitarist and vocalist Jean-Jacques Brunel, guitarist and vocalist Hugh Cornwall, and Swedish keyboardist and guitarist Hans Warmling, who was replaced within a year by Dave Greenfield. Their many legendary and iconic tracks included "No More Heroes," "Peaches," "Always the Sun," and the unforgettable "Golden Brown."

**The Undertones:** Active from 1974 to 1983 and 1999 to the present. Founded in Derry, Northern Ireland, by Feargal Sharkey on vocals, John O'Neill on guitar and vocals, Damian O'Neill on lead guitar and vocals, Michael Bradley on bass, and Billy Doherty on drums. The Undertones are the most successful band to have emerged from Derry, with tracks such as "Teenage Kicks," "Jimmy Jimmy," "My Perfect Cousin," and "Wednesday Week."

**The Velvet Underground:** Active in 1964 to 1973, 1990, 1992 to 1993, and 1996. American rock band formed in New York by Lou Reed on guitar and vocals, Doug Yule on bass guitar and organ, Sterling Morrison on rhythm guitar, and Maureen Tucker on percussion. The band was briefly managed by Andy Warhol. In 2004, *Rolling Stone* ranked the band as number nineteen on its list of "100 Greatest Artists of All Time."

**The Vibrators:** Active from 1976 to the present. London punk rock band founded by Ian "Knox" Carnochan, bass guitarist Pat Collier, guitarist John Ellis, and drummer John "Eddie" Edwards. They first were noticed at the famous 100 Club in 1976. The Vibrators appeared on *The John Peel Show* in October 1976, supported Iggy Pop on his 1977 tour, and are recognized as one of the pioneering punk bands who played at London's Roxy Club.

**UK Subs:** Active from 1976 to the present. British punk rock band founded in London by Charlie Harper, the lead singer. There have been more than seventy current and past members of the core band of four. Key singles have included "Stranglehold," "Warhead," and "Tomorrows Girls," and albums include *Brand New Age* and *Diminished Responsibility*, which both made number eighteen on the UK album charts.

**Vice Squad:** Active from 1979 to 1985 and 1997 to the present. British punk rock band from Bristol, with Bikini Bondage as lead singer. Their first single, "Last Rockers" (1981), sold twenty thousand copies and spent almost forty weeks on the UK indie chart, reaching number seven. They put out a total of thirteen singles, twelve studio albums, and two live albums and appeared on nine compilation albums over their forty-year journey.

**X-Ray Spex:** Active in 1976 to 1979, 1991, 1995 to 1996, and 2008. Founded in London by lead singer Poly Styrene (Marion Joan Elliott-Said, deceased in 2011), Jak Airport (Jack Stafford, deceased in 2004) on guitar, Paul Dean on bass, Paul "B. P." Hurding on drums, and Lora Logic (Susan Whitney) on saxophone. Their first ever single, "Oh Bondage! Up Yours!" is considered a classic punk rock track.

# ABOUT THE AUTHOR

Willy Mitchell was born in Glasgow, Scotland. He spent a lot of time in bars in his youth and into adulthood. He always appreciated the stories, some true, some imaginary, and some delusional. But these stories are true. Willy Mitchell was there!

A shipyard worker, he headed down from Scotland to Yorkshire with his family to work in the steel mills. He retired and turned to writing some of the tales he had listened to over the years, bringing those stories to life.

### Operation Argus

*Operation Argus* is a fast-paced, thoughtful, personal, and insightful story that touches the mind and the heart and creates a sense of intrigue in the search for the truth.

While sitting in the Rhu Inn in Scotland one wintry night, Willy Mitchell stumbles across a group of men in civilian clothes who are full of adrenaline—like a group of performers coming off a stage. To the watchful eye, it is clear the men are no civilians. As they share close-knit banter and beer, they are completely alert, and each of them checks him out and looks at his eyes and into his soul. Willy learns in time that the group are referred to as call sign Bravo2Zero.

*Operation Argus* is a story of fiction based on true events. Five former and one serving Special Air Service soldiers converge on San Francisco for their good friend's funeral, only to find his apparent heart attack is not as it seems. A concoction of polonium-210 has been used, as with the assassination of Litvinenko in London years before.

## Bikini Bravo

*Bikini Bravo* follows the adventures of Mitch; his daughter, Bella; and the team of Mac, Bob, and Sam as they uncover a complex web of unlikely collaborators but for a seemingly obvious common good: power, greed, and money.

Many years ago, Mitchell stumbled across a bar in Malindi, Kenya, West Africa, and overheard the makings of a coup in an oil-rich nation in West Africa. Is a similar plan being hatched today?

Lord Beecham puts together the pieces of the puzzle and concludes that the Russians, along with the Mexican drug cartels and a power-hungry group of Equatorial Guineans, have put together an ingenious plot to take over Africa's sixth-largest oil-producing nation in their attempt to win influence in Africa. The cartels desire to use the dirty money for good, and the Africans seek to win power and influence.

*Bikini Bravo* is another book of fiction by Mitchell that masterfully flirts with real-life events spanning the globe and touches on some real global political issues.

Mitch's daughter, Bella, is the emerging hero in this second book of the Argus series.

## Cold Courage

*Cold Courage* starts with Willy Mitchell's grandfather's meeting with Harry McNish in Wellington, New Zealand, in 1929. In exchange for a hot meal and a pint or two, McNish tells his story of the *Endurance* and the Imperial Trans-Antarctic Expedition of 1914.

According to legend, in 1913, Sir Ernest Shackleton posted a classified advertisement in the *London Times*: "Men wanted for hazardous journey. Small wages, bitter cold, long months of complete darkness, constant danger. Safe return doubtful. Honor and recognition in case of success." According to Shackleton, the advert attracted more than five thousand applicants, surely a sign of the times.

Following the assassination of Archduke Ferdinand earlier that year, at the beginning of August, the First World War was being declared across Europe, and with the blessing of the king and approval to proceed from the first sea lord, the *Endurance* set sail from Plymouth, England, on its way to Buenos Aires, Argentina, to meet with the entire twenty-eight-man crew and sail south.

Shackleton was keen to win back the polar-exploration crown for the empire and be the first to transit across the Antarctic from one side to the other.

The *Endurance* and her sister ship, the *Aurora*, both suffered defeat, and thirty-seven of Shackleton's men were stranded at opposite ends of the continent, shipless, cold, hungry, and fighting Mother Nature for survival.

This is a tale of the great age of exploration and the extraordinary journey these men endured, not only in Antarctica but also upon their return to England amid the Great War.

This is the story of the *Endurance*, the Imperial Trans-Antarctic Expedition of 1914, and all that was happening in those extraordinary times.

## *Northern Echo*

Willy Mitchell meets an old friend in the Royal Oak, in the northern town they grew up in, for one last blast. Tiny Tim has terminal cancer, and at the end of the evening, he makes Mitchell promise to tell their story of growing up in the north of England during the punk rock era and of their dark secret from a trip to Paris.

There were dark clouds surrounding Great Britain at that time. The Provisional IRA were actively rebelling against the English, Arabic terrorism was on the rise, and Argentina invaded one of the nation's territories in the far-off South Atlantic.

Unemployment was at its highest level since the 1930s, and whole industries were being crippled by the trade-union movement and strikes in every corner of industry. The far right was also on the rise, as was the Campaign for Nuclear Disarmament protesting the arms race that existed between the United States and the Soviet Union.

Society was on its knees; the middle class had given up, seemingly content to slide into obscurity, forgetting the victories and the pride of the past.

The youth of the time were disillusioned, with little prospect of jobs, careers, or a future, and as the punk rock scene spread across the Atlantic from New York, it changed into a movement and a commentary on the state of the country and the mood of society.

With no future and no rules, ripping up the rule book and starting again, the punk rock movement was an unlikely catalyst and contributor to change in Great Britain, with heaps of attitude, and it changed the nation for the better.

Mitchell, in *Northern Echo*, takes the reader on a sometimes humorous, eye-opening journey through one of the most interesting times in modern British history—a musical, political, and social revolution—and the story of two boys coming of age in their journey toward adulthood.

Printed in the United States
By Bookmasters